A Wave From Mama

The Slavery and Beyond Series

Volume 2

A. Robert Allen

ISBN: 978-0-578-58056-2

To everyone who wonders how we got here from there.

Part I

Weeksville
1863 - 1865

CHAPTER 1

Fort Sumter

A FEW CROSSED over Monday night, but the majority arrived on Tuesday or Wednesday, once it became apparent they were no longer welcome in New York. By Saturday morning, most who'd found their way across the river to Brooklyn took refuge in this makeshift camp in the town of Weeksville, where Black people owned most of the land. The refugees had learned hard lessons during the Draft Riots and most in the camp swore they would never again live side by side with Whites. The general consensus: there was strength in numbers, and Weeksville had numbers.

The camp became home to some complete families, as well as what remained of others. Some told stories of personal beatings they had endured, others spoke of lynchings they witnessed, but many didn't say much at all. Beyond their stories, what they had in common was a questionable future—next steps were on everyone's mind.

The refugees scattered around an open field with a variety of rudimentary shelters. Some set up proper tents, but most connected whatever materials they could find for some protection from the elements. No one prepared for such a hasty, but necessary, departure from New York.

The sweltering July heat made the stench of the camp almost unbearable. One distinctive scent, however, cut through the malodorous cloud and was immediately recognized by Ezra and Moses Brown, two brothers who worked on New York's East Side docks. Ezra called out to his younger brother for assistance, "Come on over here, I think we got some diggin' to do—someone must've passed." As Moses followed the scent, he tripped on an anchor supporting one of the tents. The occupants rushed outside to check on the disturbance and Ezra apologized for his brother. "So sorry, folks, just my fool of a brother, always trippin' on either his own feet or his own words. Go back to sleep now, you got a few more minutes before sunup."

Ezra laughed every time he passed the small sign posted by someone in the camp, which read "Fort Sumter." The symbolism was clear—the Draft Riots in New York earlier that week were the first shots fired in a new war against Blacks. Those foolish enough to think President Lincoln's recent Emancipation Proclamation marked the end of the struggle now understood it created another enemy—the Irish, who were certain the freed Blacks would steal their jobs.

The brothers continued their search for the source of the odor and entered an aisle created by four tents—two on either side. A young woman seated, legs crossed, on a blanket held her nose, and pointed in the direction of a crude tent surrounded by boxes. Moses squeezed through a small opening and found a woman lying in a pool of her own blood clutching her side, and said, "Ezra, this here that light-skinned girl from downtown, the one with the cut. Must've opened up—she bled out. Didn't want no help when she started settin' up her spot. More scared than most and didn't trust no one."

"I remember—pretty girl, but too scared for her own good. Sometimes you got to trust someone. Move the stuff behind her and wrap her in a blanket, and we'll find a spot to give her a proper Christian burial."

"Least we can do, Ezra. Hard to believe she moved all these damn boxes over here with such a deep cut. Built herself a little house—gonna take a while to clear everything out."

Moses realized most of the boxes were empty, so he started to kick them out of the way. As he kicked the largest one next to the woman's side, he heard a squeal and jumped back.

"Hold on Moses, somethin's in there."

Ezra tried to remove the top from the wooden box, but felt resistance, so he yanked harder, which caused him to stumble backward. The crash of the hatchet into the ground directly in front of Ezra made him jerk further back. The brothers gawked at their attacker, who sprung up from the crate—a tiny little boy, perhaps five years old, with fire in his eyes. The boy rocked his head from side to side and readied himself for another assault. Moses marveled at this small child with long arms that stretched below his knees. The boy curled his hands into fists, wrinkled his brow, and stared down the two men.

"Damn fool boy, you almost took my toes. Not even sure you Black—you even lighter than your mother. Give me that hatchet." Ezra grabbed the hatchet from the ground as Moses pulled the child from the crate. The youngster tried his best to escape, but Moses picked him up in a bear hug and controlled his punching and kicking. After a few moments, the boy calmed down and Moses loosened his grip. A bite to Moses's arm provided freedom. The crazed boy ran out of Fort Sumter screaming, "You killed Mama, and you're all gonna pay!"

Chapter 2

Raccoons

"Look at my eyes, and you won't see anything else. It'll all be over before you know it," the boy said to his captured raccoon as he slit the animal's throat and began the process of preparing his dinner for a slow roast over the fire. His extended stay in the woods of Virginia would serve him well—he wouldn't go hungry. A horse carriage passed on the outskirts of the wooded area where he hid behind a bush, and the sound of the whip on the horse's back made him scramble up a nearby tree, where he curled up in a ball and started counting in multiples of three: "three, six, nine, twelve…" After passing one hundred, he opened his eyes and checked on his lunch, which was about to burn, and slid down the tree trunk to eat.

His stomach full, the boy turned his attention to other matters. He thought, *Got to stay low, can't let those men spot me. I just need to make my way to the carriage. Need that rope.* He darted from tree to tree toward an unoccupied carriage on the side of the road, which had a section of rope hanging from a nail. After grabbing the rope undetected, he dashed back into the wooded area.

Traps always fascinated him and he learned how to improvise with different materials, but rope made trapping so much easier. He used a strong piece of wood to prop up a five-pound flat rock, attached the rope to the end of the wood, and placed a piece of his leftover raccoon lunch under the rock as bait. The last step—he needed to find a spot close enough to pull the rope in order to trap his kill when the moment arrived. *This will do.* He climbed high enough on a nearby tree so as not to be seen, but close enough to trigger the trap. *Yes, this is the perfect spot.*

The sun started to go down and the view of the surrounding area provided a sharp contrast to New York. He liked being back out in nature and remembered the time he spent in the woods in Virginia, when he and his mother got their chance for freedom. The boy recalled what his mother told him once they arrived in New York. "We free. Nobody gonna own us no more, and nobody gonna tell us what to do, but we got to find a way to put a roof over our heads and food in our bellies. Mama's workin' on everythin', don't you worry."

The child's thoughts remained on his mother. Tears streamed from his eyes and onto the branch upon which he rested his head. Once at the end of the branch, the tears dropped onto a leaf, like little rhythmic raindrops. The pattern mesmerized him—his head drooped, and his eyelids closed. His dream took him back to the boardinghouse in New York, right before it all happened.

The screaming and yelling from the streets made tracking the progress of the men advancing up the stairs difficult, but their arrival was imminent. The expressions of the men alternated between sneers and smiles as they discussed the punishment as well as the fun. Which should come first was the main point of contention.

"I'm gonna whip that whore and make her pay!"

"Damn fool, why do you want to whip her before the fun! I'm first!"

"I'm second!"

"No, we'll do the whipping first on her back, and flip her over for the fun. Won't make any difference to us, big difference to her, though!" They all laughed.

"What about her boy? We'll be doing the world a favor by getting rid of the little freak."

They laughed again.

With only a few more moments available to give instructions, the mother told her son, "Remember, family takes care of family and now I takin' care of you by tellin' you to go to your spot through the window. Don't worry, my little baby, they'd never kill a woman—gonna be like we back in Virginia for a spell. I know I told you to try to keep your head up to be eye-to-eye with people, but this time you can keep it down, and if you can't help yourself, lift your head, but only stare at my eyes. Understand? A few minutes of staring in Mama's eyes and it'll all be over. Like we back in Virginia for a short spell. Remember, we got through that, and we gonna get through this. Go on, jump through the window and go to your spot. I'll come for you later."

The boy jumped out of the window and landed on the rooftop next door. He crawled to his spot behind the chimney and witnessed his mother stand her ground, knife in her right hand, torso slightly crouched, with her feet shoulder-length apart. The men stormed into the room.

Crash! The sound of the falling rock jarred the child out of his dream, and he climbed down the tree to check on his catch. This animal had done him a favor and tripped the stick on its own. He lifted the rock and saw his dead catch with the bait protruding from its mouth. He dropped the rock back on top and walked away—any living thing that would eat its own was not for him.

CHAPTER 3

Crow's Hill

"MOSES, HERE HE comes. This is our chance, he's important. Do what I do," Ezra whispered to his brother as he put his right foot on a crate and his left hand in the pocket of his pants—the proper pose to greet an important person. Moses did his best to imitate his brother's movements, but when he put his foot on the crate, he pressed too hard and it collapsed into pieces. Ezra stared at his fool of a brother, but didn't take the time to point out his clumsiness, because Junius Morel was approaching their spot.

"Good mornin', Mr. Morel. My name is Ezra and this here is my brother Moses. We came across the river Tuesday night. Almost got strung up in New York—had to leave. This town, Weeksville, sure seems like the place to be. People say you the man in charge and we're hope'n we can stay. We're good Colored Americans, like you."

Junius Morel, the principal of the local school and one of the leaders in Weeksville, extended his hand to greet each of the brothers before he responded, "We welcome you to Weeksville, but I must correct you, we are not *Colored Americans*, we are simply *Americans*, and I'm not in charge—just concerned about the welfare of our town."

Ezra didn't understand the point, but nodded his head anyway. Moses offered a blank stare.

The principal continued, "We are always looking for additions to our community, especially those in a position to buy land." A strong wind whipped up the dry dirt in the camp and blew some particles into the principal's eye, which interrupted his thoughts, "So sorry, gentlemen, give me a moment."

Moses handed the principal a spotless white handkerchief and it did the job in clearing the dirt from his eye. "Thank you, Moses. As I was saying, property ownership enables Blacks to vote in New York, and we need the political power. Also, the Long Island Rail Road makes Weeksville a short ten-minute ride from downtown Brooklyn or the ferries to New York. What kind of work do you do?"

Moses cleared his throat to answer the question, but Ezra jumped in before he could respond. "Me 'n Moses work on the docks."

"Brooklyn has plenty of docks, but I'm sure you don't want more problems with the Irish. Perhaps you should consider some other kind of work. Good luck to both of you."

⤞▬◉ ◉▬⤝

Junius Morel continued his tour of the camp and came upon a handsome young man addressing a small crowd of perhaps four or five young girls, who followed his every word and movement. The principal drew closer and realized the man was reciting poetry.

"Please, one more, Mr. Heath. We love your fancy talk," one of the young ladies exclaimed. Another suggested, "A love poem!" as she tracked the movement of the charming young man's eyes. Once they settled in her general direction, she was certain he acknowledged her smile. Three other girls developed the same conclusion when his eyes drifted their way.

"Of course, ladies, just one more. Happy to oblige. What would be suitable for such an attractive group of young women?" His pause gave the girls a chance to swoon once more, which delighted Edward Heath, who appeared to have experience both as an orator as well as a ladies' man. "Ah, I have it, a Shakespeare sonnet." He cleared his throat and straightened his posture before beginning.

"Shall I compare thee to a summer's day?
Thou art more lovely and more temperate:
Rough winds do shake the darling buds of May,
And summer's lease hath all too short a date:
Sometime too hot the eye of heaven shines,

And often is his gold complexion dimmed,
And every fair from fair sometime declines,
By chance, or nature's changing course untrimmed:
But thy eternal summer shall not fade,
Nor lose possession of that fair thou ow'st,
Nor shall death brag thou wander'st in his shade,
When in eternal lines to time thou grow'st,
So long as men can breathe, or eyes can see,
So long lives this, and this gives life to thee."

The girls were satisfied after the first two lines—handsome Edward Heath told them they were more lovely than a summer's day. The poem could have ended at that point.

Junius Morel interrupted, "Bravo, Bravo. Quite a performance and what an attentive audience!" The girls scampered away as they argued over which of them was Edward's favorite.

"I am Junius Morel, the principal of the local school, and who might you be?"

"My name is Edward Heath. I just graduated college in upstate New York and came to the city to seek employment, but it appears I came at an inopportune time."

"To be sure. Can I assume literature is your specialty?"

"I am an avid reader and I must admit, Mr. Morel, I have read several of your articles."

The young man impressed Junius, and received an invitation to a meeting for potential new residents, which the principal planned to host in a few weeks at his school. A man such as Edward Heath would be a fine addition to the Weeksville community as a teacher. Junius laughed as he thought, *I'm not sure if he'll be more popular with the ladies in town or the students in class.* Either way, however, the charming and educated Mr. Heath was certain to add value to the community.

⊷⊷▬◉ ◉▬⊶⊶

Ezra and Moses also caught the end of Edward Heath's performance, but it all sounded like a foreign language to them. Fancy talk was not common on the docks, and both brothers thought it fitting such elevated speech would be used in a city literally built on a hill. The brothers gazed out toward the horizon, and Moses turned to Ezra, put his arm around his brother, and said, "This whole thing may be for the best, Ezra. We on top of the world in Weeksville!"

"You right, Moses. Top of the world!"

The brothers continued their scan of the scenery and Moses asked, "Why they call this Crow's Hill?"

"Moses, sometimes your questions are so stupid." Ezra pointed to the sky and asked, "What do you call those?"

Moses laughed, as he strained his head and shielded his eyes from the bright sun. "Right! Crows 'r all over the place! Must be the fertilizer farm with all those dead carcasses."

"Yeah, you're right. Do you think they might need some help at the farm from two strong New York men?"

"Not so sure how strong you are, Ezra. I do most of the lifting."

"Only when it just you and I, 'cause I the older brother. Otherwise, I lift as good as you."

"Don't know 'bout that, older brother. You might be showin' your age."

Ezra chuckled. "Yeah, twenty-nine, pretty old age. I better start slowin' down and let youngen's like you take over."

"Not yet old man, let's go find us a job."

The brothers walked the outskirts of the town as a first pass and started down Hunterfly Road. Ezra pointed to his left as he said, "There's another Black town called Carrsville down that way. If things don't work out here, we can try Carrsville next."

"Two Colored towns side by side…hard to believe. I know this got to work out. Make a right here onto Park and we'll start coming back around."

Clusters of houses sprinkled the bucolic setting. Shops were attached to many of the dwellings, and the brothers took note of shoemakers, tailors, butchers, and other tradesmen. After a short while, Ezra and Moses realized the businesses were run by skilled artisans who had little need of help, which led to the conclusion—Weeksville might be an excellent place to live, but they would need to find work elsewhere.

Moses smiled as they walked by an amalgamation house, and noted a few of the pretty ladies peeking out the window. One of the girls blew a kiss in their direction and Ezra cautioned his brother, "Moses, we ain't got money for girls. What we need is work, not playin' round." The smile vanished from Moses's face, but then another kiss came his way. Ezra pulled his younger brother by the back of his collar as he said, "I done told you, Moses, wipe that dumb smile off your face. Sometimes you so stupid."

The end of their walk around the perimeter of the town brought them back onto Atlantic Avenue. Moses was the first to take note of the commotion.

"Come back here, you little criminal!"

"Stop him!"

The married proprietors of a small general store continued screaming as they chased a young boy who sped past the Brown brothers with his hands full of fruit and tomatoes. After about twenty feet, the wife called off the chase. "Honey, let him go. The child probably hasn't eaten in days. We would have given it to him if he'd asked." The husband nodded and the couple returned to their store.

Ezra called out to Moses, "There's the boy who almost took my toes and a chunk out of your arm. Get 'em." Moses, the recipient of all instructions, assumed the chase.

⊹▸▬◉ ◉▬◂⊹

After wandering through the woods on such a hot day, Moses's shirt was soaked with perspiration. Broken twigs marked the spot where the boy entered the wooded area, but after one hundred feet, the trail stopped at a large oak tree. Almost forty-five minutes later, Moses wound up at the same large oak where he started, and thought, *Damn boy, it's hotter than shit out here and I'm doing all of this runnin' round. Ezra's nowhere to be found. Always got to be Moses—Moses do this—Moses do that. Damn Ezra, he probably at the 'malgamation house havin' some fun. Yeah, he snuck a peek. He calls me stupid, but I ain't no fool.*

Moses stopped his solitary rant as he sat down to rest under the shade of the oak. The first rock hit him in the leg. The next struck him in the chest and he scrambled behind the other side of the tree for protection. *There he is, that little shit.* The boy, perched high up in another oak about twenty feet away, alternated between taking bites of his tomato, and waiting for the next opportunity to hit his target.

"Come down here, boy, and stop all the rock throwin'. You want me to give you a whippin'? Come down right now!"

The sound of a rock whizzing by his head greeted Moses as he stepped out from the protection of the tree. *Damn, what kind of young boy can throw like that?* The boy scrambled in the tree as he searched for more rocks—Moses smiled as he thought, *Doesn't have enough 'munition.*

The boy climbed through the branches like a squirrel, and jumped from tree to tree—Moses followed and screamed, "What kind of five-year-old boy can climb like that? What the hell are you?" The answer: a sneer, followed by another leap. The length of the boy's jumps and the way he swung from branch to branch amazed Moses as he followed from below. Another sneer from the boy preceded an extraordinary jump to a higher branch, perhaps twenty feet in the air. Moses couldn't tell if the child's movements were evidence of confidence or stupidity, but one thing was certain—he was fearless. At the sixth tree, he missed his mark for the first time, but Moses caught him and broke his fall. The man overpowered the child and pinned him to the ground.

"What's your name, boy?"

No answer. The child squirmed his head to avoid eye contact with his attacker.

"What's your name? Not letting you up 'til you say it."

The boy squirmed some more, but the larger man immobilized him. He strained his neck to attempt a bite, but Moses kept his distance. After each of his efforts failed, he finally spoke. "My name is Venture and I told you I would get you. I'm going to get all of you, and I'm not five years old…I'm twelve! Let me up!"

Chapter 4

Esther & Mabel Washington

Moses worried as he led the boy down Atlantic Avenue with his hands bound and a rope leash fashioned around his waist. The concern wasn't about Venture getting loose again, but rather the negative reaction of the townspeople to the vision of a grown man marching what appeared to be an innocent—but bound—five-year-old boy into town. Ezra finished his goodbyes with the girls at the amalgamation house and called out to his younger brother as the crowd started to gather.

"Moses, what the hell are you doing? You're treating him like an animal!"

The married storekeepers, who chased the boy a few hours earlier, came onto the scene and corrected Ezra. "No. Not an animal, he's treating him like a slave. Not in Weeksville, you won't! Untie him!"

Moses shifted his weight from left to right and tried to choose his words carefully. "You don't understand…this boy is dangerous. Bit me on the arm. Threw rocks at me. This is the only safe way to bring him in."

The growing crowd erupted with laughter and started passing comments of their own.

"How could such a cute 'lil thing do all that?"

"What do you mean, bring him in? Is he under arrest?"

"Let him go!"

"What kind o' man are you?"

Ezra never shied away from humiliating his younger brother in public, but with this angry crowd, he stood by his brother's side.

"Moses, tell them 'bout the crate."

"Found him in a crate next to his dead mom. Almost chopped off my brother's toes and bit me. Sure, he seems like a 'lil child, but he ain't. Almost twelve and he's the devil—through and through. He blames us for his mama's death. Can't let him go and can't control him." Venture stood with slumped shoulders and his head pointed to the ground. This man touched him for the second time in as many days and he had no right. Soon he would be untied and back in the woods. *They'll never catch me again and they'll all pay.*

The crowd didn't accept any of Moses's story and the group as a whole encircled the two brothers and the boy. Ezra took control. "All right, if you want him free, this is on all of you. My brother and I are trying to help, but if you want this 'lil devil runnin' all over town hurting people and stealin' things, that's fine by us." He turned, stared at the boy, and said, "You better not come 'round us. Go and bother these other folks who like you so much. I'm going to cut you loose."

Ezra started to untie Venture, and the boy spotted a second knife on the side of the man's pants. *Almost loose,* he thought, a plan forming. *I'll grab the knife, jab him in the leg, and head back into the woods.* Ezra cut the rope and Venture put his plan into action, but when he reached for the knife, he felt the slap of a heavy hand on the back of his neck and fell to the ground. Ezra had realized the boy was trying to grab his knife and turned to the crowd and said, "I told all of you. This boy is Satan himself." The townspeople had no reaction, and Ezra asked Moses, "Why the hell did you get me involved in this?"

Little brother responded, "What do you mean, why did *I* get you involved in this? You're the one who sent me after him!"

"Moses, sometimes you're so stupid. What am I going to do with you? Let's go back to the camp."

The two brothers continued to squabble as they walked away. Esther Washington, mother of two and wife of the town's most successful shoemaker, stood over Venture and readied her heavy hand for another slap if the boy continued to misbehave. "So you're a 'lil devil, are you?" She paused for a moment, expecting an answer from the child. None was offered, so she continued, "You'll stop all of this nonsense and come with me." Venture did what he was told, and became a polite, well-behaved young man—at least during the walk with Esther Washington to her home.

Once inside the house, Mrs. Washington took Venture into the kitchen, told him to sit, and began the slow process of filling the tub with warm water. Every time she added a bucket, she gave him another treat to eat. The boy's belly was full by the time he stepped into the tub with his head rocking from side to side.

"My name is Esther Washington. My husband's name is Thomas. He's a shoemaker and we live in this here house with our two children: Horace, who's fourteen, and Mabel, who's sixteen."

Esther waited for her guest to acknowledge what she'd said and supply some basic information in return, but received no response. The boy continued to rock in a steady rhythm and sat in the water, staring at the small boat Horace had played with years ago.

"You want Horace's boat?" She got up and removed the boat from the shelf, placed it in the water, and detected the slightest smile emerging from the side of the boy's mouth.

"What's your name?"

"Venture."

Esther smiled. "Venture, that's interesting. Is there a story 'bout your name?"

Venture shrugged his shoulders in response.

"Do people call you Vent for short?"

He nodded his head and offered his first true smile. Esther enjoyed her slow but steady progress in breaking through. "Tell me about your family."

The smile vanished. Esther tried again. "Vent, it's okay. You can talk to me. Tell me about your family."

Venture jumped out of the tub and threw the wooden ship against the wall, breaking it into pieces. He screamed, "They killed Mama and I'm going to kill them all," as he grabbed his clothes, jumped out of the ground-floor window, and climbed the tree in the front yard of the house. He sat on one of the stronger limbs and continued mumbling a combination of threats about "getting every-one" and counting numbers in different patterns. First, he counted by twos, then threes, fours, and so on…always until he reached about one hundred, and then he started again with a different pattern. After a few of these counting se-quences, he would issue another general threat to everyone he blamed for killing his mother. The mumbling/counting rant went on until six in the evening, when Esther put a covered plate of food out on the porch for him.

About fifteen minutes later, Esther detected some movement in the tree. A few years earlier, Horace had tried to climb this mammoth tree and he hugged the trunk for dear life as he made his way up to the next-highest branch he could grasp. Coming down was an even slower and more arduous process. Venture stood up on the highest branch and jumped onto a larger, but lower one, swung on the tree limb for a while to build momentum, and then flipped back up to a standing position on the branch. Esther studied Vent's face and didn't pick up even an inkling of fear or doubt—either the boy was the most confident person Esther had ever met or he didn't care about getting hurt. Each movement made Esther more nervous, so she turned her back and returned a few minutes later. Venture finished his dinner while sitting on the stoop and then started another daredevil ascent up the tree.

At nine o'clock, Esther pulled up a chair next to the second-story window facing the tree. She stared at Vent and waited for him to make eye contact—as good a way as any to try and talk to the tormented child.

"Vent, what you been through must be bad and you not ready to talk 'bout it, but you can't sleep in a tree. I see how you climb and I'm going to leave this window open. If you want to come into the house through this window, you can, but if you do, you will obey me and stop all of this 'I'm going to get every-one' talk. You got my family scared of you, and until you start to talk polite, I'm blockin' the door to this bedroom on the outside. The window is gonna be your way in and out until you start talkin' better to folks. That's what I'm willin' to do, so if you like it, come on in, but if you don't, climb out of my tree and go on." After leaving the room, Esther blocked the outside of the door with a nearby bureau—she meant what she said, her family was scared. This boy with the odd name wasn't right.

After about another hour, Vent grabbed a nearby branch and swung onto the roof of the house before hanging over the ledge to come through the bedroom window. Esther heard the bump on the roof and realized the boy had accepted her offer. She smiled as she closed her eyes for the night.

Venture didn't say much for the next few days and developed a daily routine, which involved more observing than participating. He enjoyed watching the Washingtons' two children as they helped each other with their daily chores. *They family, and family takes care of each other,* he thought. Esther's husband, Thomas, joked that Vent was more pure trouble pound for pound than anyone he'd ever met. Despite his small size, the rage in his eyes never diminished and Thomas, in particular, worried what would happen when he erupted.

Mabel was the first family member other than Esther to break through to Vent. After a number of days in the household, Vent started spending time with her in the back of the house as she tended to the garden. After Mabel finished her daily work, she and Vent sat on a blanket spread over a patch of grass. Esther always assumed they talked and only became silent when she walked by.

"Mabel, what do you and Vent talk 'bout in the garden?"

"We don't talk much, Mama. First, I do my work, and then I lay out the blanket for our army game. We make soldiers out of twigs and we fight battles."

"Never expected army games. Who wins?"

"Always the North against the South. He always gets to be the North and I always let him win. When the war is over, I talk like I'm President Lincoln and free all the Southern slaves. That's when he asks me the same odd question."

"What question?"

"He says, 'Even the ones in the woods in Virginia?'"

"What's your answer?"

"At first, I just said *yes* and he smiled, and then when I said things like, *absolutely*, he smiled even more. So I mostly say, *absolutely*."

"Well, I guess we know where Vent and his family are from."

"Guess so, Mama."

"What else do you do?"

"Main thing with Vent is everything needs to be done in the right order. Once I laid out the blanket before I finished my work, and he got mad and ran off. Never did that again. After the army game, he sits and makes shapes with rocks—squares, circles, triangles, and rectangles, but that game is only for him. I'm not allowed to touch anything, so I don't."

"That's it, he plays games of army and puts rocks in different shapes, but doesn't say anythin' about what happened to him?"

"He says he's gonna get the people who killed his mama and when I told him that scared me, he seemed surprised and said nothing bad like what happened to him would ever happen to me."

"You got yourself a little protector, Mabel. Should be a good thing. How's Vent doing with Horace?"

"Don't think Horace pays him no mind, he's always runnin' in and out with all his girlfriends. You know that boy loves himself and stares into the mirror Daddy got last month. He takes it into his room and admires hisself—thinks he's the most handsome boy in the world. Unless Vent wants to hold the mirror, don't think Horace has no use for him!"

"Don't you go makin' fun of your brother. You know he's a good-lookin' boy and so smart too—he gonna do big things in his life. Worried about all the girls, though, 'cause he too young for such nonsense, but I wish he'd try to at least help Vent make some friends. Horace should take him 'round to meet other chidr'n."

"He might, Mama, but Vent only talks a little bit—just to you and me, and he doesn't like to be around lots of other people. Horace ain't said more than a few words to Vent. Could be afraid of him. I don't know. Better ask him."

"Fair, enough, Mabel. I might hold the mirror for him, so we can have a good long talk!"

Mabel laughed as she responded, "Might be the only way!"

⊷▰◉ ◉▰⊶

The next day, Mabel ran into the house after spending time with Vent out back, and called out to her mother, "Mama, Vent is going to hurt Alex. Better come fast."

Esther Washington rushed out the back of her house and found Vent on top of an older teenage boy, who pleaded through sobs and tears for mercy, "I'm sorry! I'll never do it again…never say nothin' to her again. I promise. Let me go."

Vent sat on top of the boy, waving a rock over his face with his right hand. Esther screamed, "Vent, you put that rock down and let Alex go!" Vent was confused. The boy threatened Mabel, so he had to be punished, but Vent listened to Miss Esther, and she said stop. He didn't know what to do. Alex noticed Vent's temporary loss of focus, slipped out from under, and ran away. Esther thought, *Time for a talk with Venture.*

"Vent, put down the rock, and come sit with me. Mabel, you go on inside."

He did as instructed and sat, head down, in one of the two chairs on either side of the back door to the Washington's house.

"Vent, were you going to hit Alex with that rock? What happened?"

Vent started mumbling, "I'm gonna get everyone who killed Mama, two, four, six, eight…"

Esther waited a few minutes because she understood no answers of substance could be obtained when Vent was in this condition. She called for Mabel, who stepped out from inside the house.

"Mabel, what happened?"

"Vent and me were sitting in the backyard and Alex came by and asked, 'Why you spendin' time with the crazy boy?'"

"So is that what got Vent angry?"

"No, didn't bother him at all, he stayed quiet. I told Alex Vent wasn't crazy, and he yelled back that I should be careful 'cause crazy rubs off. Vent still didn't do nothing, but then Alex threw a rock. Guess'n he wanted to hit Vent, but it almost hit me. The rock made Vent angry, 'cause he tells me, every day, no one ever gonna hurt me. Vent ran after Alex and I came inside for you."

"Okay, Mabel, I understand. Go back inside."

Vent was still counting and mumbling, "Four, eight, twelve, sixteen, twenty…" but Esther thought he'd calmed down enough to listen.

"Vent, I like you lookin' out for my chidr'n, but you went through something bad, and I don't think you can tell the difference between real bad things and something that's only a little bad. The boy you beat up, Alex, always comes 'round here. He's a little sweet on Mabel—must have been jealous of you—no reason to bash someone's head in, but you didn't understand him the right way. So this here is what we're going to do: if any of us gets hurt, and we tell you we need you to go and protect us, that's the only time you do it. We family now, but you got to be asked. You understand, Vent? That gonna be the rule. Tell me you understand, Vent."

The mumbling stopped. The rule made sense. "Yes, Miss Esther, sorry 'bout what I did."

"Okay, I'm gonna go over and 'splain to Alex's mother what happened, but remember the rule, 'cause if this happens again, folks won't want you stayin' with us in Weeksville no more, and you part of the family now. So go on, I'll take care of this."

Vent walked away and went back to sit in the garden. Mabel joined him but didn't start any conversations. He'd calmed down and they sat quietly. Vent broke the silence with a smile—the biggest and most sustained grin Mabel had ever seen. Finally, he said, "Miss Esther told me I part of the family now."

"Vent, you been part of the family since the first day you climbed into your room from the tree. You didn't know that?"

"No. Thought I'd have to leave."

"You'll never have to leave. Family is forever, Vent."

Vent started to cry and Mabel realized her mistake. She put her arm around him and rocked gently. He never explained about his family and maybe he never would, but there was no doubt he loved them. Vent ceased to be the crazy boy who jumped out of the crate—he was her new brother, valiant protector, and more than anything, a welcome addition to her family.

Chapter 5

Thomas & Horace Washington

By the end of August, Vent had developed strong bonds with Esther and Mabel, but Thomas Washington worried about the boy and the reality of another mouth to feed. One afternoon, when he was alone with Vent in the house, Thomas decided to assert himself. "Vent, you need to respect me as the head of this family and do as I say." Thomas paused to give Vent an opportunity to respond, but in his characteristic style, Vent offered no reply.

"Listen here, Vent. What you did to the Brown brothers can't ever happen again. You don't swing no hatchet at anyone and the only thing you gonna bite is food, you understand me, boy?"

Again, no response.

Thomas tried to force his head up, and realized he'd made a mistake—Vent rushed away and took refuge in the corner of the room. His downward-pointing head rocked from side to side and then all movement stopped, as the boy slowly raised his head to stare down the man who would dare touch him. The rage in Vent's eyes was so intense Thomas retreated to another corner of the room. Vent offered his standard threat, "I'm going to kill them all, everyone who killed Mama." Thomas had no doubt he would, and this time, he was the one who offered no response—time to talk to Esther.

Thomas found her later that afternoon by the stove preparing the evening meal and said, "Esther, Vent's got to go—he fights with everyone and he almost killed the Brown brothers. This boy is the devil, and even though he's only been here for a while, he's caused every kind of trouble. We need to send him somewhere else. He only listens to you, but you not always 'round—it can't work this way, Esther. Somethin's got to change."

Esther took a deep breath before she responded, "Thomas, think about what you're saying. Where we going to send him? Who is going to want a scrawny, misbehaved Black child? What you want me to do? Throw this little boy away? Why do you think he attacked the Brown brothers? Protecting himself is all, but he didn't understand they weren't the enemy. Yes, he's rough, and yes, he fights real dirty, but what chance do you think that little bitty boy has fighting fair? No one knows what he went through—he won't tell us, but I'm hopin' one day he will. Please understand, we're all he's got, and we can't throw him away, Thomas. With his light skin, he don't fit nowhere, but I promise, Thomas—he'll be better. Somethin' *is* gonna change."

In the weeks that followed, Thomas did appreciate the difference in Vent as they spent time together in the shop. Vent did what he could to help Thomas with chores and deliveries, and Thomas became pleased Esther had ignored his plea to remove Vent from the household. Vent didn't quite understand how to greet people properly or read body language, but the Washingtons understood he didn't process things the same way as most people. Despite the occasional awkwardness, Vent became a good fit with most of the family. The one exception was Horace, who never had any use for him. To make matters worse, Vent's attack on Alex brought more attention to his existence in the Washington household, and impacted Horace's standing at school; he hated the constant question, "Why is that crazy person still in your house?"

Horace also never got over the fact that he gave up his room on the second floor to Vent. Not that his new room paled in comparison, but why did *he* need to move? Was it because Vent did this weird climbing thing and came in through the second-floor window, or did the family still feel the need to block the outside of Vent's door if he went into one of his fits? Both reasons seemed either stupid or scary to Horace, who, as one of the top students in the local school, considered himself to be the most logical person in the house. By late August, everyone else in the family accepted Vent but, to Horace, he was still nothing but a nuisance.

Toward the end of the summer, Horace met his match in a competition for a girl. Despite his natural advantages in appearance and intelligence, he couldn't fathom how he seemed to be losing the battle for the young lady's affections. Horace rarely resorted to physical violence, but given his size advantage over his competition, he decided to attempt intimidation. He waited for the boy after a meeting at the school and pushed him toward the back of the building. With one last shove, the boy was on his knees in the dirt—the plan was going well.

"You gonna leave Candace be—she's mine, you understand?"

The boy stood up and answered Horace with his fists. Despite his smaller size, his first three punches bloodied Horace's face. A passerby screamed, "Fight," and ten other students rushed behind the building and witnessed Horace's beating as the boy finished up with a final flurry of punches to both the face and abdomen. All of the children laughed at Horace, who lay face down in the dirt. He raised his head in time to see the lovely Candace walking off with the boy who just delivered his beating.

When Horace came home with a black eye and bruises all over his face and arms, he grabbed the mirror and went to his room to inspect the damage—his nose appeared like it might be broken and a black bruise formed around his right eye. Horace started to cry as he thought, *I'm no longer the best looking.* Tears streamed down his face as his plan for retribution began to unfold. When he emerged from his room, he spun a different story to his family, "That boy beat me for no reason, Mama."

Esther answered, "I know his mother, I'll speak to her—"

Thomas interrupted, "Horace, stop trying to be such a pretty boy. You old enough to take care of your own business and better learn how to fight." Thomas waited for Horace to look him squarely in the eyes before continuing, "Your mama done fought her last battle for you. Now you gonna stand up for yourself and take care of this on your own." No response from Horace, other than a retreat to his room for a further inspection of the damage. The more he stared at his disfigured face in the mirror, the more he swore he would exact his revenge.

Venture listened to the story and remembered the rule—Horace was family and had been hurt, so he walked back into the woods and spent the better part of an hour scouring the fallen branches to find one sturdy enough to do some damage, but light enough for him to swing with force. Once he located a suitable branch, he whittled down one end to fashion a handle small enough for someone his size.

That evening, Venture asked Horace if he needed help dealing with his attacker. Horace answered without hesitation, "Yes, but this got to be between me and you. Understand?"

Vent responded, "Okay, but you need to point him out for me. Let's go."

Horace's chest puffed out as he made the short walk with Vent to the boy's house. *I started the fight, but he shouldn't have taken it as far as he did. If I won the fight, I would have stopped beating him before everyone started laughing, but he didn't do that for me, so I'm going to get even.*

Glancing to his right, Horace took note of Vent's confident gait and absence of fear, but after taking inventory of Vent's short, skinny body, Horace didn't like his chances against the older boy, and began to have second thoughts. *Maybe I should find another way. Vent is too small to handle this. He's not confident—he's crazy. This is a mistake.* The boy came into view, and Horace pointed him out. Vent's calm confidence became more of a determined fury and Horace lost his concern about a bad outcome. *The bastard is going to regret what he did to me.*

Vent told Horace to hide behind a bush as he put the handle of his club between his teeth and scaled a nearby tree as if he were attached to it. Vent started to mumble and count as the boy approached, "Five, ten, fifteen, twenty…" The boy passed by his position in the tree, and Vent jumped down, swinging his makeshift club before landing on the ground. He hit the boy in the lower back from behind with tremendous force.

"You killed Mama and I'm gonna kill you."

The boy tried to turn to see his attacker, but instead started to cry from the pain in his back. Vent hit him again in the same spot. The boy didn't move. Horace enjoyed the first hit and celebrated the second, but rushed over to grab the club from Vent, because a third shot might permanently injure the boy. Vent turned to Horace and screamed, "But he killed Mama. He has to die!"

"He didn't kill anybody, Vent, go home."

Horace brought the boy back to his house, left him on the stoop, and whispered words of warning in his ear. "If you want Vent to come back, you'll say what actually happened. Otherwise, you'll be smart and realize I just saved your life. I want you to tell everyone I came back and did this to you in a fair fight, and you better stay away from Candace."

Vent walked slowly back home as he considered Horace's words. *Why did Horace stop me from beating the boy? Doesn't he understand Miss Esther's rule? Didn't he himself ask for the boy to be beaten? I only followed the rule. Why did he stop me?*

The night ended in typical fashion as Vent climbed into his second-floor bedroom window from his favorite tree and continued with his other nocturnal ritual—he lay down on his mat on the floor, and then after everyone else settled in for the night, he moved the mat into the closet and fell asleep dreaming about his mama. This was the only time and place he felt safe at night, and it presented him with a daily opportunity to privately mourn the loss of his mother. Tonight, however, his thoughts focused on the events of the evening. It was all so confusing. The rule is clear and Horace is so smart. *Why did he stop me?*

Chapter 6

An Offering for Mama

Soon after sundown, Vent made his daily trek into the nearby woods. He loved the sounds of crickets and the soft songs of the few nocturnal birds that practiced their vocals at this late hour. The woods always seemed like home to Vent—he remembered the time spent with his mama camped out in the woods of Virginia until their contact arrived to take them up north. Mama kept talking about the joy of being free, but to Vent the woods already provided freedom—he wondered why his mama wanted to keep running. Every time he offered a suggestion along those lines, his mother responded, "Fool boy, *civ'lized* people don't live like animals in the woods," which made Vent wonder what *civ'lized* meant, and whether it was something he wanted to be.

After thirty minutes of dedicated work, five traps were set—all in their regular locations. Vent climbed a tree, which sat in the approximate center of the traps, so he would be close to the action. The lack of light made observation difficult, but the devils only came out at night, which gave Vent little choice as to when to do his hunting.

A loud clanking sound—rock on rock—signaled the first action of the evening and the squeal provided evidence of success. Fifteen minutes later, the second clanking sound, followed soon thereafter by the third, fourth, and fifth—so closely grouped, they almost appeared to be simultaneous. Tonight, Vent achieved his quota in record time. The daily goal, five kills, because after ten nights, fifty would be dead—this seemed like a good number of devils to rid the world of. *How many more could there possibly be?* But after twenty nights and almost one hundred successes, there didn't seem to be an end in sight.

Vent climbed down from his perch in the tree and visited the first trap. Much to his surprise, the trap held an injured squirrel rather than a dead raccoon. Some nuts in close vicinity to the raccoon meat he left as bait provided the attraction. Accidents did happen from time to time. He didn't mean to catch the injured squirrel, and spoke softly to the animal, "Look at my eyes, and it will all be over in a second." The squirrel complied and as their eyes met, Vent slit the animal's throat, and dug a shallow grave for his mistaken kill.

On to his second trap. This one contained a dead raccoon, with a piece of the bait protruding from its mouth. An enraged Vent stabbed the already dead animal to ensure the absence of life. Vent dropped the devil into an empty burlap bag. The third trap contained an incapacitated raccoon; Vent flashed his knife as he taunted the animal. "See this knife? Imagine the pain when I dig it into your body. Any animal that eats its own doesn't deserve to live." His speech complete, he waited for the raccoon to comply, but the animal's eyes never opened—devils were often uncooperative. His knife began to dig, and the second dead raccoon joined the first in the burlap bag.

The fourth trap contained another squirrel, which was afforded a merciful death, but the fifth, another devil, which took its fatal stabs after hearing Vent's words of admonition. Three dead raccoons now rested in Vent's burlap sack.

The clearing reminded Vent of the camp he and his mom stayed in while in Virginia. He lay down on the ground—burlap sack at his side, and admired the stars as he began his conversation. "Mama, you said they wouldn't kill you. You were wrong, but don't you worry, I'm going to get them all. Until I do, I offer you these raccoons, which are the lowest of low. These raccoons are in honor of you, Mama."

Vent started a fire and threw his burlap bag into the blaze. He counted by threes, fours, and then fives. By the time he got to sixes, all that remained was ash and his night's work was done.

CHAPTER 7

Colored School No. 2

COLORED SCHOOL NO. 2 was a tremendous source of pride for the residents of Weeksville. Entering this building as a student meant the beginning of a journey denied to most Colored people—a journey to a better future. Junius Morel, the principal of the school, enjoyed a national reputation as a writer and understood better than anyone the kind of opportunity a good education could provide. In addition, his role as a member of The Committee of Thirteen—an influential group of Colored New Yorkers who represented the Black population in matters of importance, added to his prestige. Junius appreciated how his education made all of his achievements possible. Often, Principal Morel reflected on each of his various roles of leader, writer, and educator, and always came to the same conclusion: the simple but essential task of teaching was his most important work.

Principal Morel often walked the halls, remembering past students who went on to bigger and better things. He passed a framed essay, mounted in a prominent position on the wall and remembered the author. *John Sampson, a most remarkable German child. What a marvelous piece about the founding principles of the United States. So hard to imagine a White boy appreciating the irony of the concepts of freedom and liberty within a society based, at least in part, on slavery. This is one White man who will make a difference.* He smiled as he continued his tour.

Other exceptional essays written by Colored students outnumbered those penned by Whites, but the disparity in numbers simply reflected the racial balance of the school. These essays represented public proof of the high standards at Colored School No. 2, which ensured that the children of Weeksville would be literate—reason alone to believe the next generation would be more prosperous than the last.

Junius struggled with the issue of educational segregation. He thought, *Is it possible for Whites and Blacks to learn together with equal treatment?* This was the case at Colored School No. 2, but under White control, Blacks would not receive equal treatment. *Perhaps being separate, but equal, like the community of Weeksville, would be a better option?* The principal's mind started to drift as he considered this basic question yet again. The knock on his door brought him back to matters of the day. Esther Washington wished to speak with him about a potential new enrollment.

Junius greeted his guest. "Esther, how are you? How are things in your husband's shop? I hope he's doing well."

"Yes, everything is fine, Mr. Morel. Thank you for asking. How are things at the school?"

"We're getting ready for the start of another year. Busy as always, but how can I help you, Mrs. Washington?"

"I took in a child over the summer from the refugee camp. The one found with his dead mother in the camp after the riots. He caused some trouble a few months back, but he's settled down and should be in school. I'm guess'n you might know 'bout him."

"Yes, Esther, my understanding, however, is that he hasn't settled down yet. I don't need problems like that at the school. Are you sure he's calm enough? Is he ready to be a student?"

"I think so, but he's still high-strung. Seems younger than he is. He's going on thirteen."

"Let's chat with him. Is he outside?"

"Yes."

"Please bring him in."

Vent walked into the principal's office wearing some of Horace's old clothes. Esther did her best to shorten and tighten both the pants and shirt, but Vent still swam in the outfit. He took the empty seat next to Miss Esther. Principal Morel smiled at his potential new student and opened with, "I understand your first name is Venture, an unusual name. What is your last name?"

Venture didn't answer and didn't raise his head.

"Venture, what is your last name?" the principal repeated.

Esther decided to intervene. "Vent, Principal Morel is a good man and I want you to raise your head, look at him, and answer his questions. Tell him your last name."

"My mama said it didn't matter, just the name of the folks who used to own us as property."

Esther took Vent's trembling hands into her own and counseled him. "Vent—that ain't no way to speak to Principal Morel. He is an important man in Weeksville. Now tell him your last name."

"Simmons."

The principal smiled. "Fine. Venture Simmons. Will this be your first time as a student in school?"

Vent couldn't believe this man had asked another question and he kept his head lowered. He offered no response.

Esther Washington whispered, "Vent, please answer all the questions, ain't gonna be so many more. Principal Morel is a good man."

The principal repeated his question. "Venture, will this be your first time in school?"

"Yes, but Mama taught me how to read and write. Math I just always understood."

"Venture, nobody naturally knows math. What do you mean by that?" the principal asked.

"Always could add, subtract, multiply, and divide for as long as I can remember."

"Vent, is it?"

"Yes."

"If I had a hundred apples and I needed to give them equally to twenty people, how many apples would I give each person?"

Vent answered without hesitation, "Five."

"Excellent!"

The approval from the principal, along with the introduction of one of Vent's biggest interests, mathematics, cracked the boy's armor ever so slightly. The principal offered a second, more difficult question. "If it takes six apples to make a pie, how many pies can you make with ninety-five apples? I'll give you a piece of paper to work on this one." The principal reached for a sheet of paper from the corner of his desk.

"Don't need no paper. You could make fifteen pies of the regular size you want, and one smaller one with the leftover five apples, which would be just right for someone my size," Vent offered with both a smile and a giggle, because his mama taught him a long time ago that any statement about his small size would be considered funny. Vent never attempted a joke before as far as Esther understood. *What a surprise*, she thought. *Maybe school will be good for him.*

"I think Vent will do just fine in school, Mrs. Washington! Welcome to Colored School No. 2, Vent! You start on Monday."

The sound of a whip coming from the street disturbed the feel-good moment, and Vent rushed into the corner and curled up in a ball. He repeated his mantra, "I'll get them all, they killed Mama," and then started to count. "Five, ten, fifteen, twenty…"

Esther rushed over to check on Vent. "Ain't nothing to worry about outside. Everything is fine. The school is a safe place. Principal Morel is a good man. No one out there trying to hurt you, Vent."

Vent's eyes rolled back in his head. "Gonna kill them all. They killed Mama. Gonna kill them all. Fifteen, thirty, forty-five, sixty…"

Esther pulled up a chair and sat as close to Vent as possible. She knew he didn't want to be touched, but felt better when close to someone who cared. They sat together as Vent continued his mumbling rant.

Junius Morel got up from his desk, shrugged his shoulders, and walked toward Vent, but stopped when he saw the child tense up. He directed his comments to Esther. "He is a remarkable child, but he still needs to adjust a bit more—Monday might be too soon. Give him some time. I'm going to leave the two of you here in my office so I can prepare one of the classrooms for a meeting tonight. Take all of the time you need."

"Thank you so much, Mr. Morel, but don't give up on this boy. He'll be a good student. I promise you, he'll be okay."

"Don't worry. I hope to welcome him into the school in the near future, but first he needs to be ready. Let's give him time. Good day, Mrs. Washington. Good day, Vent."

The principal stopped by his bookcase on the way out of his office and searched the top shelf for a few moments before pulling out a book. "Here, encourage him to read this math book. I'll leave it on my desk. Also, please remind your husband about my meeting tonight at the school for the visitors in the camp."

"You mean the Fort Sumter folks?"

Principal Morel didn't much like the name given to the camp, but in the interest of clarity, he responded, "Yes, Fort Sumter."

"I'll let him know, Principal Morel. I'm sure he'll do his best to be there. Thank you for the book and your time."

"Good day, Mrs. Washington, and Venture, please enjoy the book."

Esther and Vent sat for another fifteen minutes in the principal's office. As suddenly as it began, it ended—Vent stopped his chant, stood up, and sat at the principal's desk. He held the book up to the sunlight and admired the way the light passed through the thin sheets of paper. One page, in particular drew his attention, and he smiled. Another page made him laugh. He started to write on the blank piece of paper the principal had left behind, tucked the sheet into the book when finished, and placed the book on the principal's desk.

"Let's go home, Miss Esther."

"Vent, you can take the book with you. The principal wanted you to read it."

"All done, Miss Esther. Let's go home."

Vent headed out of the office with a bounce in his walk and a smile on his face. Then the crack of a whip from a passing horse carriage triggered another bad episode and Vent ran home to the safety of either his tree or closet. Esther followed and pondered the same questions she'd asked herself since meeting Vent weeks before. *What happened to this boy? At least now I know his last name, but what made him like this?* Esther wondered if she would ever get answers because Vent refused to talk about what had happened, and appeared downright scary when he repeated his endless threats of retaliation for the total loss of his family. *Who knows, maybe he had brothers and sisters as well. What am I going to do with this boy?* The question, simple, but the answer, complex.

Principal Morel returned to his office about an hour later, found the book still on his desk and assumed Vent was too upset to take an interest—not so unexpected—but then took note of the paper inserted at the end of the book. He removed the sheet and realized that Vent submitted his first homework assignment. The paper contained answers to a series of ten questions, which involved the kind of mathematics with which some of Principal Morel's most advanced students might struggle. *What a remarkable, but troubled boy*, the principal thought to himself. *I'll be sure to check on him over the next few weeks.*

Chapter 8

The Meeting

"Is this the place for the Fort Sumter folks?" the first guest asked. Junius Morel forced a smile and decided not to object to the characterization of the meeting, "Yes, please join us." The town's temporary guests began to stream into the largest classroom in the school for an orientation of sorts about the town of Weeksville. The final guests to arrive included the Brown brothers, Ezra and Moses, and the recent college graduate, Edward Heath. Junius hoped to convince at least a few of the guests to remain in Weeksville, and given his current need for a teacher at the school, he hoped Edward Heath, in particular, would stay.

The guests enjoyed the lemonade and cookies Principal Morel provided for the occasion, but since people didn't understand what to expect at the meeting, the small talk was subdued, except for the two brothers.

Moses whispered a question to his older brother, but Ezra didn't consider it worthy of a response. "Moses, why you ask me somethin' like that? Not sure you got anything in your head other than stupid. Sit down and try not to talk. Okay, Moses?"

Moses shrugged his shoulders at his brother, who often called him stupid, but rarely disparaged him in public. *You better be careful Ezra, because I'll go off on my own—I don't need you. As a matter of fact, you need me more than I need you.* Moses smiled as he finished his thought, but wondered if he would ever deliver that message out loud. Noting his brother's smile, Ezra mumbled under his breath, "Damn fool, doesn't even understand when he's being insulted."

Junius Morel took his position at the front of the room and reviewed his unusual class. Several of the larger men, including Thomas Washington, the shoemaker, along with the Brown brothers, opted to stand in the back because the school's small seats and desks were not designed for students with their dimensions. A light breeze cooled the room and the shimmering light from the lanterns struggled to provide adequate lighting for the large space—Junius checked the level of oil one last time, and called the group to attention.

"Good evening, everyone. Thank you so much for coming tonight. I thought it would be fitting to bring all of our newcomers together to learn a little about Weeksville. I'll start off, but any of our townsfolk who would like to add to my description can say anything they think is appropriate. Please pardon my lecture style, but as you can see from our surroundings and the nameplate on my desk, I am the principal of the school, and lecturing is something with which I am familiar."

A few people chuckled, but many didn't get the joke, and Junius wondered if he'd selected the appropriate level of vocabulary for his audience. Most of the Weeksville residents were illiterate, and many of those in attendance were likely much the same. Junius realized he was pandering to the educated Edward Heath, and made a mental note to tone down his language as he moved forward. The principal continued.

"In 1835, a Colored man by the name of Henry C. Thompson bought thirty-two plots of land from John Lefferts south of the new Long Island Rail Road line. The purchase of this land by a Colored person, so close to the railroad, made it the perfect location to build a Black community. One of the first few people who bought a parcel was James Weeks, followed by his brother Cesar, and the properties around their homes began to be called Weeksville. The idea of Weeksville is simple—it is a haven for Colored people. Any Black man is welcome to buy land, which will entitle him to vote. That's right, we're building a voting, political base here, and we encourage all like-minded Colored people to join our ranks."

Junius paused for a second to check if anyone had any questions. Moses raised his hand. Ezra nudged him with his elbow to encourage him to shut up, but little brother would not be deterred.

"Mr. Morel. This is Moses Brown. How much the land cost?"

Ezra couldn't stay silent, "Moses why you askin' this man such a stupid question? You ain't got no money. Put your hand down."

"Oh yeah? My money is more than you think, Ezra, and we'll see who's stupid."

Junius needed to regain control of his group. "Gentlemen, perhaps you can finish this discussion after the meeting, but modest lots with a low cost are available, and as long as you spend at least $250, you will be able to vote."

Moses responded, "Thank you. I'll see what I can do."

Ezra whispered to his brother, "You'll see what you can do? What money you got? Silly fool."

Moses responded, "I'm not wasting all my money on 'malgamation house girls and I'll show you who's stupid." *Yes, I said it and it felt good!* A more confident Moses returned his attention to the host, and Ezra didn't understand what to make of his last remark.

"Let me continue. Weeksville sits atop a hill with a pronounced physical separation from surrounding areas. The first and foremost goal of the town is to define ourselves as a community of free people where those fleeing slavery can feel safe and protected. Beyond that we wish to assert our rights through voting and provide as many economic opportunities as possible for Colored people. Our last major goal is to oppose all of the societies who would force free Blacks to leave our country and go to places like Liberia in Africa."

Junius spotted Edward Heath waving his hand in the back of the room. The principal acknowledged the question with a nod and Edward Heath rose to speak.

"Mr. Morel, thank you so much for inviting us all here this evening. As I told you a few weeks ago, I know of you and your position on this matter from a number of your published articles, but isn't it true that one of these societies you say the town opposes is based in Weeksville? Isn't the home of the African Civilization Society right here in this town?"

"Why yes, young man, you are correct—an upsetting development, to be sure. They opened their doors about five years ago."

"So isn't it fair to say that consensus on this point of organized migration may not be as complete as you imply? As a matter of fact, I myself am considering a move to Liberia."

Junius took a moment to process his disappointment. He had hoped this young man would share his views and perhaps stay on as an instructor at the school. The process of reflection did not take long, however, and Junius prepared himself for a scholarly debate with his young adversary as he responded, "Please tell us why you like the idea of organized emigration."

Edward Heath stood again, cleared his throat, and offered his argument. "Here in the United States, a few towns like Weeksville made an effort to separate themselves from the surrounding White communities out of a recognition that Black people will never be given a chance for a full and free life in this society. The problem is that when you leave Weeksville and board the Long Island Rail Road, you step off ten minutes later in a place where we are considered less than human…a place where we will never matter. Do you want to know what the Whites think of us? I carry this newspaper clipping from the *Brooklyn Eagle* around with me as a reminder. When our own Frederick Douglass suggested two years ago that Black men be given the right to fight for their country in return for citizenship, *The Eagle* wrote:

> Douglass is trying to get the Darkies to take a hand in the war. He says that the war is for slavery and to let the Blacks, with their sinewy arms, fight the battle. We can only put down insurrection, he adds, by putting down slavery. The gen'man of color don't take the hint. If there is any fighting to be done, Sambo, as a general thing, desires to be counted out. The genius of the Darkey is of a culinary and not a military character. He takes to waiting on tables, whitewashing, barbering, cooking, and other useful and honorable occupations as naturally as a duck to water but he has a wholesale dread of gunpowder."

Edward Heath paused for a moment to let the full impact of the horrible passage sink into the group. Much to Edward's surprise, the piece shocked only about half in attendance. Many seemed immune to the hurtful nature of the words. He continued, "If we send our educated Colored people to places like Liberia to act as cultural missionaries, we can lead the indigenous people economically, spiritually, and politically and build a place where we will all matter."

Moses turned to Ezra. "What he say, *indigeenus*? What that mean? I sure hope he didn't cuss out Mr. Morel. That boy better mind his manners." Ezra offered no answer to his brother, because half of the words used by the young man did, in fact, sound like a foreign language.

Junius Morel reflected for a moment and straightened his posture before offering his retort. "Excellent remarks, Mr. Heath, but let's go into some greater detail. First, I'll clarify a few of your points." Junius took a momentary break and offered a wink to Moses. "I believe some here tonight found a few of your terms to be confusing. When Mr. Heath says 'indigenous people,' he means the local tribes. So his plan is to join other educated men of color to go over and lead the local tribes in Liberia—I believe he said economically, spiritually, and politically. Am I correct, Mr. Heath?"

"Well, yes…that is what I intended to say," the young man responded, sensing a turn in momentum.

"Excellent. So let me ask you a question. No…let me ask the group a question. How many tribes do you think will welcome these educated Americans as their leaders? Even better, how many tribes do you think would even welcome them as regular members—forget about leadership positions?"

Thomas Washington raised his hand. "Not a one. Folks like you will go all the way over there and find out you're even less accepted there than you are here."

Junius embellished that point. "You're right, Mr. Washington. They were born there, their children were born there, and their parents died there. In other words—they have roots in Liberia. Who are we to tell them what to do? Where were we born?"

The whole crowd chanted, "America."

"Where were our children born?

"America!"

"Where did our parents die?"

"America!"

"Where should we have a voice to say what to do?"

"America!"

"That's the opposing argument, Mr. Heath, and by the way, I also carry around a little piece of paper with me, but mine states the original motivation for the founding of the first emigration society, the American Colonization Society. Let me tell you why they supported emigration to places like Liberia:

Freed Blacks must leave because they present a 'perpetual excitement' to those still in slavery and encourage unrest and runaways. Freed Blacks can never be allowed to mix with the White race. Blacks are mentally inferior and prone to criminal activity and will never be good citizens, and finally, Blacks will take jobs from working-class Whites in the North."

The principal scanned the room and took note of all of the heads nodding up and down affirming his position. He concluded his thoughts. "This is why they want us out. They don't care about leading the 'indigenous' people spiritually or any other way. This is our home as much as it is theirs and I'll have you know, Mr. Heath, one day in the not-so-distant future, Blacks will matter. We're not going anywhere."

The assembled group cheered Junius Morel's animated delivery of his compelling argument. Moses, in particular, enjoyed the back-and-forth dialogue as much as the excited chants of "America" and turned to Ezra as he said, "Mr. Morel is one great man!" His brother responded, "For once, you got somethin' right!" The brothers shared a laugh.

Junius Morel gave his guests a moment to calm down before addressing Edward Heath one last time. "I hope we changed your mind with regard to emigration and, if so, there is a place for you in Weeksville; but if not, I don't think you convinced anyone in this room of the strength of your position. Now, I would like a few of the other townspeople to come up and speak."

As the remaining speakers organized their thoughts and delivered their remarks, one man in the back of the room had become convinced to emigrate to Liberia, but not because of the young scholar's argument. This man, who had been the occupant of a boardinghouse in the Five Points section of New York, and who went by the name of Mackie Johnson, needed to find some place to relocate. What he witnessed a few weeks earlier at the boardinghouse during the Draft Riots was unconscionable, and what happened to the little boy who crawled out of the crate was something he would never forget. The boy would have been better off dying with the rest of his family. While Liberia might not be the perfect place, according to Junius Morel, Mackie was certain he could convince some tribe in Africa to take him. He didn't need to be in charge of a thing and didn't need to convert anyone into anything; he just needed to be safe and more than anything, needed to get away. *With or without you, Mr. Heath, I am off to Liberia.*

Chapter 9

Berean Baptist Church

"Hard to believe Vent has been with us for two years," Esther Washington mentioned to her husband, Thomas, as they made their way to services at the Berean Baptist Church. "I'm not his natural mother, but he's my boy now. The war is over. Things are getting back to normal, and Vent needs some normal too. I believe he'll never be right until he tells us what happened during the riots, 'cause we can only help him if he tells us. Thought he might tell Minister Sundick, but he hardly ever goes to services."

"Vent doesn't talk to anybody 'cept the family and Mr. Morel. Thank God he's enrolled in school. Junius says he reads and writes okay, but his math is out of this world. Maybe his numbers will help him get a job one day. One thing, though, he'll need to come out of the damn tree and talk to a few people for anythin' good to happen."

"You right, Thomas, but I guess God has a plan. Just wish he'd get goin' with it!"

Minister Sundick stood at the door with his wife Joanna and greeted all of the worshippers as they arrived. The forever-bickering Brown brothers—often heard before they were seen—approached.

"What you say, Ezra? If I'm so stupid, how come I'm the one who saved my money and bought us property? Because of my money, I'm the one who can vote."

"Damn fool, you don't even understand who's running."

"Neither do you, so what *you* talkin' about? I just need to spend some time to find out what each of the candidates is sayin' is all, and I'll figure out what to do."

"What *you* talkin' about? You'll vote Republican 'cause it's them got us free. Unless, of course, you want a few dollars to vote the other way!"

"I'm not selling my vote, Ezra. I'm an honest, God-fearing man."

The minister waited for a logical moment to interrupt. "Yes, Moses, you are an honest, God-fearing man. Why don't you both go inside and settle down? The service is starting soon."

The Brown brothers advanced to some other topic of disagreement as they entered the church and took their customary seats in the third pew.

The five-person choir began to perform a hymn called "Amazing Grace," which had spread from the South to the North as a result of the Civil War. The enchanting hymn, brought to life by the entire congregation along with the choir, provided a wonderful beginning to the service. After some time and a few more hymns, Reverend Sundick delivered God's message.

Sundick's fiery oratory roused the crowd, as always, and he made sure everyone appreciated the progress of the last few years. A few indirect references to the role of the Berean Baptist Church in the Underground Railroad gave the crowd a sense of purpose and fulfillment. Some smiled as he still spoke of the church's role in secret terms. The minister continued as he stated with tremendous pride, "We can all walk the streets without fear of a slave catcher invoking the Fugitive Slave Act and transporting us down South into a life of slavery." His most important message, however, celebrated the end of the war and a future filled with the potential for respect and prosperity.

Moses and Ezra loved hearing the minister preach and took a moment to survey their fellow worshippers and neighbors. Jobs in downtown Brooklyn as laborers gave them sufficient income, and Moses's surprise savings made them property owners for the first time in their lives. The Brown brothers lived a life they didn't think possible a few short years ago. In a rare moment of camaraderie, Moses turned to his brother and hugged him. Ezra accepted the hug, but cautioned Moses about, "Acting like such a stupid fool in public."

After the Invitation, during which Minister Sundick invited all the parishioners to accept Christ in their heart, join the church, or rededicate their life to God and Christ, the service neared the end. Sundick proceeded to acknowledgements and housekeeping issues, and offered prayers for a few ill members of the congregation. Next—a dedication to a longtime member, Henry Miller, who had passed away the previous week at the age of ninety.

"At the end, we sat together every few days to pray and prepare, and Henry shared with me the unexpected surprise of his life—living to see the end of slavery in the United States. After ending in most of the civilized world years ago, the terrible institution of slavery did come to an end in America with Henry present—he thanked the Lord for giving him the ability to bear witness to this momentous event. Old Henry said, 'Minister, I'm ready to meet my maker. I'm moving on fulfilled and ready for all the afterlife has to offer.'"

The minister announced his final piece of business before wishing everyone a blessed day. "My friends and neighbors, I received a letter from someone we met two years ago by the name of Edward Heath, a refugee who lived in the camp after the riots. Mr. Heath sent us greetings from Liberia. This is what he wrote:

To the Wonderful People of Weeksville,

This is Edward Heath, the young man who spent a few months with you back in 1863. I'll never forget the way the people of Weeksville welcomed me. My time assisting Principal Morel at the school and worshipping at the Berean Baptist Church were the highlights of my stay. Principal Morel was disappointed with my decision to leave, but it was something I needed to do. I realized within moments of my arrival, his assumptions about Liberia were correct, but we are persevering, and doing our best to make this a decent place to live.

I never thought I would miss New York winters, but the eternal summer in Liberia is only disturbed by months of rain. Many other people came from America and we all tend to stay together. I remember the good fun you all had with my reference to the 'indigenous' people or local tribes. Again, Junius Morel proved to be correct—they do not accept us as their legitimate leaders and fight us at every turn.

I made a commitment to play a part in giving Liberia a chance to succeed, but I do long for the day I return home, with my preferred destination being lovely Weeksville.

By the way, Mackie Johnson, who shared a tent with me in the camp, also sends his regards. You may not remember him so well because he kept to himself, but he too is most appreciative of the help he received while a resident of Fort Sumter.

Greetings and Godspeed,

Edward Heath"

Esther turned to her husband and whispered, "Fine young man—sounds like he misses home and I do hope he finds his way back here one day. A lot of the pretty young girls in town would like to settle down with him." Thomas snorted and his head jerked back when Esther elbowed him in the side. "Thomas, Thomas, wake up, I'm talking to you. The minister is talking to you. God is talking to you!" The groggy worshipper took a moment to gather himself and told his wife, "Do me a favor and tell them all I'm busy right now." He then put his head down and returned to his dreams.

CHAPTER 10

Rules to Live By

CLANG! CLANG! CLANG! Principal Morel kept his hand on the drawstring for the school bell, as he gave the children time to reenter the building after recess. Venture crawled down from the top of the fence, which separated the back of the schoolyard from the neighboring property. Most of the other children finished playing games, sharing final laughs, and headed inside. A few stragglers needed more encouragement—Clang! Clang! Everyone started heading upstairs for reading classes.

Principal Morel addressed the students, "Hold on, children. We're doing something different today. We are switching the order of the subjects. Today, we will cover math before reading, so let's separate into our math levels. The advanced group, go to Room 1, the middle group to Room 4, and the beginners, please report to our biggest classroom, Room 6."

Vent started to perspire and rocked back and forth. Principal Morel walked to his side.

"What's the matter, Vent?"

"We don't do math after recess. We do reading. The first group goes to Room 6, and everyone else in the second group goes to Room 4."

"Not today, Vent. I'm changing things today."

"No. We do reading after recess. We do math after reading—always."

Principal Morel chose to ignore Venture's last comment and addressed the students as a whole once more. "Students, please follow my instructions. Mr. Simmons, come to my office."

Vent focused on the floor as he followed Principal Morel to his office. His rocking became more noticeable—Junius thought he might be on the verge of one of his counting/mumbling fits, which had become rare of late.

"Vent, this is your second year in school, and I understand math normally follows reading, but today, I changed the order for a reason."

"Can't change the order, Principal Morel. We do reading first, math next. I'm in the second group with reading and the first group with math."

"Venture, let's talk about something else for a moment. Tell me about your mornings. What do you do first when you wake up?"

"I put my mat away in the corner."

"What comes next?"

"I wash up and dress."

"Do you dress in a certain order?"

"Yes."

"Would you please tell me how?"

"Bottom to top, first inside, then outside. My shoes come last."

"Interesting. Vent, give me an example of this morning."

"Put my socks on first, my underwear second, pants, third, and my shirt, fourth. My shoes come last."

"Do you always dress in the same order, Vent?"

"Yes."

"Do you understand why?"

"'Cause that's how I do it."

"Vent, you're fourteen years old and you'll be in school for another three or four years. Do you want a job when you finish school?"

"Yes, sir. I want money to give Miss Esther."

"Excellent answer. So this is why I changed the order today."

Vent stared at the principal as if scrutinizing his eyes would help him understand. The rule about taking turns in conversations demanded he say something, but he didn't understand how changing the order of subjects would help him with a job. After a prolonged silence, the principal clarified. "Vent, when you work at a job, you might find out most mornings you do one thing and most afternoons you do something else, but when you start working, you won't be the boss, and the boss is the person who gets to decide the order. Understand, Vent?"

"Yes, but why would he change the order? One thing goes first, the next thing, second."

"Not always, Vent, but my point is if you don't do whatever the boss says, in the order he says it, you'll lose your job and have no money to give Miss Esther. At work, you must do what your boss says. Who do you think the boss is at school?"

"Principal Morel."

"So, what could I have done before when you refused to do what I said in the order I demanded?"

"Made me lose my job as a student."

"Yes, now you understand. No one can tell you how to dress, Vent, because dressing is a personal thing. You want to dress bottom to top, inside to outside, shoes last—that's your business, but at school or at work, you must to listen to the boss. Understand?"

"Yes, sir, should I write this rule down with the other important ones?"

"Yes, Vent. I'll give you a minute to write the rule at the end of your list. When you're ready, read the new rule back to me."

Vent opened his notebook and turned to the back and added his most recent rule. "Do you want me to read only the one new one or the others also?"

"Please read my rules, along with the ones provided by your mother and Miss Esther."

Venture cleared his throat and started to recite his social rules, beginning with the ones Principal Morel gave him.

"People don't like people who keep their head down and they also don't like people who always stare in their eyes, so I should try to do a little of each, but not too much of either."

"Good. Keep going," the principal offered.

"If someone says something and other people laugh, it could be a joke, and as long as they aren't talking about me, I should laugh too. If they're talking about Vent—they're making fun of me."

"Excellent. Tell me about what you learned today."

"At work or at school I must do what the boss says in the order he says it, or I might lose my job and have no money for Miss Esther."

"That's correct, now tell me the rules your mother and Miss Esther taught you."

"My mama taught me if I say something about how small I am to people I know, they might laugh and think it's a joke. If they say it to me, they making fun. My mama also taught me, family takes care of family."

"How about Miss Esther?"

"Miss Esther taught me I should only fight for the family if one of them gets hurt and asks me to help. She said sometimes I don't understand things right."

"Good job, Vent. I think you learned an important new lesson today, so go on ahead to math class with the rest of the students."

"One more rule. Principal Morel—learned this one long time ago, but you never asked me about it. This one I learned myself."

The principal took the notebook from Venture and read the last rule out loud to his student. "Any animal that eats his own kind is the devil, and got to be killed." The principal smiled and took note of Venture, who nodded his head up and down—affirming this final, self-taught rule. The principal, at a loss for words, took a moment and said, "Vent, we're going to come back to this rule at a later time. I'm not sure what you mean, but we'll talk about this rule another day."

"Principal Morel, I'll do what you say because at school you the boss, but you got to know, the last rule is the most important one."

Principal Morel appreciated long ago the many contradictions that were all rolled up in Venture Simmons—socially awkward, but mathematically brilliant; undersized, but physically gifted; slow to make friends, but deeply committed to the few he possessed. Junius found these paradoxes to be both fascinating and confusing, but this most recent revelation of Venture's one personally developed rule was something altogether different…it was alarming, and all of the possible interpretations—equally frightening.

Part II

Brooklyn – 1869

Chapter 11

Monkey Boy

"Moses, why you keep bringin' him 'round? I stay as far away as I can. Crazy don't go away—may hide for a spell, but always comes back. He's pure crazy."

"No, he's all right, Ezra, and he ain't no boy no more—he's a grown man. We help each other. I talk to him 'bout not killing people and he's teachin' me to read and write."

"Not killing people. I told you, he's—"

"Only jokin', Ezra. He calmed down a lot. Here he is now."

Moses spotted Vent running full speed with his shirt off from the window of his small house. The boy, a shade under five feet tall with extraordinary muscular development, had the longest arms Moses had ever seen. "Ezra, come to the window. Wait until he gets to the fence."

Vent jumped headfirst over the fence, landing in a smooth somersault, barely breaking his stride. Given Vent's athleticism, Moses encouraged him to join the Weeksville Unknowns, the local Colored base ball team, but Vent never wanted to be in any public place with lots of people gawking at his small size. He arrived at the house and opened the door without knocking.

"Hey, Moses, hey, Ezra."

Moses responded first. "Damn, I never seen anyone run and jump like you. You must be trainin' for something."

"No. I just like to stretch my *long* legs every once in a while." Vent chuckled as he offered one of his well-rehearsed jokes.

Moses turned to Ezra and said, "Vent even got a sense of humor. No reason to be afraid of him no more."

"I'm not afraid of some tiny little boy."

Moses laughed as he asked the obvious question, "So why you hidin' in the corner?"

Ezra bumped into a chair as he hurried out of the house exclaiming, "Never you mind, I got chores to do!" Vent noticed Moses's laugh, so he offered a brief giggle of his own.

Vent and Moses sat down and started talking about Vent's new job and the latest developments in the neighborhood. Moses, now an uncle of sorts to Vent, thought back to the day, right before he started school in 1863, when he helped Vent put things in perspective.

Vent had run into Moses when he exited the general store with supplies for Miss Esther. Instinctively, he started to move away from his nemesis as fast as possible, but Moses called out, "Venture, stop." Vent didn't want another confrontation with Moses, and kept moving in the other direction, but his bulky bags slowed him down. Moses caught up to him and grabbed him on the back of the shoulder.

Vent protested, "Don't touch me. I didn't steal these things. You got no right to stop me. Let me go."

"Never said you stole anything, I want to talk," Moses responded.

Venture considered running, but felt trapped. He turned to Moses. "Talk? I think you want to tie me up again and walk me around town."

"No. I didn't even want to tie you up when I did. You still plannin' to kill me and everybody else?"

Vent didn't answer, but lifted his head up and offered a furious glare.

"Yup, what I thought—you can't keep threatening people. Ezra says I'm stupid, but even I understand you can't keep doin' this. I tried to help you and I think I did. Seems like you're doin' all right with Miss Esther."

Vent didn't want to answer, but offered, "Yeah…she treats me good, but why do you care?"

"Because you sayin' all of this 'I'm going to kill everyone stuff.' If you knew who killed your mother, I could understand, but you sayin' you want to kill everyone no matter what they did or didn't do, and lots of us only tryin' to help."

"You helped me when you held me to the ground? You helped me when you tied me up and walked me into town like a slave? Don't need no more help from you."

"What would have happened to you if I didn't bring you into town? Would you be livin' with a roof over your head? Would Miss Esther be takin' care of you? Would you be walkin' down this here street like a normal person buying supplies from the store? I think the answer is *no* to all those things. I'm not even sure you'd still be alive."

When Moses started his last thought, Vent couldn't wait for him to stop talking, so he could say something else, anything else, to further make his point, but by the time Moses finished delivering his message, Vent started to realize Moses was right.

Venture didn't say anything, but lifted his head and stared at Moses, who didn't turn away because a question mark replaced the typical Vent glare. After a few moments of silence, Vent shuffled his feet and said, "Mr. Moses, sorry about the bite, and tell your brother, I'm sorry 'bout the hatchet."

"Now you're talkin' the right way, Vent. Thanks for the 'pology, but you can tell Ezra yourself. I still got one last thing to tell you and like anything I say, you can listen or not, but I'm gonna tell you anyway. Okay?"

Vent nodded.

"You don't want to talk 'bout what happened to you. I understand that… lots of us don't like to talk 'bout what happened during the Draft Riots, but some folks think when you talk 'bout bad things, somehow they get better. This is why everyone keeps askin' you. Thing is, all the bad stuff is in the past—bad then, and still bad now. My brother, Ezra, keeps sayin' I'm the stupid one, but to me, thinkin' and talkin' about old bad stuff, just makes you keep feelin' bad. It's all right to keep bad stuff to yourself, but you got to stop thinkin' 'bout it all the time, 'cause you'll miss out on some good stuff that could come your way. Now that a big mouthful for me—almost made my head spin. I hope you got my meaning."

Moses's speech changed Vent for the better. He still slept in the closet and continued his counting rituals, but the general threats stopped. Venture's improved public demeanor enabled him to become more accepted in the neighborhood from that point forward. The speech also marked the beginning of what would become a great friendship.

⊶⚬ ⚬⊷

Horace graduated at the top of his class at the Colored School No. 2. He set his sights on an office job, and soon became an office assistant for a construction company in downtown Brooklyn. When he learned the company needed people comfortable climbing beams on high floors, he recommended Vent and the two brothers began working together in early 1869. In the morning, they waved goodbye to Miss Esther and made the short walk to the Long Island Rail Road. Horace also took the train home at the end of the day, but Vent needed his exercise and ran an obstacle course of sorts back to Weeksville, involving sprints, tree climbing, several leaps over fences—both high and low—and some tumbling, just for show. People loved cheering him on as he traveled the three miles from downtown Brooklyn to Weeksville.

Vent became a legend on the job site, but hated the nickname his Irish co-workers gave him: Monkey Boy. Horace and Vent were the only two Blacks at the site, but most of the Irish claimed one and a half Blacks worked the job, referring either to Vent's size or light color. Others said the job was mostly Irish, but they had one Black and one monkey. Vent didn't like either characterization, but understood he needed to bite his tongue.

"Vent, I need you up on the fourth floor to guide the beams into place," the supervisor, Harold Reems, instructed.

All of the Irishmen stopped working, because no matter how much they hated the Blacks, watching Monkey Boy climb was something to behold. Vent opted for a flashy start to his climb, and decided to forgo the use of the ladder to reach the first horizontal beam. He started with a sprint and jumped with his long outstretched arms in order to grasp the first girder. The force of his movement caused him to swing back and forth a few times—something Vent enjoyed. Next, he hoisted himself onto the connecting vertical beam, and started scaling the vertical columns. Once he arrived on the fourth floor, the Irish applauded. They all started chanting "Monkey Boy! Monkey Boy!" Vent could have done without that.

Venture Simmons was no longer the scared but furious boy who jumped out of a crate wielding a hatchet in Fort Sumter. The Washingtons had become his immediate family, Moses, a trusted uncle, and Weeksville, his home. Vent's employment enabled him to fully utilize his physical gifts as well as his facility with numbers, as he often helped the office staff estimate the quantities of materials required for each job. Moses was right—when Vent stopped obsessing over bad stuff in the past, some good stuff came his way. He learned to direct his anger and his new self-control was confirmed each night, when he pulled his mat into the closet and began his mumbling and counting. Vent's new mantra supported the fact he was no longer after *everyone*, but he still pledged to kill the specific bastards who murdered his mama.

Edward Returns

THE DUO ARRIVED at the site of the old Fort Sumter and tried to remember the location of their tent six years earlier. Roads had sprouted up in the intervening years, which made pinpointing the exact spot where the two men resided a difficult task. The sense of Weeksville as a town resting on a hilltop was nothing more than a memory—Edward Heath and Mackie Johnson barely recognized a thing. New roads dissected the land, connecting numerous properties and structures, which hadn't existed a few short years earlier. The most impressive aspect of the change, however, appeared to be a general consensus that this was only the beginning.

Edward and Mackie had become a team during their time at Fort Sumter and remained close throughout their years in Liberia. Edward was the brains, and Mackie, the brawn—both skills of the utmost importance during their time in Monrovia, the capital of Liberia. The intelligence of Edward put them in good stead with the transplanted Black elite from the states, and Mackie's muscle kept them safe from any number of perils, which included violence from the local tribes. Edward thought of Liberia in the past tense. He hoped that Weeksville would become both his present and future. Mackie, always by Edward's side, remained confident his association with the brilliant Edward Heath would continue to be a smart move.

The two men found a place to stay as boarders in the home of a widow not far from the heart of the old Weeksville—close to both Colored School No. 2 and the Berean Baptist Church. They decided to pay their respects and check in with a few of the folks who had treated them so well years before. As they walked the short distance to the church, they passed the field where the

Weeksville Unknowns, the local base ball team, practiced. Base ball had caught on around the time they left for Liberia, and the men paused to observe the team going through their drills. Mackie was intrigued with the sport and told Edward he would catch up with him later.

Edward rounded the corner and glanced in the direction of the Berean Baptist Church. "My God. The church must've burned to the ground," he mumbled. Edward was surprised when he received a response to his solitary observation.

"Yes, back in 1865. Folks are worshipping where they can now, but the re-building is already underway. My name is Esther Washington and I remember you well. All of the young ladies took a fancy to you a few years back. How you been, Mr. Heath?"

"Very well, thank you. How remarkable for you to remember me after all of these years! How are you, Mrs. Washington?"

"Fine as well. Folks still talkin' 'bout how you and Junius went back and forth in the meeting for the Fort Sumter folks at the school. Nobody can outtalk Principal Morel, but we reckon you came about as close as anyone so far. 'Scuse me one moment." Esther raised her hands to her mouth and formed a cone to better project her voice. "Vent, over here. Come on over and say hello to Mr. Heath. He met you long time ago."

Edward remembered the slight boy and the story of him jumping out of the crate—he had grown a bit, added lots of muscle, but was still abnormally short. His arms, however, stretched to his knees. Edward figured Vent to be about eighteen years old, but if not for the slight stubble on his face, he might have passed for thirteen. Vent sprinted over with an athletic burst as he dashed in front of a passing carriage, drawing the ire of the driver.

"Damn foolish boy, are you trying to get yourself killed!" the driver yelled.

Vent paid him no mind and Esther shrugged her shoulders as she made the introductions, "Vent, this here is Edward Heath. You met him years ago when you both came to Weeksville in '63."

Edward held out his hand, but Vent left him hanging. Miss Esther took charge. "Vent, shake Mr. Heath's hand, he's an old friend." Vent obliged and sur-prised Edward with the strength of his grip. *My God! This boy is all muscle*, Edward thought. Vent caught a glimpse of Mackie Johnson turning the corner. Mackie spotted him at the same time and stopped in his tracks. The chance encounter triggered a mumbling and counting episode—Vent started with eights. "Eight, sixteen, twenty-four, thirty-two, forty…"

These attacks had become few and far between over the last several years and Esther said her goodbyes in order to get Vent back home. Edward headed for the Colored School No. 2, and Mackie Johnson headed back to his rented room to think. *How could he still be in this town? What am I going to do?*

⊷▬◉ ◉▬⊶

"Junius, how are you? I wanted to come and say hello as soon as I arrived."

Principal Morel smiled as he greeted his old friend with a hug. Their frequent exchange of correspondence made discussions about Edward's Liberian experience unnecessary. The local tribes didn't accept the Americans. Junius wished, for Edward's sake, he'd been wrong on this point. The flawed plan to send transplanted Americans to a capital city in Africa named after a former U.S. president never had a chance for success—but Liberia was the topic of another day. Junius decided to update Edward on some important political changes closer to home. "Many developments since your departure, Edward. Voting rights for Colored folks should be the same as the Whites, without the requirement of $250 in property, within a year or two."

"Welcome news, my old friend. I'm surprised at how fast this happened."

"You may consider this fast, but let me tell you—long, hard work generated this result, and from my perspective, this is years overdue."

Edward didn't want to begin another debate with Junius Morel and responded, "I guess things seem fast, especially when you return from spending six years abroad."

"Excellent point, Edward. Things are booming in Brooklyn—we are the third-largest city in the country and construction on a massive bridge, which will span the East River, is about to begin. The bridge is being built by John A. Roebling and his son, Colonel Washington Roebling, who distinguished himself during the war. All of the political powers lined up to make this tremendous undertaking happen. The bridge is all the talk these days."

"How exciting, Junius! I can only imagine the scope of this project. Is this the largest bridge of this type that has ever been attempted?"

"The short answer is, yes, but Roebling built large suspension bridges in other parts of the country, so if anyone can accomplish such a feat, he is the man."

"What about all of the changes in Weeksville?" Edward asked.

"Most consider the changes to be progress and, in many respects, I agree—lots of new roads and buildings, but the flattening of the hills has permanently altered the character of the Weeksville you visited in '63. We've also had a large influx of Europeans—not the same percentage of Black ownership we had a few short years ago, but with suffrage for Colored males right around the corner, we will achieve political influence. I'm optimistic about that, my young friend."

"Superb news, Junius, but you may no longer be able to refer to me as your 'young friend.' I'm not as young as I used to be."

"Neither am I, Edward, and retirement looms for me in the not-so-distant future. If only there was someone to follow in my footsteps..." Both men laughed and shared a hug. Edward felt like he was home.

CHAPTER 13

Irishtown

THE POLICE SERGEANT continued his orientation tour with his new recruit and walked the blocks nestled next to the East River between Tillary Street and the Brooklyn Navy Yard—the part of Brooklyn referred to as Irishtown. He instructed the new officer on the basics of the neighborhood. "Goddamn Irish. All they do is drink and fight. We spend all our days locking up the Paddies."

"My father told me they're not all bad, though, sir. Lots of them started with me as officers."

"Sorry to say, John, I think your father became a little soft on the job. The damn Irish are all bad—I understand them better than anyone. The bosses think putting drunken criminals on the job will make things better? I don't think so, and I'll never trust the damn Paddies and neither should you. Most of the people we arrest are Irish. They're the scum of the earth—like this piece of shit over here."

A drunken man with urine-soaked pants gawked at the officers as he raised his head off the curb.

The sergeant continued, "What a poor fuck…thinks he's having a good day. Drunk before noon—some life, I tell you. His buddies would say he's 'pretty well over the bay.' Listen, you drunk bastard, move on!" Sergeant Herbert Anderson punctuated his sentence with a kick to the man's side and wiped his shoe with his handkerchief. "Better to step in shit than touch an Irishman. Lowest form of human being."

The sergeant's orientation ended as he bid the trainee farewell and headed back to his carriage. The young officer, happy his time with Sergeant Anderson had come to an end, reflected on his father's advice—the police department was filled with people who viewed policing in a way that wouldn't serve him, as well as others he should seek out as mentors. Anderson was in the first group, and John planned to meet with someone in the second group as his last stop for the day.

Herbert Anderson took note of several young Irishmen approaching his carriage and hoped they would do something—anything—that would give him cause for a confrontation. He glared at them, daring them to make eye contact. The sergeant's well-known reputation in the neighborhood made them all keep their heads down as they passed.

Ah, drunk and stupid as always, but spineless, that's something new, Anderson thought as he ducked into a small storefront bakery.

"Good afternoon, sergeant," offered the clerk behind the counter.

"Keep your good afternoons to yourself. Is my order ready?"

"Yes, sir. Here it is." The clerk handed Anderson a small pastry box, and the sergeant shook the box a few times to check the weight. "This better be the size cake I ordered or there'll be hell to pay. Make sure you tell Devlin—hell to pay, understand?"

"Yes, sir. The cake is the right size, sir. Not to worry."

Anderson nodded, handed the man a small rolled-up piece of paper, and headed out to his carriage. The clerk went to the back room and delivered the paper to John Devlin, one of the Whiskey Kings of Irishtown, who unrolled the paper and read out loud to his two associates, "Raid tonight at seven o'clock—Front Street distillery. Federal and local. Be ready."

Devlin barked instructions, but his men understood what to do with no additional clarification—all evidence of their illegal distillery on Front Street needed to be cleared out over the next five hours. Devlin's sweet poteen had become one of the most popular illegal brands in Irishtown, and as a result, he was among the richest men in the neighborhood—where whiskey was for drinking and water for washing.

Outside, Sergeant Anderson peeked at his cake, and flipped through the stack of bills, which did, in fact, appear to be the right size. He headed back to the station.

⋯▸▅ ▅◂⋯

John Singleton found the address a few minutes after leaving the sergeant's side and located the apartment toward the back of the first floor. No one responded to his knocks. *Should have been here by now,* John thought as he flipped open his pocket watch. After being on his feet all day, John took a seat on the small stool against the wall and glanced out the hallway window for something of interest, but his view was limited to the back of the adjacent building. *Where is he?* John checked the time again and realized his father's old partner in the department, The Professor, was now twenty minutes late.

John's mind drifted as he admired the ornate design of the watch, which featured the flowing wings of an angel, and he thought back to the day his father gave him this special timepiece as a gift at the age of fourteen.

"John, I need to take care of a little police business across the street. Sit here and wait for me. This is a friend of mine, Sally McCloskey. She'll take good care of you. As much lemonade as he can drink…right, Sally?"

"Yes, sir, and even though he seems old enough for something stronger, we'll try to stick to lemonade," Sally responded while offering a wink to John, who smiled. She put her hand on Officer Singleton's shoulder as she explained, "You know this was hard for me and I don't want any trouble."

The elder Singleton patted the top of her hand and responded, "This is no trouble and there will be no trouble. Not to worry."

"I can't thank ya enough for trying to help my son, Connor. The gangs get what they want around here and they want Connor because of his size—but he's a good boy. Yes, he's got a bit of a temper, and I'm worried what will happen if they keep pushing him to join. My giant of a boy would just as soon beat the hell out of the bunch of them, but no amount of size can stop a bullet or a knife. He can't refuse them—they won't let him say no. We need your help and can't thank you enough…"

John's father interrupted the rambling explanation and expression of thanks. He had all of the information he needed and pulled Sally off to the side as he whispered, "Nothing to thank me for yet, but I'll be back in a minute. Keep an eye on John for me. No need for him to hear all of this. I'll be right back."

John heard every word.

Sally headed back to the kitchen to pick up her next order, which gave John the opportunity to follow his father across the street. The elder Singleton walked through a group of drunken men who were harassing a young woman. The moment he approached, the men let the girl go and tipped their hats. Despite the absence of his uniform, John's father was afforded tremendous respect, which didn't go unnoticed by his son.

The elder Singleton began to speak to a man who also demanded a good deal of respect, and a firm handshake followed their brief exchange. John's father headed back toward the restaurant. Everyone stepped aside and tipped their hats again as he passed. John arrived at the restaurant a few moments after his father and anticipated the obvious question. "I took a little walk, Dad."

"Ah, no matter…wait here for me. I need to speak to Sally again before we go."

John had no intention of missing the explanation and followed his father inside.

"Good news, Sally. They'll leave him alone and they'll leave his friends alone as well. These Irish gangs have enough willing members, so we can't let them draft others who have no interest. Especially your son Connor—we've got to keep all of the giant Irishmen on the right side of the law! Once the criminals become the size of Connor, we'll all be in trouble! Listen, I understand there are lots of law-abiding Irish, and your boy is one of them. He'll be all right. The matter is resolved."

"Thank the Lord! No, thank Officer Singleton and his lemonade-drinking boy! You saved Connor! Please wait here. I'll be right back."

Sally ran back into the kitchen and returned with a finely engraved gold pocket watch, which she pressed into the officer's hands. "I'm not a lady of means, Officer Singleton, but I want you to accept this gift because you saved my boy's life. I insist."

Later that day, John asked his father about what he did for Sally McCloskey and why he accepted the watch from her in return. His father explained that he did what police officers are supposed to do—he used his authority and power to prevent something bad from happening. As for the watch, he said, "John, sometimes in life you'll be offered something you must accept because if you don't, you'll be disrespectful. This was one of those times. Maybe one day someone will offer you a gift like this, but until then, why don't you hold onto this for me."

John put the watch in his pocket with the understanding his father earned it, and he couldn't wait to earn one of his own.

John heard the cough as soon as he heard the hallway door open and it shook him out of his daydream. The Professor greeted John and invited him into his apartment.

"Sit down, John. How fitting—following in your father's footsteps—not surprising, though. Your dad was one of the few honest cops, and you always seemed like a good *gossoon*. I hope you follow his example."

"I plan to. I want to thank you for coming to his funeral last month. He suffered at the end. Maybe it was for the best."

"Yes, John. I think you're right—probably for the best. Your father and I worked together for such a long time, I considered him to be an elbow relation. How did the first day on the job turn out?"

"Well, I did the tour of the neighborhood with Sergeant Anderson. I'm sure you can imagine how that went."

"Yes, yes, he hates the drunken Irish and kicks some ass for show, but how do you think he affords the fancy house he lives in? I hope you took no mind to his senseless tattle—he's one of the most corrupt policemen on the force."

"My dad told me you would give me better background than him. Been here since the fifties, right?"

"Yes, long time. I moved to Vinegar Hill soon after I arrived in the states. I prefer to say Vinegar Hill as opposed to Irishtown—for me the name is a symbol of what could have been."

"What do you mean?"

"The American Revolution inspired my grandfather and his generation to fight for independence from the English in 1798. Our revolution, however, ended badly and the last battle, a tight scratch, was called Vinegar Hill. We went at it all hammer and tongs, but we failed. Many in the first wave of Irishmen fleeing further retribution from the English settled in these blocks, and we named the area Vinegar Hill. We can't forget what almost was, because one day, independence will come. Although I'm not sure in my lifetime."

The Professor paused for a moment and John realized a possible rationale for the nickname—the history lesson seemed quite complete and was delivered in excellent English with only a few odd Irish phrases sprinkled in for effect. The Professor spoke like an educated man. A deep rattle emanating from his chest accompanied the next coughing fit, and The Professor reached for his medicine. "No sweet poteen for me, John, this is true Irish whiskey. Jameson is the brand, best there is. I wouldn't insult you by offering one to you on your first day on the job." He took his first sip and the cough settled down.

The Professor continued, "Yes, many came after the failed revolution, but I came with the next wave of Irishmen after The Great Famine in the 1840s. Most of my family died of typhus on the way over, but I somehow survived. We've been laborers for years. Right now, things are a little on edge for two reasons. Both things you should be aware of." He paused to take another sip.

John waited a few moments and after The Professor offered his standard Jameson sigh, he asked, "And what would those two things be?"

"I don't want to insult my brethren with such a basic explanation, but the Irish value two things above all else: their ability to work and make a living, and their need for a few drinks at the end of the day. Be it what it would, both of these things are at risk."

"How so?"

The third sip, a long one. The Professor smiled and offered his requisite "Ahhh" before he continued, "The Irish understand they are viewed as the shit of society and as much as this is distasteful, it provides a kind of guarantee for the lowest-paying jobs requiring manual labor. The Blacks, though, created the pinch of the game, and the Irish view freed Blacks as a threat because they'll work for even less. I'm sure you remember the Draft Riots six years ago—even though you must've been a wee bit of a lad. Despite the fact the Germans, Italians, and Polish might be viewed in much the same way, the Irish consider the Blacks as the primary threat to their livelihood."

"So how is their need for drink being threatened?"

"Your sergeant is the expert on this topic, but the basic facts are simple. Proper whiskey is taxed, and that tax is built into the price of the drink, which makes for more expensive whiskey. This, in turn, creates an opportunity for dozens of illegal distilleries in the neighborhood to produce the *sweet poteen* we learned how to brew in the old country. Nowhere near as good as the Jameson whiskey, but once a lad has a bit of a seasoning, taste is not the primary concern. These distilleries pay no tax, use the cheapest ingredients, and the drinks are both plentiful and inexpensive. The government raids the distilleries whenever they find out about a location, but between people pelting them with rocks and tip-offs from folks like your sergeant, the distilleries survive and make certain men wealthy. We call them the Whiskey Kings."

"So I should keep an eye out for possible conflicts with Blacks and try to find these illegal distilleries?"

"Don't be an eejit! Be an honest cop, but learn how to survive. I'm not telling you about these two things so you can do anything about either one. I'm telling you so you stay the hell away from both issues in the interest of a long career as a police officer and a healthy life."

Not the orientation he expected from his father's old partner, but critical information, nonetheless. John Singleton accepted the advice and headed home for the day, determined to find some way to make a difference where and when possible. The rookie officer wasn't comfortable with The Professor's advice to *look the other way*, and didn't think his father would have been either.

Georgia

"'Scuze me, ma'am, my name is Florence Johnson. My husband works over at the docks as a stevedore and we moved to Weeksville a month ago. I stopped by your husband's shop the other day with some shoes needed fixin' and spotted you standin' out back. Mrs. Washington, right?"

"You can call me Esther. I thought I recognized you. How you like Weeksville?"

"Much better than where we came from down south a few years ago, but that'd be true for almost anywhere!" Florence Johnson snorted and slapped her leg as she appreciated her own humor, as she often did. Esther smiled and offered a polite laugh.

"We remembered Weeksville, 'cause when we came all the way up from Georgia, we spent a night at the Berean Baptist Church. Those folks treated us like family. We went up to Canada next, but came back now 'cause we can, and it too cold up in Canada, anyway. We used to Georgia heat, not Canada cold."

"Well, it gets cold here too, but I hope you'll like Weeksville, though."

"Changed a lot since we left. Lots of White folks now—more streets, too."

"Still a good place to be. I used to always say, 'Welcome to Weeksville,' but now I mostly say, 'Welcome to Brooklyn.' Things are changing for sure. In your case, I think I'll just say, 'Welcome back!'"

"Thanks, Miss Esther, but I wonder if you might do something for me? Nothing much, only an introduction."

"Introduction?"

"Yeah, my daughter's standin' over yonder. I named her Georgia—made sense at the time!" After giving Florence time to recover from several snorts and thigh slaps, Esther offered a brief, but sincere giggle—she liked this new arrival to the area.

"Sweet little thing, my Georgia, but I need for her to meet the right young man. Hope'n you don't mind, but we walked by you the other day when you were talkin' to the handsome boy right across from the Berean Baptist Church, and wondered if you might help Georgia meet him in some ladylike way."

"Oh, you want me to be a matchmaker! One of my favorite things!" Esther blurted as she did a thigh slap of her own. "Yes, Edward Heath is a handsome one, but I'm afraid lots of young girls have their eye on him. He's such an educated man, graduated college, spent the last six years in Liberia—didn't work out so well, according to what I understand. He's back now, and we're all hopin' he'll stay."

"Hard to believe such a young boy done graduated college and spent six years anywhere. We thought he might be 'round Georgia's age—eighteen. Such a strong boy, and can he ever run and jump! We both started giggling every time he left the ground." Florence felt compelled to demonstrate the giggle, but, as always, it drifted into a snort and some thigh slaps. This latest remark from Florence was news that was worthy of celebration, and Esther offered her broadest smile yet as she realized Florence Johnson wanted to fix her daughter up with Vent.

"Oh my, I'm so sorry. I thought you meant Mr. Heath, the man with the hat."

"No, he too old, too fancy, and a little too tall for my Georgia. We talkin' bout the handsome runner with all those muscles."

Esther took a moment to appreciate this opportunity for Vent, as well as to reflect on her personal disappointment in assuming Edward Heath was the *handsome boy*. She didn't worry about Vent lacking an interest in girls, but suspected he needed help with his social skills in order to ever approach anyone. In any case, light-skinned, long-armed, tiny men did not fit the ideal profile in most circles. Perhaps Vent might like this young girl with the funny mother. A broad grin preceded Esther's response. "Oh, he's my boy, Venture—sure does run fast, jump high, and he can he climb anything God put down firm in the ground—a special boy. Your Georgia want to meet him?"

Two snorts and three knee slaps later, Florence responded, "That's why we talkin', Miss Esther! Don't need no more help with my shoes—they all been fixed!"

Both ladies shared a long laugh and Florence waved her daughter over. Georgia understood this meant the conversation went well and arrived by her mother's side. She exchanged greetings with Esther, who thought, *She's perfect for Vent. Cutest little smile, respectful, and barely five feet tall!*

Esther started to make plans. "Here's what we'll do…first, though, let me ask, how many Johnsons are in the family?"

Florence responded, "Only the three of us, we live over on Hunterfly Road."

"Okay, the three of you are invited over to Sunday dinner—five o'clock. Our house is right above the shop. Pleasure meetin' both of you."

Esther headed home to begin preparing the house for their guests. Sunday was only two days away.

⊷⊷⊷ ⊶⊶⊶

Esther and Mabel cleaned and prepared the house on Saturday and spent all of Sunday afternoon cooking. The men, tasked with straightening up the outside of the home and making themselves presentable, thought they were given the tougher assignment.

Vent was uncomfortable with the idea of special guests, or special *anything*. He liked for all daily routines to play out exactly as they always did. He asked, "Miss Esther, since when we invite all new folks over for dinner?"

"Never you mind, Vent, we doing it today, and I don't want you wearing those old rags you wear every day. Remember, I'm the boss of this house, and you'll do as I say."

Vent remembered the rule Junius Morel gave him. *The principal was the boss of the school, but who was the boss of the house? Miss Esther or Mr. Thomas?* The screaming interrupted Vent's thoughts. "Vent, don't make me lose my temper. I done told you, I'm the boss, and I bought you a proper shirt and pants for tonight. We're all going to be proper in every way."

She sure does sound like the boss. Vent withdrew his opposition to dressing up. "Where my new clothes, Miss Esther?"

"Thank you, Vent. I laid everything out in your room. You go on up and change. Trust me, Vent, this is going to be a special night for you."

"Special night for me? I'm just gonna eat real fast and go over to Moses's place, like I always do—teaching him more reading and writing."

"Moses can wait, Vent. Tonight you'll be here until I say you can go. Understand?"

"Yes, Miss Esther, you the boss."

"You're a good boy, Vent. I like when you listen to me."

The preparations complete, the Washingtons sat around the table dressed in their Sunday finest, awaiting their guests. All three men tugged at their shirt collars because, according to Miss Esther, shirts needed to be buttoned all the way to the top for this special dinner. Everyone understood the reason for all of the fuss, except for Vent. Esther didn't want to scare the boy because an opportunity to meet an eligible girl like Georgia might not come around again for a long while. Miss Esther warned Horace he better not even smile at Georgia—tonight was about Vent. Horace reluctantly agreed.

Vent noticed all the smiles around the table and asked, "So what's the big joke? Why everyone so happy?" No one answered, but Thomas gave Vent a hearty slap on the back, as they heard the knock on the door.

Thomas Washington escorted the guests to the table and Esther helped with the introductions. Georgia presented her hand to Vent, and Miss Esther worried he would not reciprocate, which would trigger awkwardness as she offered direction to her child. Vent didn't understand why, but he immediately extended his hand, but not quite far enough, so Georgia moved a step closer and inserted two of her petite fingers into Vent's slightly cupped right hand. Vent stammered, "My name is Venture, but people call me Vent."

"I know, silly, Miss Esther just told us!" Georgia answered, punctuating her comment with a snort. Georgia made sure she sat next to Vent, took care of the small talk, and avoided all awkward silences. Within minutes, Vent understood that Georgia and her mom watched him run one of his many obstacle courses, and were impressed with his abilities. The two families enjoyed their meal and reminded Vent and Georgia to take a bite or two now and again. Vent hoped the night would never end, as did Georgia. After the Johnsons left for the evening, Vent sported the same silly smile his family had before their arrival.

CHAPTER 15

The Velvet Caps

THE LEADER OF the Velvet Caps assembled his men at their headquarters on the Little Street Docks in Irishtown. The somewhat mysterious and premature death of the former head of the gang prompted his rise to power. While he had nothing to do with the demise of his predecessor, Sean O'Malley suppressed the need to clarify that fact as he paced in front of his men like a general reviewing his army. O'Malley checked for adherence to the Velvet Cap dress code: skintight pants, blue shirts, and caps made of velvet. He nodded his approval. Time to address the troops.

"All right, fellas, something's happening tonight. The orders came straight from Devlin, who's back in Irishtown after his short vacation upstate." The group chuckled at the reference to Devlin's time in the penitentiary in Albany. O'Malley continued, "No jail can hold John Devlin—friends in high places, I tell ya!" The gang leader paused to take a sip of whiskey from the flask in his pocket. "We've got a bit of a scrape tonight at the Front Street distillery—the one in the basement of the corner tenement house—should be local police, and some marines from the Brooklyn Navy Yard. We need to vent our gall as only we can, boys. Let's slow them down so everything can be cleared out in time and make them wish they never messed with the Velvet Caps!"

The men cheered in response and marched toward Front Street. Once they got close to the distillery, they dispersed, and groups of two or three men entered each of the buildings in close proximity. Given the likely involvement of the marines, the Caps understood the general direction from which the authorities would arrive. Women assumed positions on the rooftops, from which they would hurl rocks down at the officers as they approached. Next, alley gangs of teenage boys organized into units would dash out from their hiding spots, pelt the officers with rocks, and run back to the safety of the meandering backstreets. The officers hesitated to chase anyone into these back passages for fear of never returning to the main road.

The scheduled time of the raid passed, and O'Malley wondered if they'd received a bad tip. After all this work, there would be dire consequences for whoever supplied the faulty intelligence—but at about seven thirty, a group of twenty men led by a federal revenue officer came marching down Front Street from the direction of the Navy Yard. O'Malley whispered to one of his gang members, "Damn wiseacres, they think they can take on the Velvet Caps with only twenty men?"

The raid of the first alley gang signaled the beginning of the attack as ten teenage boys ran onto Front Street and pelted the soldiers with rocks. The commanding officers told their men to hold their fire and only use bayonets. One sixteen-year-old boy took a jab in the leg, and limped back to the safety of a nearby alley as the rocks and bricks descended from the rooftops. The officers moved faster toward their target and then another alley mob attacked, followed by more aerial bombing. The soldiers, bruised, bloodied, and frustrated by the time they got to their location, stormed down the stairs to find an empty apartment, with the distinctive odor of a distillery.

Officer John Singleton was part of the raiding party and fared better than most. He caught a few rocks in the back, but was more angry than hurt. The Caps had known they were coming—someone on the force had tipped off the gang. John Devlin called out to the harassed officers from the protection of a nearby window. "Top of the evening to you, Officers! Welcome to Irishtown."

⊷⊨◉ ◉⊨⊷

Devlin's homecoming turned out to be a grand affair as he arrived in time to thwart another raid and reassert his position as the most prominent of the Whiskey Kings. He began his career in the whiskey business as a poor Irishman, but his combination of determination, persuasion, and penchant for violence soon placed him among the elite in this obscenely profitable illegal trade. Once

Devlin established firm connections to the City Halls on both sides of the river, he'd arrived in terms of prestige and power. The final confirmation of his position as the premier Whiskey King took place a few days earlier, when the president of the United States, Andrew Johnson, pardoned him after serving only a few months in the penitentiary.

Earlier that night, Devlin's instructions to O'Malley—harass and injure, but do not seriously hurt the officers—proved to be good strategy. *Always better to win a series of small battles than do anything that would cause an all-out war,* Devlin thought as he held up his whiskey flask to the portrait of the president he'd installed on his office wall, and said, "Andrew, thank you for the pardon; I hope I didn't beat up your boys too bad tonight! Cheers."

Now that the president had been properly thanked, he took a big step to his right, stood in front of a full-length mirror, and admired his colorful suit, gold chains, and gold rings. He hadn't been able to wear his favorite clothing and jewelry during his *vacation* upstate, and wanted everyone at his grand homecoming party to not only understand he was back, but to take note he was as rich and powerful as ever. He gave himself a nod of approval as he thought, *Irishtown royalty at its best!*

His parties on Adams Street were lavish and tonight would be one of the best ever—the highest quality booze, girls, gambling, and music. Everyone would remember the night John Devlin came back home. One last piece of business needed to be conducted before he began the festivities—a brief meeting with Sean O'Malley.

"Ah, the new leader of the Velvet Caps! Excellent work tonight, O'Malley. How do you like the new job?"

"Very much, Mr. Devlin. Happy we did well tonight."

"Yes, you got the job done. The Caps came out all hammer and tongs—not like your last boss. I lost two distilleries because of him while I was away. He had to go, so he did. Do you understand what I'm saying?"

"Yes, sir."

"This new job of yours will be yours as long as you deliver by protecting my business interests. Every time you do, I'll toss you one of these." Devlin threw O'Malley a stack of bills rolled up in a bundle. "Every time it goes arseways…I guess a smart man like you understands, but let's not worry about that now, we've got a party to go to!"

O'Malley found it difficult to go back and forth so quickly between compliments and threats, but with a wad of bills in his pocket and his men waiting for their payoff, he shook it off, put a smile on his face, and eliminated failure as an option. He understood where his predecessor went wrong—he became a little soft toward the end. *Won't happen to me*, O'Malley said to himself, as he made his way back to the Little Street Docks.

The men were waiting for him on the rooftop. This time, no inspection, no speeches, only a toast after everyone was flush from both the cash and their first round of drinks. O'Malley raised his flask and offered, "That'll teach the revenuers to stand between an Irishman and his drink! To my messmates!"

"Here, here!"

CHAPTER 16

Base Ball

VENT MADE A compromise with Miss Esther and wore his fancy pants, but refused to button his shirt all the way to the top—breathing was hard enough around Georgia. The walk to Hunterfly Road also enabled him to follow through on Mabel's suggestion, and he picked a lily from an open field. Today, his routine would be different, and for some reason, different was okay. Vent resisted the temptation to jump fences and climb trees. *Can't sweat, got to be calm, but it sure does take a long time to get somewhere walking this slow. Not sure how people do it all the time.* Despite his sluggish pace, he soon found himself knocking on the Johnsons' door.

"Good afternoon, Mr. Johnson. Afternoon, Mrs. Johnson. Perfect day for a base ball game."

"Sounds like a good plan, Vent," Florence answered as she reached for the lily before continuing. "Thank you so much for bringin' me this here pretty flower. I thought you took a liking to me. Let's ask Georgia to stay home and you and I will go for base ball!" Vent didn't know what to say, and started to stammer, "But Mrs. Johnson…" Snorts and knee slaps followed as Florence Johnson assured Vent she was joking—she found it odd, however, that Vent didn't understand her humor. The awkward moment ended when Georgia came out from the backroom wearing a pretty summer dress. She directed her subtle smile toward Vent, which froze him in place.

Mr. Johnson slapped Vent on the back to shake him out of his funk and said, "You two youngen's go and have some fun. Vent, I know you're a gentl'man. Make sure she gets home 'fore dark."

"Yes, sir, Mr. Johnson."

"Hello, Vent," Georgia offered with a second, more public smile, along with a curtsy—something she'd seen a White woman do in New York.

"Hello, Georgia," Vent responded while making an effort to do a curtsy of his own. All the Johnsons started snorting and thigh slapping as Georgia exclaimed, "Boys don't curtsy, silly. Let's go do some base ball, or whatever you call this thing!"

Georgia snuck her hand into Vent's as soon as they left the house and the couple strolled across town to the field next to Yukaton Pond. Vent pointed out some of the sites along the way. "This pond is where we skate in the winter. Did you ever ice skate?"

"Not in Georgia! But I did skate once in Canada. Kept fallin', though. Not as much fun as I thought."

"You got to be balanced the right way. Mr. Thomas made me a pair of ice skates from some old shoes. I skate all the time."

"Vent, why you call your parents Miss Esther and Mr. Thomas, when your brother and sister call them Mama and Papa?"

Vent didn't answer.

"Vent?"

Vent removed his hand from Georgia's and said, "Not supposed to think 'bout bad stuff no more. Moses told me; otherwise, I miss out on good stuff. You good stuff, Georgia. Don't ask me no more."

Georgia, confused by the answer, thought to herself, *Why is this such a tough question, and who is Moses?* She decided to focus on the positive and grabbed Vent's hand as she offered, "So happy I'm good stuff, now tell me 'bout this base ball." Vent relaxed, but took some time to regain his composure.

"Okay, this here team is called the Mutual Base Ball Club, which is their new name—used to be called the Weeksville Unknowns, most folks still like the old name better. They playin' against the Brooklyn Monitors. Basic thing is running around the bases 'til you make a full circle, which is one run. These teams score lots of runs. Last game, the score was forty-three to twenty-nine. We lost."

"Well, today, we're going to win and do lots of base circles. Is that how I say it, Vent?"

"No. Not exactly, but you'll learn."

Vent and Georgia found a good spot to sit on the grass behind third base. Miss Esther had suggested that Vent bring a blanket along, so Georgia wouldn't mess up her dress. A crowd of about seventy-five Colored folks found their own positions on the outskirts of the field as the players warmed up in preparation for the game. One White man with a folding chair sat close to the couple by the third base line. He held a notebook and started scribbling something as soon as he sat down.

Mackie Johnson arrived as the game began and sat on the grass behind the first base line. He had enjoyed watching the team practice a few days earlier and wanted to experience his first base ball game. The teams took the field, and the first hit, a foul ball down the third base line, headed toward Georgia. Vent reached out with one hand and caught the ball before it struck her chest. He tossed the ball back onto the field and the crowd, along with a few of the players, applauded. Georgia gave Vent his first kiss—square on the cheek, after whispering, "My hero!"

Mackie got up and left. *No way to avoid this boy.* He needed to leave town.

The game progressed and Vent pointed out more of the rules, while Georgia nodded and cuddled closer to her new boyfriend. The White man in the chair moved closer as well and asked the couple, "Would you mind keeping an eye on my chair and notebook for a moment? I want to go across the field for some water."

Vent kept his head down and offered no response, so Georgia jumped in, "Yes, sir. My name is Georgia and this here is Vent. Happy to oblige."

"I'm George Rhodes, a reporter for the *Brooklyn Eagle*. I'm doing a story on the game. Thanks so much. Please hold onto this so my notes don't blow away." The reporter handed his notebook to Georgia and made his way across the field.

"What a pleasant White man! Don't you think so, Vent?"

"I guess so."

Georgia started to read the man's notes and put down the clipboard in disgust as she exclaimed, "He's makin' fun of us…he wrote, 'the players and the spectators are as Black as the ace of spades' and we all on our best behavior trying to act like ladies and gentlemen. What a terrible thing to say!"

Vent responded, "He like all the other White folks. Some are bad through and through, but others seem all right, but still bad, like the reporter."

After George Rhodes returned and collected his notebook, Vent and Georgia picked up their blanket and moved further down the left field line. Once settled in their new position, one of the Brooklyn Monitors hit a deep foul ball over the couple's heads and the ball rolled toward the pond. The left fielder didn't seem interested in saving the ball, so Vent sprung up, dashed toward the water, leaping over a fence along the way, and caught up with the ball in the nick of time. He trotted back to the field, but instead of tossing the ball to the left fielder, who would relay it to the pitcher, Vent reared back and threw the ball from deep left field straight to the catcher—a perfect strike. The crowd roared and the manager of The Mutuals said to one of his players, "Find out who he is—a little on the small side, but seems like a natural."

The game, as high scoring as ever, was tied thirty-two to thirty-two at the end of the thirteenth inning. Vent promised to bring Georgia home before dark and didn't want to upset her father, so the couple packed their blanket and left hand-in-hand for the walk back to Hunterfly Road. Georgia glanced over her shoulder at Vent and smiled. She was both surprised and concerned when she first discovered Vent's special challenges and listened to lectures from her parents, who told her to go slow because she could likely find a better match. Georgia's father thought *someone* who could protect her would be best and her mother wanted *someone* who would be a good provider, but Georgia didn't want *someone* at all—she wanted Vent.

She had picked out the spot earlier, assuming things would go well, and as they passed a large willow tree close to the turn for her street, she pulled Vent behind the tree.

"I got some questions for you, Venture Simmons!"

"What? What do you mean questions, I told you…"

"Hush, I'm in charge now. Question one—do you promise to always save me from flying balls and other bad things?"

"Well…yes, I do."

"I'm not done yet, Venture. Question two—do you also promise to be my boyfriend and not pay any mind to other girls?"

"Yes."

"Last one. Question three…do you promise…now, listen here, I mean promise…you will always, and I mean always, kiss me just like this…" Georgia leaned in, and Vent hoped she would never lean out.

After the embrace, Georgia whispered, "You never answered question number three," and Vent screamed, "Yes, yes, yes, Miss Georgia!" He was in love.

Chapter 17

You Bet

Captain Arnold Johnson sat back in his chair and stared out his window. Given the location of his office in the center of the station, the window didn't open to the outside, but it did transport him to another time and place. The bright painting of a glass window with a farmhouse, barn, and horse stable in the distance took the captain back to his childhood days in upstate New York, and made him wonder how different his life would have been had he stayed to work the land. As the eldest child, the farm was his for the taking, but Arnold Johnson decided on a city life and turned over ownership to his younger brother. The varied challenges of managing the police station in Irishtown stood in sharp contrast to the standard routine of managing a small farm—Captain Johnson often yearned for a simpler life.

A knock on the door brought him back to the present and another problem to be solved. The captain wished knocks could be followed by good news, but rarely, if ever, was this the case.

"Captain, John Singleton is a problem. I understand he's second-generation police, but even though Sergeant Anderson gave him the orientation, he doesn't seem to be catching on."

"All right, O'Reilly, tell me about the problem with the kid."

"Well, he's brought in more bullshit arrests during his first few days than most of us do in a year, and he is actually enforcing our 'public disturbance' ordinance in Irishtown! Hard to believe—if we're going to arrest the Irish for being drunk, we'll need to lock up the whole neighborhood, myself included!"

"What else is he doing?"

"He's reported the locations of two of Devlin's illegal distilleries. Not news for us, but also not a local problem. We need the Whiskey Kings' help from time to time, and he doesn't understand that we leave those distilleries alone."

"My God, after being broken in by our resident criminal, Anderson, this is how he goes about his job?"

"Seems so, Captain. Check the desk, he's got another drunk he's bringing in for making a public disturbance. He's the laughingstock of the station, Captain, and father or no father, he's going to cause more trouble than he's worth with his idea of what makes a good cop. I think ya better talk to him."

"Okay, O'Reilly. I'll chat with him. Keep him in the station for a while and give me a chance to gather my thoughts."

"Will do."

Arnold Johnson took another long gaze through his window. This time his mind wandered back to his days as a young policeman, when he discovered the line between true crime and things that must be accepted as a cost of doing business. Johnson's captain at the time, John Singleton's father, taught him the rules. *Perhaps I should offer my own little orientation to set the young officer on the right path.* Captain Johnson called out through his doorway, "Singleton, come in here."

"Yes, sir, Captain."

"John, you and I need to talk. Only an hour left in our shifts, so let's talk where all meaningful conversations take place in Irishtown. Follow me." The new officer followed his captain without asking questions or passing any remarks, but became surprised when they entered a bar about a block away from the station house.

"Welcome to Murdock's House of Merriment, Officers," the elderly barkeep offered.

"Such a pleasure to be back, Mr. Murdock. I wonder if you wouldn't mind asking those four fellows at the end of the bar to find another place to sit?"

"Anything for you, Captain." The bartender walked toward the end of the bar and whispered a few words into the ears of the four men, who appeared to be well beyond their first drink. The men turned, ready for a fight, but once they realized Captain Johnson made the request, they tipped their hats and moved to the other side of the bar.

John asked the Captain, "Why did we need to sit in these particular seats and aren't we still on duty?"

"John, this is your problem, you ask all of the wrong questions at all of the wrong times. If your captain wants to take you out for a drink at nine in the morning, you go without uttering a word, because the captain makes the rules, and four in the afternoon is not an ungodly hour for a drink, my young man… we've got a lot to talk about."

"Why these seats?"

"Well, these are the two seats your father and I sat in when he took me out for similar discussions."

"My father came into bars during his shift?"

"John, again, always asking the wrong questions. Your father was one of the greatest officers I ever worked with, but right now, we are here to talk about you, and I want you to listen."

"Okay, Captain."

"We are about to drink some illegal whiskey made in an illegal distillery, which everyone in the station understands is located in the basement of this bar. The bartender will serve us and we'll drink as much or as little as we want and he will not charge us. This is one of the ways they say thank you for ignoring the distillery, and also one of the ways we show we can be trusted. Trust is important, John, because sometimes we need to go to them for help solving real crimes."

"Real crimes? Isn't this a real crime? Drinking illegal whiskey on the job with the full understanding an illegal distillery is in the basement?"

"No, John, this is the point. Whiskey can never be *the crime* in Irishtown. Never stand between an Irishman and his drink and never arrest him for having a few too many. The crimes we care about are major burglaries, murder, assault—things of a greater magnitude. All of these people you call criminals help us solve those serious matters because of the trust we've built by never making whiskey the crime. We demonstrate our trust by having a drink or two, on the house, with them. Your father understood this and you need to make sure you understand from this point forward, or your time in Irishtown will be short."

The captain waited for the young officer to respond, but Singleton only offered a glare. Johnson raised his glass and said, "We drink this glass of Devlin's best sweet poteen in tribute to the fine balance between true policing and things that don't matter!" The captain offered his toast as a final opportunity for Officer Singleton to demonstrate his understanding. For Johnson—bottoms up, for Singleton—a sip, a sneer, and a goodbye.

The barkeep walked over to the captain to offer a refill and stated the obvious, "He's a problem, isn't he?"

"You bet."

CHAPTER 18

Little Street Docks

"MR. REEMS, I thought the bill needed to be paid next week. Irishtown isn't safe for a Colored man at night," Horace explained to his boss.

"Listen, Horace, you're doing a good job, but paying bills on time is important. You're the bookkeeper and you should understand the payment dates for all the bills. I shouldn't be the one telling you."

"Sir, Irishtown at night…I can't…"

"Goddamn, Horace. My wife warned me about this—hiring a Darkey for a White man's job. You take this payment over to our supplier before they close, or we can't do our work tomorrow. This is your job, and either you'll do all of it, or you'll do none of it. Your choice."

Horace resigned himself to making the trip in the interest of maintaining his employment, and headed out to the work area, but Harold Reems called him back. "Don't bother trying to track down Vent to go along with you. Guess why? Not enough supplies to keep the work going today. I sent most everybody, including Vent, home. You're on your own, Horace. Either you drop the payment off, or don't come back tomorrow. Now go."

Horace started to make his way over to Irishtown and stayed on main roads as much as possible, but with the sun going down, he became worried—the Irish would soon be imbibing their first end-of-the-day drink, and with each subsequent cocktail, the probability of a safe exit decreased proportionately. The manager of the supply house, located next to the Little Street Docks, made Horace wait thirty minutes before accepting the envelope and promising to deliver the materials as scheduled in the morning.

Horace sensed the trouble as soon as the large Irish boy approached him. Jimmy McGreary planned to make an example of this stupid Black man, who dared to walk the streets of Irishtown after sundown. The circumstances were perfect as all of the Velvet Caps, including his older brother, Aengus, planned to enjoy the show. The gang gathered on the rooftop of their typical meeting place—separated from the supply house by a narrow alley.

"Pay attention, boys, my brother Jimmy will show you what he's made of. He'll sure take care of the Darkey. I'm telling ya, he should be one of us. You'll be impressed," Aengus suggested as he tipped his hat to his brother, a bear of a boy but, at only seventeen years old, a bit on the young side to join the gang.

The Caps went to the roof of their headquarters, peeked over, and made room for their leader, Sean O'Malley, so he would have the best seat in the house. Almost time for the show.

Young Jimmy McGreary used too much force, and Horace was knocked backward into the wall of the alley. His head struck the wall first and he collapsed into a heap on the ground. His attacker sensed the audience on the roof demanded more action, so he became creative and picked Horace up with his left arm while continuing to pummel him with his right. The boy screamed, "Irishtown's not for your kind—not your kind. You understand? Do you understand?"

Sean O'Malley called down from the rooftop, "Jimmy, you damn eejit, he understands nothing—he's out. You can't gull us into believing he hears a word you say. Leave him in the alley and go on home. Come back when you understand how to give us a good show." A disappointed Jimmy McGreary let Horace drop to the ground and walked out of the alley with his head down.

O'Malley turned to Aengus. "He's not ready yet—doesn't understand his own strength. Remember, most of the time we want to hurt, not kill. The killing brings on too much trouble. Talk to your beast of a brother about controlling himself, and stop all the tattle about him becoming a Cap right away. Yes, he'll be a Velvet Cap one day, Aengus, but not today." Aengus nodded in agreement, pleased to receive some assurance of future membership for Jimmy. He responded, "I think you're right, Sean. Jimmy's too strong for his own good, so I'll teach him how to hit half as hard."

Another gang member liked the sound of the name. "Yeah, let's call him Half as Hard Jimmy." The men laughed and got down to gang business.

⊸⊷

"Vent, where's Horace? After seven o'clock. Not like him to be this late."

"I left work early, Miss Esther. Didn't run into him much at all today."

"I'm worried, Vent, not like him to be so late. Go and try to track him down."

Vent never liked to break any routines, but in times of emergency he found an inner strength, which helped him to protect those he loved. Miss Esther noted the transformation—his head rose and he took on a more confident gait as he exited the house.

Vent checked the few places in the neighborhood where Horace might have stopped, but no luck. He thought, *Something is wrong, got to go back to the job to check if anything happened.* The next train for downtown Brooklyn was scheduled to leave in thirty minutes, so Vent opted to run the short three miles to save time. He entered the building expecting to encounter the men on the late shift, but given the light workload of the day, the late shift had been canceled. The boss, Harold Reems, was alone at the construction site putting away some materials.

"Mr. Reems, you seen Horace? He never came home."

"Not since four o'clock, when I sent him to drop off a payment. He never got home?"

"No, never did. Not like him."

"We had a big problem earlier today with supplies. Maybe I shouldn't of sent him, but I made him go over to Irishtown. I hope nothing happened to him."

"Irishtown at night? Not safe, Mr. Reems. Where did you send him?"

"Grunding Supplies by the Little Street Docks."

Vent's eyes began a further transformation—the fury was back. Tonight, he would need to violate all of his routines. Tonight, he would do whatever was necessary because Horace was in trouble, and Horace was family. Vent ran into the shop and grabbed one of the oversized jackets and hats the men wore outside when they worked in the rain. He figured with his small size, light skin, and concealed face he might pass for White, especially at night. He covered up and headed over to Irishtown.

John Singleton worked his beat in Irishtown from two in the afternoon to ten at night, Monday through Friday, and always made a point to walk by the Little Street Docks. The Caps gave him no respect and displayed no fear when in his presence, but Singleton still made it a point to walk by their location several times each shift. The officer took note of the gang members on the roof of their building, and tipped his hat as he walked by.

O'Malley called out from above. "Good evening, Officer. Some odd sounds are coming from the alley, for aught we know, it might be an injured animal—you may want to take a peek." All of the Caps started to laugh. As Singleton got close to the alley, he spotted the bloodied man crawling toward the street. The officer rushed to his side and blew his whistle, hoping someone in the area would respond and stay with the man while he went for more help.

Vent arrived at the docks a few minutes earlier and found Grunding Supplies closed for the night and took note of the boisterous gang on the roof—he worried they might have crossed paths with Horace. After climbing up the side of the building, Vent found a spot on a windowsill close enough to the rooftop to listen to the gang's conversation. The sound of the whistle jolted Vent into action and he jumped down from his spot onto a pile of garbage, which caught the attention of both the gang and the policeman. The gang wondered where this tiny man came from, but the limited light only permitted them to make out the outline of Vent's small frame. After being startled himself, Officer Singleton realized the little man knew the victim of the brutal attack. Vent hurried to his brother's side. "Horace, are you okay?"

Singleton and Vent carried Horace out to the carriage of a nearby storekeeper, which they commandeered for police business. Vent convinced the officer to head for a doctor on the outskirts of Weeksville who treated Colored folks.

Singleton didn't understand what to make of this man who seemed to jump from the skies. They rode in silence with Singleton driving the carriage, and Vent cradling his brother's bloody head in his lap. Horace drifted in and out of consciousness during the ride to the doctor's house. Singleton finally broke the silence. "Your brother was attacked, but Irishtown is no place for a Colored man at night."

Vent didn't want to talk. He wanted to kill, but this officer did help, so he answered, "Never happen again. Won't be pressin' no charges."

"What's your name?"

"Vent."

"Okay, Vent. You make sure he never heads back there."

The two men carried Horace into the doctor's house and laid him carefully on the examination table. The doctor came outside a few minutes later and whispered into Singleton's ear and returned to Horace's care. Singleton turned to Vent. "The doc says he should be all right in a few days, but he needs a little more time to make sure. I'm going to head back to return this carriage. You'll be able to get him home?"

"Yes."

"You're a man of few words."

No response from Vent, only an air of pure determination and resolve. Officer Singleton became worried and cautioned Vent, "I hope you realize you shouldn't go back to Irishtown either. You understand?"

Again, no verbal response from Vent, but he did offer a nod, which Singleton accepted. The officer headed back to Irishtown and Vent started sprinting toward Moses's place.

An hour later, Vent and Moses carefully placed Horace in Moses's carriage. After hearing the doctor's advice not to ride too fast, Moses responded, "No worries, Doc. This here horse only goes at two speeds, slow and slower." Despite his injuries, Moses detected a slight smirk from Horace. Vent, however, made no effort to acknowledge Moses's attempt at humor, and flashed the same crazed look he displayed the day he arrived in Weeksville.

Moses drove, while Vent sat in the back whispering with Horace. "Who did this to you?"

Moses interrupted, "What you boys saying? Don't be plannin' no trouble."

All conversation ended for a few minutes until Horace motioned for Vent to lean closer to his face. He whispered, "A big monster of a boy. They called him Jimmy and I think he has a brother in the Caps called Aengus. He did this to me for fun."

Moses didn't like the muted conversation between the two young men and said, "Stop the whispering. I'm tellin' you both, this is the end of all of this. No sense plannin' any revenge against White folks—we may not be slaves no more, but we sure ain't free enough for this kind of nonsense. So hush up, and let's go home."

Vent didn't say a word, but the fire in his eyes returned. Horace remembered the time Vent brutally beat the boy years before when they were children. What happened in Irishtown demanded revenge, and this time, Horace had right on his side, and would insist on being present—not to control Vent, but rather to make sure he finished the job.

CHAPTER 19

Another Tip

"Betrayed again! Someone leaked word about the raid to Devlin. We need a better way," the frustrated federal revenue officer lamented. "So this time, no one gets the location until an hour before we act. I want a group ready, but only the three of us will know the address for now." The local police captain, Arnold Johnson, and the colonel commanding the marines in the Brooklyn Navy Yard both nodded. "I may be paranoid, but I'm not even going to say the location out loud—these walls may be thinner than I think." The revenue officer wrote the location on a piece of paper, showed it to his two colleagues, and ripped the sheet into several small pieces, which he tossed into the garbage can.

The secretary outside the door cursed under her breath, *Shit, he wrote the fuckin' location! What am I going to do? Maybe they left the note with the address somewhere in the office.*

A few hours later, the captain left early to take care of some personal errands, and the secretary seized the opportunity to search the office. Thankfully, her boss was an organized man—all documents filed away, his desk clear, and nothing at all out of place. This made the desk drawers and garbage the most likely places to find the sheet with the location of the raid.

A quick glance at the garbage bin brought a smile to her face and Roberta McGurt gathered up all of the pieces of torn paper and went into an empty interrogation room to try to reassemble the sheets—the raid would be tonight at seven at John Devlin's Adams Street distillery, so there wasn't much time. She wrote the location on a clean piece of paper, threw out all of the other scraps, and went to find Sergeant Anderson.

John Singleton sat at an empty desk filling out some paperwork and took note of Roberta McGurt seeking out Anderson. John maneuvered his location and arrived within earshot as she said, "Hard to believe, they're going after the same one they failed with in the spring. Here, take a peek." The secretary began to show Anderson the paper, but stepped back, laughing, as she commented, "Oh, sorry, I forgot you can't tell an 'r' from an 'a,' you illiterate bastard. Take my word for it and make sure I get my money tomorrow."

"Be careful with your insults, you little Irish whore. Never forget, I know you from the days you spread your legs for pennies by the docks. Remember your name in those days, BOB? Not so long ago, Bent Over Berta, yeah…BOB—a good name for you. Never forget who cleaned you up and made you Roberta McGurt, the respected secretary to the captain. Are you bending over for him? I guess once a whore, always a whore. You Irish are all the same. Careful how you talk to me, BOB, or you'll be back to spreading your legs for spare change, and I'll get my information some other way."

"Always need to have the last word, you Irish-hating illiterate bastard. I think you're jealous I never bent over for you, but even a whore has standards. Shut the fuck up about all of this ancient history, and don't kid yourself, I'm the only source. Take my note and do your job with Devlin."

Anderson hated taking shit from BOB—he took little crap from anyone— but dealt with her bullshit because she was, in fact, the only source. Of all the sergeant's scams over the years, which created his special retirement fund, this one—tipping off the Whiskey Kings about raids—proved to be the most lucrative. The secretary walked back to her office and Anderson placed the folded paper in his top drawer, cleared his throat, and addressed his men. "Listen fellas, seems to be a slow night here in Irishtown, the damn Paddies may have run out of whiskey to drink. I'll be back in an hour or so. Keep an eye on things for me."

The staff in the office cleared out within minutes of the sergeant's departure. Officer Singleton took a seat at Anderson's desk and found the note in the top drawer. The address for the raid was written on standard issue police letterhead, so John rifled through Anderson's drawers to find a blank sheet of paper, and wrote the location of the address of another Devlin distillery on a new sheet.

He made an effort to match the writing style of the secretary, but realized the illiterate Anderson would never be able to tell the difference.

An hour later, Sergeant Anderson returned to the same Irishtown bakery. He issued his standard warning that the cake better be the right size, and after receiving assurance it was, the piece of paper with the tip was in the hands of Devlin's men. Within ninety minutes, the Velvet Caps assembled both the rooftop women and the alley boys, and everyone readied for mischief. The allotted time arrived, but the raid never materialized—at eight o'clock, the Caps received word the authorities had raided another distillery—the main one on Adams Street.

Devlin smashed his favorite whiskey tumbler into the wall and threw a dagger into the head of his portrait of the president of the United States. He alternated between yelling, "Fucking revenuers," and, "fucking Anderson." O'Malley walked into the office, but maintained a safe distance by standing by the door. The Whiskey King demanded a meeting with the sergeant, who would be lucky if the bakery accepted a simple return of the cake. All of the Irish hated Anderson despite his usefulness, and as much as O'Malley mourned the loss of any Devlin distillery, he liked the idea of Anderson being on the business end of Devlin's stick.

Waiting for Horace

Hours of sleep followed Horace's brief lucid moments in the back of the carriage. The family kept a vigil by his bed, and Mabel, who had left home two years earlier to marry her childhood sweetheart, Alex, wouldn't leave Horace's side. Georgia came over in the morning to help out with cooking and other chores, which would make the family comfortable during their time of need. Horace's long rest started at about ten the night before, and when his sleep continued past noon the next day, the family sent for the doctor.

"I worried about this—he may be suffering from internal bleeding. We won't be sure about any lasting damage until he wakes up."

Esther and Thomas responded in unison, "Doc, what you mean 'bout lasting damage?"

"Head injuries are hard for us to treat. Horace is a sharp boy, and I hope he's still sharp when he wakes up. Thank God you found him when you did. From what I understand, if he'd stayed in the alley and received any more damage, he'd be a goner. No need to worry about things you can't control—I've also seen things like this heal well. We need to wait."

Vent came down from the tree when Georgia arrived, but climbed right back up after offering his greetings. Esther picked up on her concern as Georgia stared at Vent, who returned to his old mumbling and counting routine.

"Miss Georgia, I want to thank you for coming on over and helpin' out, and I don't want you to worry 'bout Vent. Bad things happened to him as a little boy and every once in a while he finds comfort in this here tree when new things go bad. He and Horace are close, but the only way we'll find out what happened to Horace is if he wakes up and tells us. Vent will never talk 'bout bad things from the past—it's one of his rules. So don't worry he's mad at you. This is his way. He's a good man and he's worth the effort—he saved Horace's life—no one else could have gotten in and out of Irishtown at night 'cept him. Seems like an upset little boy up in a tree right now, but he can also be the most ferocious kind of man when his family needs him. You gots to work with both sides of him and never give up, if you want to be his woman. Hopin' this doesn't scare you away."

"No. Takes more than a little tree climbin' to scare me away, Miss Esther."

"Good girl! I'll show you a trick I first learned when Vent came here years ago and wouldn't come down from the tree. Come upstairs with me."

Esther and Georgia climbed the stairs and Esther placed a chair in front of the window in Vent's room. "Child, you sit here and wait 'til he spots you. Don't say much, and he'll come to you when he's ready."

Georgia sat for fifteen minutes until Vent raised his head and their eyes connected. He swung out of the tree and through the window, and they sat together without saying a word. Georgia began to sing "Amazing Grace"—Vent's favorite hymn. His eyes drifted off and Georgia realized Vent was no longer fully present.

After singing the hymn twice, Georgia rocked her boyfriend and kissed his forehead as she considered his three distinct sides—she fell in love with the shy, sweet, and smart Vent. The Washingtons appreciated the loyal and tough Vent, but understood this side needed to be managed. No one understood Vent's third side, which involved his unusual social behaviors, but Georgia hoped one day she would and she whispered, "Vent, we all a mixed bag, and when I reach into your bag, almost everything I take out is real good, but a few things I'm gonna help improve. You gonna help me too, like with all the base-circling stuff in base ball. Never understood why people run so hard just to get back to where they started. Seems like you could save a whole lot of time by standin' still!" Georgia found her last comment to be hilarious and started to snort and slap her thigh. Vent smiled.

Miss Esther called out from downstairs, "Vent, Georgia! Horace is waking up. Come downstairs!"

The couple raced to Horace's bedside and found him sitting up. The bruises darkened on his face, but he smiled and thanked everyone for being by his side.

Horace paused for a moment, turned to Vent, and offered special thanks for saving his life.

"It wasn't just me, Horace. A police officer, John Singleton, found you first. You lucky to be alive, Horace. You real lucky."

"Vent, ask him something so we can check if his brain is workin' right," Miss Esther said.

"No need. This is Horace. He's okay. Spoke to him a bit in the carriage before he took his long sleep. You remember what we talked about, Horace?"

"Sure do, Vent. Every word."

Vent responded, "Miss Esther, he's fine." Horace nodded.

The group dispersed and took a moment to reflect on this moment in their individual ways.

Esther and Thomas walked across the hall to their bedroom, thrilled their brilliant son would be okay.

Mabel and Georgia decided to walk home together because Mabel's new home with her husband, Alex, was on Hunterfly Road, close to the Johnsons'. They each became lost in their own thoughts as they walked. Georgia, happy the family accepted her help in their time of crisis, but concerned about Vent's return to his old troubled behaviors. Mabel worried because she noted the return of the fire in Vent's eyes when the boys discussed their conversation in the carriage— bad things happened after Vent went into that state.

Horace examined his brutalized face in the handheld mirror by his bedside and became furious. After some time, he calmed down as he thought of what Vent would do to his Irish attacker. *This time, revenge will be so much sweeter, because it's fair.*

Vent retired to his room and spent the first night in a long while in the closet. Miss Esther's rule was clear—he prepared for war.

CHAPTER 21

The Untouchable Sergeant

HERBERT ANDERSON BANGED on Roberta McGurt's door at a little before midnight. After receiving no response, the sergeant walked to the window of her first-floor apartment and noticed candlelight glimmer coming from inside. He returned to the front door. The resumption of the banging disturbed Roberta's interactions with her two lady friends, and she lost her focus. "Goddamn it! Got to go to the door. Remember, I'm throwing this party, nothing else happens 'till I get back." Her two guests nodded and one offered a giggle—Roberta's take-charge personality, arguably, was one of her sexiest traits. After donning a robe over her otherwise naked body, Roberta excused herself, and walked toward the door with a hammer.

"Who the fuck is banging on my door!"

"Open the door, you stupid whore. Herbert Anderson is banging. Open up!"

Roberta decided holding the hammer took precedence over covering up, and let the beltless robe dangle open as she opened her door. The sergeant rushed in, and dismissed her somewhat provocative dress because the ability to pass another BOB joke was the least of his concerns.

"Roberta, what the fuck happened?"

"What are you talking about?"

"You gave me the wrong address. They hit the main distillery on Adams Street."

"The exact address I gave you. I wrote Adams Street, clear as day. I even told you they were hitting one that they raided before. Don't you remember that?"

"But you didn't tell me which one and you wrote the Front Street distillery."

"Exactly how much do you want me to announce in front of your men, Anderson? If you weren't such an illiterate bastard, we wouldn't have this problem. I wrote 234 Adams Street. I remember the exact address."

Anderson maintained his focus on finding answers. "Somebody fucked up here. If not you, who could it be? I passed the same note you gave me to Devlin's man."

"Can't be true. What did you do with the note after I left?"

"I put the paper in my desk drawer for safekeeping."

"You got a lock on the drawer?"

"No. No need. No one would dare go in my desk."

"Well, I guess someone dared this time. Someone must've seen me pass you the note and picked up on some of what we said."

Anderson paused for a moment and tried to remember the names of those in in the area during the time of his conversation about the raid. He dismissed the theory. "Can't be, Roberta. Who would dare fuck with me?"

"Listen, you say they call me BOB. Well, you should understand your nickname is 'The Criminal Cop.' Someone could be trying to put you in bad standing with Devlin—to fuck with you or try to take over the business. Either way, you better figure out who."

Anderson took another minute to consider the possibilities, and said, "You may be right. No other explanation."

"All right, you figure out how to make things right with Devlin and we'll find a way to catch who's messing with our business. Let me go back to my friends."

"God, you're still such a fucking whore."

"Yeah, yeah, but now I fuck for fun. I'm becoming a lady of means. Don't mess this up for me, Anderson. Good night."

Sergeant Anderson walked away from the apartment building, considering the possible candidates. The likely scenario—someone else thought of the same scam and wanted to discredit him in order to take over the business with Devlin. *Who would dare do such a thing?* Anderson thought—he'd made examples of anyone who crossed him in the past, and the group in his inner circle didn't contain any aggressive types. *Only a couple of young officers, a few small-time hustlers, and one or two honest cops. Who could it be?*

Anderson headed out to find Devlin—no reason to avoid the eventual confrontation. A few rights and lefts and Anderson turned onto Adams Street heading for the site of the raided distillery. The police, no longer in the vicinity, but Devlin's men blanketed the area and spotted Anderson right away.

"Sergeant Anderson, Mr. Devlin wants a word with you. Follow me."

Anderson noted an absence of fear on the part of the four burly Irishmen who encircled him while flashing confident grins. *Do these assholes think they can use force on me?*

"Listen, you stupid Irish fucks. Lay a hand on me, and you'll regret getting out of bed this morning. I'm looking for Devlin myself."

"Isn't this a wonderful thing, Officer? We're all working toward the same goal! Follow us, Sergeant Anderson."

The group marched down Adams Street, entered a corner tenement, and went downstairs to the basement. Devlin sat at a plain table in a simple wooden chair, wearing the clothes of a common Irishman, with none of his bawdy jewelry.

"Sit down, Anderson."

The sergeant took a seat and each of Devlin's men retreated to a different corner of the small room.

"I thought I would meet you tonight dressed the way I began my career in the whiskey business—didn't start out as a Whiskey King. In the beginning, I dressed like all of the Irish peasants you insult every time you come into Irishtown."

Anderson didn't understand where this conversation was headed and shrugged his shoulders.

Devlin continued, "But you not only insult us as you walk our streets, but kick a little Irish ass from time to time based on the uniform you're wearing. Am I correct, Sergeant Anderson?"

"Well, from time to time, I need to put some fellas on the right path," Anderson offered with a chuckle, which abruptly ended when Devlin jumped to his feet, and rushed over, taking hold of the sergeant by his shirt collar.

"Understand what is happening right now, you cocky fuck. I am dressed the way I did when *I* needed to put some people on the right path. Do *I* need to put *you* on the right path, you Irish-hating bastard? Do I? Answer me!" Devlin demanded as his four associates came toward the sergeant as added backup.

"Hold on. Hold on. No need for any of this. Let's keep our heads, here. Seems like someone switched the note. The original note said Adams Street, not Front Street," the sergeant offered in an effort to defuse the situation.

"So, when you handed the Adams Street note to my man, he switched the paper in the twenty seconds it took him to walk to me in the back of the bakery? Come on, Anderson, this is your explanation?"

"No. Not what I mean. I think someone who is trying to mess with our business arrangement switched the note at the station."

"An opportunity to steal the business may exist if you make another mistake like this."

"No other mistakes. I promise you."

"So, this is what's going to happen. First, you are going to return the cake to the bakery as a start to make this right and the next tip will be for no payment at all. Once everything is back to normal, we return to our old arrangement."

Anderson's face became red and he jumped up and tried to pull out his revolver. All four men converged on him and took away his gun. The largest of the Irishmen put Anderson in a chokehold and he struggled to free himself, but to no avail. "How dare you take a police officer's gun! How dare you demand repayment? You're lucky I let you do business. Why I…"

The first and only punch from Devlin hit Anderson in the stomach. He stepped back and nodded to his men, who began to pummel the sergeant into submission. Once the brief but furious beating ended, the four men propped the officer up on his wooden chair with his cap placed at an odd angle on his head. The sergeant's eyes were blackened and he bled from both his nose and mouth.

Devlin walked over and straightened the sergeant's cap and said, "I'm hoping you understand my point and no further explanations will be necessary. You are nothing but an aging, crooked cop. My connections go so far over your head, those people don't even know who you are. The president of the United

States personally pardoned me—I am untouchable. Do you feel untouchable, right now, sergeant?"

No answer from Anderson.

Devlin concluded, "I'm pleased you understand our arrangement. The cake must be returned tomorrow, and the next tip, which better be correct, is free. As you leave, tip your hat to each of my Irish countrymen and offer them a smile. Off with ya."

The sergeant wobbled as he stood, and while he did tip his hat, he substituted a sneer for the smile. Devlin's men wished him a collective, "Top of the evening," as they laughed at the disheveled officer. Anderson swore to himself he would find the person who double-crossed him and, Whiskey King or not, Devlin would pay for fucking with him because there was absolutely no doubt— Sergeant Herbert Anderson was the very definition of *untouchable*.

Chapter 22

Dying Every Single Day

Moses pushed against the door to his barn, but found it locked from the inside. After pounding several times, Vent opened the door, and said, "Hey, Moses, what you want?"

"What I want is for you to let me into my own barn."

"Moses, you said the barn was mine for a few days when I asked you yesterday. Remember?"

"Vent, I remember, but what you doin' in *my* barn?"

"Workin' on some stuff in my free time."

"What kind of stuff, Vent?"

"Not sure yet, but when you gave me permission, you never said you needed to understand what for, and I started this morning. Anyway, I'm not big on questions."

"You not *big* on lots of stuff, Vent!"

"Did you go and make a joke on me?"

"You gettin' smart, Vent—you picked up the joke on your own, but back to what you doin'—what you working on?"

"Listen, I realize this here your land. You becomin' some kind of big landowner in these parts, but you never asked what I wanted to do—not fair to ask after I started. So let me be, Moses. Let me finish up."

"Worried 'bout what you're finishing up, Vent. I think you're plannin' to do something to those Irish folks who hurt Horace. Remember, no Black man can do anything to no White man. Leave this one alone."

"I never said I'm plannin' anything."

"You never say anything, Vent—that's the problem."

Moses realized his approach needed to change. He bent down and searched for a rock with some decent size and weight, and threw it at a tree about forty feet away. "Damn, I missed," Moses remarked.

Games involving throwing and catching always interested Vent, and he stepped out from inside the barn, picked up three bigger rocks, tossed them in the air to check their weight and fired all three at the same tree, hitting his target twice, and missing by a few inches with his third attempt.

"Always thought you a natural base ball player, Vent. You need to try out for the team. Base ball is the kind of thing you should be doing with your free time."

"Not so sure 'bout base ball for me, Moses, but I like watching the games." Vent smiled as he remembered taking Georgia to her first game. Moses decided to try one last time. "Remember when Horace asked you to beat up the neighborhood boy, and later you found out he was wrong in asking? Horace, mostly a good boy, but he got a thing about revenge—seems to like it, but doesn't want to get his own hands dirty. Guess that's why he likes you."

"Don't understand nothing 'bout what you're sayin', Moses. Workin' on stuff is all. Let me be."

Moses persisted. "Vent, don't you realize things are good right now? You got a job, a girlfriend, a family, and friends like me. You go and do something foolish and you'll wind up a dead man."

"Everyone winds up a dead man, Moses; might happen any day, no sense worrying."

"What do you mean, no sense worrying? You taking too many chances every time you jump from tree to tree, or do flips onto roofs—if you fall and break your neck, you're done. Now, you plannin' to go off and do something to some big Irish fella 'cause you need to fight for Horace? You takin' too many chances, Vent. Things good for you now—listen to me, stop all this foolishness."

"Moses, you taught me something a long time ago—helped me live better. You said, don't keep thinkin' about bad things from the past 'cause you'll miss out on good stuff, like Georgia, but if you let me, I'm gonna teach you something, too."

"What a young crazy boy like you gonna teach a grown man like me?"

"So, first you call me short, and now you call me crazy. Mama told me when people say those things 'bout me, they makin' fun. Are you sure you a good friend?"

"Best ever, Vent. Only lookin' out for you."

"Okay, let me teach you Vent's lesson. Some people go up on a big building and they look down and they scared they gonna die, even though lots of people done been up high before and they holding onto a rail. Other people afraid every day about what somebody gonna tell them, even though they listen to the same stuff all the time and life goes on. Other people won't even take the ferry over to New York because Black folks got killed there during the riots a few years back—even though lots of Colored folks go on the ferry every day. What I'm sayin' is, those people worry 'bout everything, and don't believe they can do something other people done or even they did themselves. I jump from tree to tree, walk on building beams every day, and I don't worry 'bout a thing, 'cause I done all these things before, and I understand what Vent can do. People who worry all the time are dying every single day of their life 'cause they always afraid—I understand I'm only gonna die on one particular day, so what's the sense in worrying all the time? I'm not saying I'm doing anything about what happened to Horace, but if I am, I'm not worried, and I'm not doing anything I'm not sure I can do. So that's your lesson from a short, crazy boy."

"Not sure if your lesson is the smartest or dumbest thing anyone ever told me, but after listening to Ezra all these years, I understand how bad being called dumb feels, so I won't say which one I think. You be careful, boy, I hoped to be your friend for a long time to come, not so sure 'bout the *long* part anymore."

"Moses, you done found another thing you just don't need to worry 'bout."

Chapter 23

A New Partner

"Listen, I need you to do a special favor for me, and you understand what happens when you do a favor for Sergeant Anderson, right?"

"No, sir. I do not," answered the Irish cleaning lady.

"Well, let's say they'll be a little extra pay for you. All you need to do is stay in this general area for about an hour or so after I leave tomorrow afternoon and tell me who sits at my desk or opens my desk drawers for any reason. Not so much to ask, right?"

"No, Sergeant, not so much. I'll tell you what happens after you leave."

Step one of Anderson's plan was in place and step two required BOB to play along by repeating the exact sequence of events that led to the note being intercepted a few days earlier. Step three involved the report of the cleaning lady after the sergeant left the building. Anderson viewed the problem as bigger than a missed payday with Devlin—he ruled this station with an iron fist. *No one goes against me without paying the price. No one fucks with Herbert Anderson.*

The next afternoon, Roberta McGurt marched into the open station house work area and asked for the sergeant. After their discussion, Anderson placed the note in the same drawer. A few minutes later, the sergeant announced that the Irish appeared to be taking a day off from their mischief, so he planned to leave early.

Anderson and McGurt left the precinct around the same time. The sergeant headed around the corner to a bar he liked to frequent and winked to the cleaning lady on his way out. Roberta told her boss she needed to leave for personal reasons.

The cleaning lady emptied all of the garbage and swept the floors for the next hour. Two people stopped at the sergeant's desk. The captain visited first, and appeared to be searching for some paperwork. The second man, the young officer whose father was also a cop, shuffled papers around the desktop and dropped something on the floor. The cleaning lady couldn't be sure, but he may have opened the top drawer when he bent down.

The sergeant came back into the station and motioned for the cleaning lady to follow him into the hall. After hearing the names of the two people, he became concerned. He dismissed Singleton as the person who intercepted the note, because the kid barely understood where to report to work every day. The captain, however, was another matter and a major concern.

Many tried to catch Anderson doing something illegal, but the sergeant always sensed the captain was not part of this group. The more likely scenario—the captain smartened up and wanted in on the action. Anderson, much better with numbers than words, started to do the math in his head. *Yeah, I'll be happy to cut the captain in for 25 percent, BOB's percentage—no need for her to be in the mix any more.* Now pleased with this turn of events, Anderson imagined the moment he'd tell the whore to fuck off. *Things have a way of working out,* he thought. The sergeant had a new partner and just needed some time to cultivate the relationship.

⊷⊷▣ ▣⊷⊶

BOB reached the tenement house after a short walk—the time had come for this next logical step. Roberta outgrew the illiterate Anderson long ago. After all, her relationship with Devlin began years before in her prior occupation—time for a reintroduction to the most prominent Whiskey King in Irishtown. Devlin's men started joking with BOB as she arrived.

"We thought you went straight, are ya here to make a little extra money? Happy to bend you over the couch right over here for old time's sake. What do ya say, BOB? How about a go?"

All of Devlin's men started laughing, which made the Whiskey King walk to the outer area to check on the commotion.

"Roberta McGurt, my little sweetheart, how are ya? Are these lousy bastards troubling you in any way? We understand you're working for the captain now, and we'll give you all the respect you deserve. Right, boys?"

The men nodded in agreement, despite their smirks.

Devlin continued, "Roberta, please come in and we will catch up on old times."

Roberta held her head high as she walked into Devlin's office—they settled in for a chat.

"Mr. Devlin, sir, I'm so sorry to disturb ya, but I need to discuss a matter of some importance."

"I'm happy to be of service."

"I doubt you realize it, but we've done some business together before."

"Yes, I believe about five years ago, at one of my parties, when—"

"No, no, no. I'm not talking about my old occupation, although I must say, I found your company quite charming." BOB blushed as she tilted her head downward. Devlin smiled.

Roberta continued, "I'm the one who gives Anderson the tips on the raids. The stupid fuck let someone switch the last note I gave him with the address and because he can't read, he gave you the wrong address."

"Oh my God, Sergeant Anderson, who shits on all of the Irish, is as illiterate as the lot of us, what an interesting development! What does he pay you?"

"He says he gives me half of the hundred you pay him for each tip."

"Ah, he remains true to his nickname, The Criminal Cop. I pay him two hundred for each tip, which means, you're only getting a quarter."

"The lying fat fuck!" Roberta exclaimed.

"No reason for him to take advantage of you anymore. Tell him you lost your source of information, and you come straight to me. I'll give you a hundred and fifty for each tip. Better for both of us. What do you say?"

"It will be a pleasure to do business with ya, Mr. Devlin, but I must be on my way. Hope you don't mind. I must attend to a pressing social engagement." The Whiskey King's imagination got the better of him, and his smile broadened as he considered the possibilities of her *social engagement*. Roberta McGurt got up and exited, while Devlin stared out the window at his beloved Irishtown. *Things have a way of working out,* he thought. The belligerent sergeant could now be dealt with in a different manner. Devlin had a new partner.

The Plan Takes Shape

"THE DOC SAID you shouldn't be movin' around so much 'cause head injuries are tricky, so back to bed, Horace."

"Okay, Mama, I only wanted to stretch my legs. Hopin' to go back to work soon. We need the money."

"Your boss, Mr. Reems, came by the other day, and said he shouldn't have sent you to Irishtown so late. Mr. Reems got some good in him and said you can take all the time you need."

"All the time I need? Didn't seem so understanding the night he sent me over to the docks, but all right, Mama, back to bed."

"Good. Your sister is coming over later to visit a spell. Rest up, so you can spend some time with her."

"I'll take a nap, but wake me up when Vent comes in."

"He's been going straight over to Moses's place after work. Told me he's working on something, but he'll be here later. I think he's still teachin' Moses how to read and write, but I'm sure he'll check in on you later."

"Okay, Mama. I need to talk to him."

"Why?"

"Stuff, Mama. Nothing special."

"Open your drawer next to your bed, Horace. I know what you keep in the drawer—the damn mirror your daddy bought for me, but I ain't seen it in years. Take a good look at yourself. What you see?"

Horace paused and didn't need to go through the exercise of looking at himself in the mirror to provide a response. "A face so beat up and bruised, it will never be the same. More than anything, my mirror shows me what the big Irish bastard did to me for fun!"

"No, you wrong, Horace—you too old to be worried 'bout being handsome. You handsome enough to marry any girl in Weeksville, even with those bruises. What you should be seeing is *alive*. Horace, you should be praising the Lord for sparing your life and getting you back home safe to your family. If you make Vent go into Irishtown to hurt the Irish boy, it'll mean you care more 'bout being pretty than keepin' your brother alive. Don't disappoint me, Horace, do the right thing. I'm counting on you."

⊷▬◉ ◉▬⊶

Vent spent each of the last few nights in Irishtown. He figured out how to sneak in undetected, covering as much of his face as possible. Finding Jimmy McGreary proved to be easy enough based on Horace's description of him as a "monster of a boy." Jimmy was more than twice Vent's size in weight and a foot taller. Success in this fight would require both speed and dirty tactics. Vent worried about Jimmy's size.

At this point, Vent followed the giant Irish boy around long enough to understand his evening routine, which began with a meeting of his own gang of teenagers, who hung out in an alley between two warehouses related to the same business. Garbage was stored in the space between the two buildings and no windows overlooked the alley. A catwalk about fifteen feet above ground connected the second floors of both buildings and gave the alley more of a closed-in sense. Once the business closed for the day, the alley became the perfect place for Jimmy's young gang to conduct their affairs undisturbed. Vent found a spot in the back of the alley close to the gang hangout and overheard many of their conversations over the past few nights. Tonight's dialogue included the same basic topics and ended in the same predictable way.

"Jimmy, are you gonna get me into the Caps after they take you?"

"Listen, I told you, I got to be accepted first, which means I need to build up my reputation, so remember to call me, 'Half as Hard Jimmy,' 'cause I hit that Darkey so hard, I knocked him out with one punch. Anyway, that's the name the Caps gave me—you think they give names to everybody? I don't think so. I'll be a Cap real soon and I'll try to help all you guys become Caps when you're old enough."

Jimmy's young group of five associates, ranging in age from twelve to fifteen, started chanting "Half as Hard Jimmy—Half as Hard Jimmy." Jimmy smiled as he spotted Katie Fitzpatrick turning the corner and instructed his friends, "Now leave me be, all of you. Let me do my business with Katie." The boys all laughed as they moved away from the alley.

"Top of the evening, Miss Katie. Right on time as usual."

"Listen, you big piece of shit, I promised to do this ten times for ya just to leave my little brother alone. He never did anything to anyone. Now, this is number five, and I got two other customers—payin' customers, I'll have you know—after you tonight. So no more talk, let's go."

Jimmy waved Katie into the alley as he said, "Step into my office, Miss Fitzpatrick."

"Oh, shut the fuck up with the Miss Fitzpatrick bullshit. I fuck for money and you're only getting these free rides a few more times." Katie pulled up her dress, pulled down her knickers, and leaned over a short barrel in the alley. Jimmy went to work. A few minutes later, Katie was gone and Jimmy stood with his pants down, beating his chest to celebrate his great conquest. This celebratory moment would give Vent the perfect opportunity to strike. If their deal involved ten free rides, only five remained after today, so Vent would need to act soon.

Fighting fair was never an option for Vent—he barely weighed a hundred pounds and stood an inch shy of five feet tall. He needed the element of surprise, along with dirty tactics, to beat this mountain of a boy. The fight needed to be fast and in the dark, because if anyone identified Vent, they'd hang him for sure. Moses was right, they might not be slaves any more, but they certainly weren't free.

The plan was set, but Vent avoided sharing any details with Horace and snuck into his second-floor bedroom via the tree to avoid questions. Despite Horace's request to be present, Vent couldn't allow his involvement because if things went bad, they would both pay the ultimate price for failure. No Colored man could attack a White man, even if he was Irish.

CHAPTER 25

Final Preparations

"HEY, BOYS, DIDN'T realize you became a moving company. What are all these boxes?" Officer John Singleton asked.

Four of the Velvet Caps glanced at each other and shrugged. One offered, "Not for us to say. We do as we're told."

"I think I'll take a peek to satisfy my curiosity," the officer replied.

Sean O'Malley noted the exchange from the window of the newest Devlin distillery being built in a vacant apartment, and ran into the street to take control of the conversation. "Officer Singleton, whatever is the problem?"

"No problem. I'm asking about all of these boxes. Your men don't appear to understand what's happening with them."

"Ah, Officer Singleton. Such is the plight of the Irish. We never understand the why's, all we need is the what's and the where's. So all these lads need to know is that these boxes should be moved into this building. Bogging them down with more information is too much for a simple Irishman. Right, boys?"

All of the Caps started laughing. "Yes, of course, Boss, everything else is tattle. We're simple Irishmen helping out with a move."

Singleton decided not to push any further and mentioned as he walked away, "I guess this building may be one we'll keep an eye on. Hope we don't start smelling any sweet poteen, because if we do, I'll be back."

"Understood. Fellas, please go inside the building for a minute, I need a private word with the officer."

The men moved toward the building and Officer John Singleton straightened his back and asked the obvious question, "What do you want, O'Malley?"

"I understand how hard surviving on a policemen's salary can be. Be it what it would, you protect us against all of the bad elements in society and do all of this for such small pay." O'Malley paused for a second to take an envelope out of his pocket. "Perhaps, if I gave you an envelope like this every month, you might forget about this location and stop snooping around the Velvet Caps building by Little Docks?"

Singleton grabbed O'Malley by the collar and said, "I'm not Anderson—you can keep your dirty money. I should bring you in for bribery."

"Bribery! This is a simple payment, and if you don't want this money, the officer you bring me to will, and he'll let me go. If he's not interested…well, that's impossible, all of you coppers are interested, it is only a matter of price. Don't think you'll be taking me anywhere, and you won't last in Irishtown if you don't learn how to play the game. Good day to you, Officer."

Singleton, at a loss for words, turned and walked away—the unfortunate fact was most of the officers did accept bribes. *How did my father manage so many years in this kind of a system?* Singleton headed to The Professor's apartment. He needed to talk.

⋆⟫⟪⋆

"John, been a while since we've chatted. How's the first few months on the job?"

John started unloading everything—the incident with O'Malley, all the issues with Devlin, switching the notes about the raids, the beating of the Black man by the Velvet Caps, and all the rampant corruption within the force.

The Professor poured himself a tumbler of Jameson whiskey and after a brief hesitation, poured another one for his young friend.

"On your first day on the job, I didn't offer you a drink, but by now you understand a little Jameson helps after a tough day. You made some mistakes, John. Your job is about choosing between the lesser of evils. Things like murder, serious robberies, and rapes are the major crimes, but many other offenses, what I'll call nuisance issues, require finesse."

"What kind of finesse?"

"Irishmen need their drink and the booze can't be expensive, so the Whiskey Kings actually serve a purpose. If the Caps offer you a bribe, you accept the money, because this will make both O'Malley and Devlin friends instead of enemies. One day you'll need a favor from them to solve a real crime. You may not like the system, but this is the way of the world as a policeman in Irishtown."

"So what happens next?"

"The gangs don't come after policemen, but what they do is go to the boss, who will be connected through one or two intermediaries with your boss, and young John Singleton will likely find himself transferred to another area far away from Irishtown, where he will be a smarter officer the next time around. Those officers who don't play along to any extent, don't last. John, if this describes you, save yourself lots of time and effort, and quit."

"You're saying my father took money?"

"I'm saying your father understood how to separate the true bad guys from the shady businessmen. He was a terror with the bad guys, but he did build relationships with the businessmen."

"I'm disappointed in my father, Professor, and to be honest, I'm also disappointed in you."

"Ah, John, everything is disappointing before you finish your first tumbler. Things improve after the second, and by the third, you're on top of the world! Drink up and go back to work!"

⊷═◌ ◌═⊷

"Good morning, Miss Esther, I came over to talk to Horace for a spell."

"Sure, Moses, he's in his room. Go on in."

Moses walked down the short hallway and knocked on Horace's door before entering. "How you doin', Horace?"

"Hi, Moses, doing a lot better—healing up okay, I guess. I don't think Vent is here."

"Don't want Vent, I want to talk to you, man to man, 'bout what's goin' on."

"What you mean? Moses?"

"I mean you got Vent risking his life to go after some Irish giant. Do you understand what gonna happen to Vent, if he fails? Do you understand what happens to Vent, if he does this for you but gets caught after the deed is done?"

Horace didn't answer and sat up in bed, straightening his back.

"Okay, Horace, you don't want to say, so I will. They goin' to kill Vent if things don't go perfect."

"Vent won't be caught, Moses, and I'm gonna help."

"Horace, you ain't gonna be anywhere near the fighting—you nothing but a coward—smart coward, though, and not 'cause you read and write so well. You smart 'cause Vent does your dirty work. Unless you tell him to stop, he's gonna do this, and I'm not so sure it will go well. You understand me? What you gonna do?"

"Moses, I understand what you sayin', but what they did to me can't stand. Vent's not scared, he's gonna be successful. I'm not tellin' him to stop."

"Goddamn little coward—if things go wrong, the blame is all on you. This time, I can't stop him, but I'm tellin' you, anything else happens to him, I'm gonna tell everyone, including your mother, what a coward you are. Vent's life is worth as much as yours, but you willin' to risk his life 'cause what they did to you 'can't stand.' You not welcome no more on my properties and you stay away from me in general. I don't like cowards—never did, never will."

Moses stormed out of the house and headed back to the barn, kicking the dirt every few feet. Horace got Vent into all this trouble and he was gonna need help. *Well, Vent, Moses gonna be your help. I just gotta make sure there's some chance this all gonna work out.*

⌁

"Captain, thank you for taking some time to meet with me today. I understand what a busy man you are."

"What can I do for you, Sergeant Anderson? You don't consult with me much as a rule."

"I'm tryin' to take care of the details for you, Captain. No need for a man of your stature to be involved in the little things required to run a precinct. Least I can do."

"Okay, Anderson, enough of the bullshit, what do you want?"

"Well, sir, a sensitive matter of some importance. We need to talk."

"Sensitive?"

"Yes, I understand you went through my desk the other day and I wanted to know if you needed something from me?"

"Yes, I searched your desk for a report I gave you a few hours earlier. Odd thing, though, my secretary told me I might as well take the report back from you because you don't read a lick."

Anderson jumped up from his chair. "She's nothing but a little cunt, how dare she say I can't read!"

"Sergeant, please sit back down. How have you managed to hide not being able to read for all of these years?"

"I read, but I need better spectacles, is all—hard for me to read the fine print."

"Oh, so it is more of an age thing—perhaps you should consider retiring, Anderson. Let's give a younger man a chance to run things for a bit."

"Don't overstep, Captain, my friends are in high places, but I'll be certain to work on those spectacles."

Anderson stood up, straightened his uniform, and walked out of the office, returning moments later with the words, "Sorry, Captain, I forgot to close the door." He slammed the door so hard, the portrait of the farm fell from the wall. The sergeant stomped away from the office as he thought, *That little cunt, BOB. She'll get hers—and soon.*

The biggest surprise, however—the captain was looking for a report, which meant young Officer Singleton was the one coming after him. Hard to imagine—a green kid, son of a longtime fellow officer, making a move like this. Anderson planned to teach the kid a lesson.

◆━◑ ◐━◆

Vent pushed his creation out of the barn and imagined how difficult it would be to roll his device over three miles to Irishtown—not only would the task be physically exhausting, but the idea of slipping in and out unnoticed seemed almost impossible—but he needed to find a way soon.

Moses came out of nowhere. "So what is this here *thingamajiggy* you done spent all this time building in my barn?"

"Not sure I want to say."

"Vent, who your best friend in the whole world?"

"You, Moses."

"Don't you think the time has come to trust your best friend with whatever this plan is you put together?"

"What plan?

"Vent, stop. I know you going into Irishtown. Time to tell me what you plannin' to do"

"Okay, Moses. I'll tell you because you asked and also because I might need some help."

"I promise I'll listen and try to help, but if it sounds like we both gonna get killed, I'm out, and if only you gonna get killed, I'm gonna try and change your mind. If the plan is good and safe enough, I'll give my best friend a hand. Show me what this thing does."

Vent spent the next fifteen minutes explaining what his trap would do, and Moses started laughing. "Okay, Vent, I think this crazy contraption will work, and all you need is a ride to move this thing into Irishtown. Here's what we going to do—I never told you I started a carting business. I do it a couple of days a week. I'm okay going into Irishtown during the day, 'cause I'm doing deliveries, and we can cover your *thingamajiggy* up in the back of my carriage. My last delivery is on the other side of the alley you talkin' 'bout."

"Perfect, Moses, but how many businesses you in? Never heard about the carting."

"I got lots of things going on, trying to buy up as much land as I can. This is my plan, but back to yours—one last thing you gotta build, 'cause I can't be seen with you. You go and build a little box on the bottom of my carriage, big enough for you to squeeze into."

"No problem, Moses. Thanks for your help."

Moses understood Vent would go through with his plan with or without his help, and appreciated the trust Vent showed by confiding in him. Vent's mom might still be alive today if she had trusted someone enough to help her with her wounds when she arrived at Fort Sumter. If Vent failed, and had a similar fate, Moses's conscience would be clear. Moses patted Vent on the back and said, "What a perfect way to even the score with big Jimmy McGreary!"

CHAPTER 26

Moving On

"JOHN DEVLIN! HOW did you enjoy your little upstate vacation? We missed you—much too quiet without you. Welcome back to Brooklyn!"

"Such a warm welcome means a lot coming from Hugh 'Boss' McLaughlin. With all of Brooklyn to worry about, I appreciate you taking the time to come back to Irishtown to sit with an old friend."

"Never forget your roots. I started as a simple ropemaker in the Brooklyn Navy Yard a few years ago."

"Now you're the boss of all Brooklyn Democratic politics—a long way from ropemaking!"

"Sure is. Tell me, though, why are we meeting in the back of a bakery?"

"Well, I try not to draw too much attention to myself or call in any more favors than necessary…"

McLaughlin's laughter interrupted Devlin. "Good one, John. All you *do* is draw attention and *ask* for favors, but I must say, you give your fair share of favors in return. What do you need?"

"First, I need a little break from the raids. I understand this is more of a federal thing, but I lost my main distillery last week."

"Okay, you're right, it is a federal thing—the revenue officers are tight-lipped about their plans for raids of late, but I'll talk to a few people—I can't make any promises, though. Anything else?"

"Yes. Two other things I know you can help with."

"Tell me. Whatever you need, John."

"I need Sergeant Herbert Anderson retired. He fucked me big-time and he's no longer part of the future. Been on the job a long time, causing some trouble right now. I want him gone."

"Done. He's drawn too much attention to himself over the years. They all call him The Criminal Cop, so we can spin this as an effort to clean up the ranks of the police. What's the second favor?"

"Also relates to another transfer—a recently hired officer by the name of John Singleton. I don't care where you put him, but I want him out of Irishtown."

"Done. Remember, John, I may need a few favors of my own down the road, and I do keep score."

"You're not the only one, Boss. We all keep score."

The Democratic machine in Brooklyn proved to be efficient as ever. One stop at police headquarters and both the retirement and transfer were arranged. The issue of the raids, however, presented a difficult challenge because of the involvement of the federal authorities, and Boss McLaughlin needed time to develop a possible approach.

◄►▬◑ ◐▬►◄►

Sergeant Anderson planned to take Singleton into an interrogation room and find out who put him up to his treachery—no inexperienced officer would ever go against Anderson; someone else had to be behind this bold move. The sergeant spotted John Singleton coming through the door of the station, but before he had a chance to call out his name, Roberta McGurt arrived at Anderson's desk with a smile on her face and a message—the captain wanted to meet with him. Roberta remained at Anderson's desk as the sergeant walked away.

"Sergeant Anderson, please sit down—interesting how things work out. We discovered your corruption a long time ago, and this week, we also found out you're illiterate. Those issues made you a constant topic of conversation and, earlier this morning, I received a visit from my bosses. Guess what, Herbert? They also wanted to talk about you. What a popular fella, you are, Sergeant Anderson! Guess what? The bosses all agree and the plans are all set—you're being retired as we speak. If you put up a fuss, we'll bring charges, and believe me, the proof will not be hard to find. Roberta is packing up your personal belongings, and these two officers will escort you out." The captain motioned to two officers standing outside his door. They walked Anderson back to his desk, where

Roberta McGurt handed him one small box, along with the message, "Such a pleasure serving with you!"

Anderson's reply, "Fuck you, BOB, fuck all of you." Retired Sergeant Anderson left the building. Next, Roberta walked over to John Singleton and told him he, too, needed to meet with the captain.

"Singleton, sit down. This is going to be hard for you to understand, because you seem to be one of the good cops, but you haven't found the right balance with how you go about your work. I'm going to give it to you straight. You made some enemies in Irishtown—some important people—and they want you out. But I'm going to put you on one of our best details, though, because of what your dad meant to this department. You're going to become part of the police contingent securing the construction site for our new bridge. This will be exciting, John—this bridge is the biggest ever. Try to learn from your Irishtown experience—do the right thing, but go slow and find better ways to move things in the right direction. Understand, John?"

"Yes, Captain, I think I understand, but couldn't I have one more chance to make things work for me in Irishtown?"

"No, sorry, John, the decision is made. Report to the new job right away, head over and ask for the captain—my old friend, Helmut Dill. Good luck, John. Don't give up—just be a more selective with your interpretation of the law. Understand?"

"Selective interpretation…I'll do my best."

CHAPTER 27

Half as Hard Jimmy

"ALL RIGHT, VENT, we can talk as long as no one else is on the road, but if I say, 'Shhh,' you stop talking. Understand?"

"No problem, not much of a talker."

"No shit!"

Vent curled up in his customized shelf on the underside of the carriage and settled in for the ride. The plan set—Moses would pull up to the alley at four thirty, unload his delivery, wait for the right moment, and give the signal, "Go." Vent would then crawl out from down below and wheel his special cargo into the alley while Moses waited with the carriage about a mile outside of Irishtown. Vent calculated he would need about ninety minutes to set everything up before the action took place.

Moses made his first stop and delivered some materials to a general store and Vent prepared for his exit. The second and final stop was only about two blocks away. The carriage came to a halt and Moses took a long time to unload his materials. Vent waited and considered beginning one of his counting sequences, but resisted the urge. Moses said, "Go."

Vent jumped out from under the carriage and hopped up to the cargo area. The first problem, easy to solve—Moses placed a long board as a ramp to the ground and Vent wheeled his heavy trap down the ramp and into the alley. Once inside, he concealed all his materials.

Moses's carriage pulled away and Vent began to prepare the alley. First, he formed a wide and loose noose with rope in the general area where Jimmy would celebrate his conquest of Katie Fitzpatrick. He covered the rope with garbage and leaves, and took a step back to admire his work. *Yup, hid this real good.*

The end of the rope ran along the side of the wall and up and over the el-evated catwalk above Jimmy's celebratory spot. One final step—Vent opened the heavy box and removed a few of the sandbags, which provided added weight. He needed every ounce of strength in his body to lift the box about three feet in the air onto a metal chest someone discarded long ago. Vent returned the sandbags one at a time, covered the box, slid into his hiding spot, and waited for the sun to go down.

For the first time in a long while, Vent lacked total confidence in a physical activity—his crude trap only worked in theory, but he felt good about protecting his family and living by Miss Esther's rule. As soon as the sun went down, Jimmy and his crew began to congregate outside the alley.

"Jimmy, are you sure you'll get us into the Caps after they take you?"

"What did you call me?"

"Sorry, *Half as Hard Jimmy*, you gettin' us into the Velvet Caps?"

"I'll do the best I can, fellas. Ah, a little early tonight—goodbye fellas, and good evening, Miss Fitzpatrick."

The boys' laughter became faint as they walked away from the alley to give their leader his privacy.

"I told you, enough with the Miss Fitzpatrick, sounds like my ma…you want to fuck her?"

"No, you're more my type."

"Fuck you, I may be a whore, but don't insult me by calling me *your type*. This is number six. Thank God we're near the end. Let's go, you big piece of shit."

Katie headed straight for the barrel, pulled her dress up, her knickers down, and Jimmy did his thing, finishing within a few minutes. Katie made her quick-est exit yet. The customary pants down, chest beating commenced as Jimmy celebrated yet another conquest of the lovely Katie Fitzpatrick. One shove from Vent pushed the heavy box off the trunk, and the weight of the box falling toward the floor yanked the rope into a tight noose, which lifted Jimmy—legs first—into the air. Vent underestimated Jimmy's weight, so while his legs were up, his head still rested on the ground, and the box dangled a few inches from the floor. A single shot to the head with a club knocked Jimmy out, and Vent went to work.

He tied Jimmy's hands together and put a gag in his mouth and a hood over his head. Next, Vent cut Jimmy's pants off, sliced off his shirt, and cut the rope so both he and the box would fall to the ground. He removed a few sandbags in order to retrieve his supply case, which contained a brush as well as pine tar, which he started spreading all over the front of Jimmy's body. Once he achieved full coverage, Vent dropped a bag of chicken feathers on top of the tarred Irishman, cut his legs free, and threw water on his hooded face. Jimmy woke up disoriented and started walking into walls in the alley. At this point, Vent retreated to another of his hiding places on the other side of the block.

Jimmy screamed as he wandered out into the street and a crowd started to gather. Big, bad Jimmy McGreary had been tarred and feathered. The chants started coming from the crowd, "You big idiot, we see why they really call you *Half as Hard Jimmy*!" The crowd roared with laughter. After about five minutes, someone removed the hood from Jimmy's head, and he realized what had happened to him. Jimmy's brother, Aengus, arrived on the scene, rushed to his brother's side, covered him up, and tended to his bloodied face.

When Aengus directed three fellow Caps to search the area, Vent jumped out of his hiding spot, leaped over a fence, and did a flip at the peak of his ascent out of force of habit. The run to the meeting place with Moses didn't take long—Vent crawled into his shelf beneath the carriage and Moses started to head back to Weeksville. Horses approached from behind and Moses took control. "Vent, don't move and don't say nothin'. I'm gonna handle this."

Aengus and three of the Velvet Caps stopped Moses's carriage and asked if anyone had run past him. Moses responded, "No, not past me, but someone did run real fast down the hill." He pointed in the opposite direction. "Seemed like a big guy, but hard to tell in the dark."

The Caps went down the hill and found no one and gave up their search. After arriving back in Irishtown, one of the Caps said, "I got a look at him when he leaped over the fence—not a big man at all, more like a small boy."

Aengus responded, "I don't want you repeating your story to anyone. Gonna be tough enough for Jimmy to join the Caps after being made a fool, and if people think a small boy did this, he'll never be accepted. Probably was a gang of guys, yeah that's right, a gang. That will be our story."

Moses stopped the wagon as they got close to Weeksville and let Vent crawl out from under to tell Moses what happened. The two men exchanged nervous smiles as they considered the night a success and hoped their getaway was undetected. Once in Weeksville, they spotted Mackie Johnson standing alone on the side of Hunterfly Road.

"Moses, stop the carriage. Got to figure out who this guy is—I met him somewhere and he runs away from me every time I cross his path."

Moses pulled over and called Mackie over to the carriage as Vent put his head down and turned in the other direction.

"What you want?" Mackie asked.

Vent raised his head and faced Mackie, who became spooked. Vent didn't say a word—Moses controlled the conversation. "What your name?"

"Mackie Johnson."

"Why you so afraid of this here boy?"

Mackie turned to his side as he considered whether he should run or try to talk his way out of this predicament. The moment Vent caught Mackie's profile, he remembered. Venture stood in the carriage as he said, "You nothing but a damn raccoon, you eat your own. You were there when my mama was attacked."

"I didn't touch her, though. I was nothing but the lookout, downstairs. The others wanted to have a little fun, we all thought we'd die at the hands of the Irish mobs. Just wanted a little fun—they said your mother only slept with White men and needed to learn a lesson. No one said anything 'bout killin'. You gotta believe me, I only the watchout…"

Moses refused to let things play out on Hunterfly Road and knocked Mackie Johnson in the back of the head with the same club Vent used on Jimmy McGreary. The unconscious man was then bound, covered with a blanket, and placed in the back of the carriage. *This is bad*, Moses thought. *Vent is going to want to kill this man. Need to sort this out at the barn.*

Chapter 28

The Dues of a Coward

"Moses, what the hell you doin'? You can't be draggin' no tied-up strangers into our barn. Sometimes you so stupid! Crazy Vent, leading stupid Moses…whatever this is, seems like big trouble. Mind my words, Moses. Big trouble. What your stupid brain done got me involved with now!"

"Ezra, ain't no reason for you to be involved, but if you want to understand what we doin', you come inside and find out. Remember, though, this here my barn, and this here my land, so older brother or not, I'm not gonna take no more instructions from you. You comin' in or stayin' out?"

"Damn fool, course I'm comin' in, need to keep *crazy* and *stupid* under control."

"Okay, Ezra, but you ain't controlling nothing—you don't understand what going on here. I do. This time, little brother gonna take care of things. You right, Vent got to be controlled, but I'll control him. You understand?"

"No, but I'll do what you ask at first, but if this thing starts goin' the wrong way, I'm speaking up and I'm steppin' in."

"Fair 'nuff. What we 'bout to do is tricky. Little worried myself."

A rag, stuffed in his mouth, muffled Mackie's pleas, and the blanket, wrapped around his upper body, limited his movements. Vent's outward silence conflicted with his intense stare, taut facial muscles, and twitching shoulders—a nod to Moses preceded a quick climb up the center beam of the barn to an upper storage compartment. A short leap from the highest point of the beam put Vent in position and the counting commenced in multiples of two, "Two, four, six, eight…"

The bound man sat in the far corner of the barn with his hands still restrained, but the brothers decided to remove the rag from his mouth. Moses and Ezra, stood over him while Vent's counting evolved to fours. "Four, eight, twelve, sixteen…"

Moses cleared his throat so his voice would carry to the upper compartment. "Vent, this night gettin' more complicated with every passin' minute. We gonna talk 'bout all of this later, but first we'll ask this man, Mackie, what he says 'bout your mother's death. Everything we ask gonna be calm, and if he smart, his answers will be the same. Mr. Mackie, you a big man, but I'm even bigger, and my brother here ain't no one to be trifled with neither, but I got to tell you, this boy countin' numbers up yonder is the one you wronged, and he the one you got to fear. Right before I hit you over the head, you 'splained somethin' about being the *watchout*. Tell us the whole story and, Vent, I want you to stay up where you are. 'Cause we listenin' 'til we hear his story."

A nod to Mackie Johnson triggered the first of many pleas. "You makin' a mistake, let me go. Talk to Edward Heath, he'll tell you I'm a good man. Let me go, ask Edward Heath…he'll tell you."

"We not sending for anyone 'till we listen to your story. I ain't gonna ask you again, so start tellin' us your story and we want all of it," Moses replied.

Mackie Johnson started from the beginning. "The Irish mobs controlled the streets in Five Points, and I didn't want to be on my own, but I needed to go to the ferry or find some other way to cross the river to Brooklyn. These three men told me they wanted to do the same thing. Even though I knew they were bad as bad can be, I thought my chances would be better with them than on my own."

The background was the easy part. Mackie paused to find the right words to present the next part of his story. He looked up at Vent in the upper compartment and continued. "The men saw you and your mother walk into the boardinghouse, and she made a mistake when she came to the window, 'cause that made finding her easier. I think she realized this 'cause she closed the curtains real fast. They started sayin' bad things about you and your mother and I asked them why they talkin' about all this 'cause we had to go, but they paid me no mind. Remember, I needed them more than they needed me. All three of them didn't like your mother, said she had to be reminded she Black—she slept with White men for money, said she's nothing more than a whore, with a midget freak for a son." Vent stopped counting and glared at Mackie the moment he referred to his mom as a whore. Mackie realized he didn't present this critical part of the story well.

Moses attempted to calm the growing tensions in the room. "Vent, let the man tell his story. Mr. Mackie, I think you better be more careful with the words you use. You understand me?"

"I'm only tellin' you what they said!"

Moses repeated himself, pausing a little longer between each word while raising his voice. "Mr. Mackie, do—you—understand—me?"

Mackie answered, "Yes."

Vent started counting in sevens. "Seven, fourteen, twenty-one, twenty-eight…"

Mackie paused for a moment to assess his situation—the boy, pure crazy, Moses, more reasonable, but Ezra remained silent, which gave Mackie no sense of where he stood on the crazy/sensible scale.

Moses got things back on track. "Okay, Mr. Mackie, you gonna finish this story."

"The men planned to whip her with a leather strap they found in front of the boardinghouse, and then take turns rapin' her, but they never said anything 'bout killin'. Most things goin' on during the riots would be blamed on the Irish, but none of them cared about being caught anyway because they didn't expect to live through the night—only wanted some fun 'fore they came to their own end. One of them wanted to whip your mother and the other two wanted to rape her. I pleaded with them to forget 'bout your mama 'cause we needed to head to the water and stay clear of the mobs. They ignored me and told me I should go off on my own, if I didn't want no fun. But I didn't like my chances on my own, so I became the *watchout*."

Moses thought Mackie started to repeat himself, and while he wanted Vent to understand what happened, he didn't want him to suffer through the story twice, so he interrupted. "We understand, you stayed downstairs as the *watchout*. What else happened?"

"My head spun every which way when I watched out for the mobs, and I spotted the boy jump out of the window. Craziest thing—seemed like he flew. I realized he saw me too, and this is why I been avoidin' him ever since we been back. The boy saw all the terrible things those bad men did to his mother from his hiding spot on top of the roof next door."

"What happened to these men after they left the boardinghouse?" Moses asked.

"They wanted to find the boy 'cause they wanted to do something to him too, not sure what or why, but they hated him—kept callin' him a freak. Said he deserved the same thing happened to his mom." Mackie struggled to stand up and stared at Vent as he finished this part of the story. "I never told them you up on the roof. I protected you and never told them!"

Vent screamed down from above, "You think protectin' me makes you a hero. I'm gonna kill you, and I'm gonna make sure you see it coming, like my mama did!"

Moses called up to Vent, "Enough. You go and sit back down. We're gonna finish this story without no more interruptions. You understand me, Vent? Mackie, what happened to those three men?"

"Not sure, because they decided to steal some stuff from a store before we headed to the water. I realized they would keep makin' stops and one of those stops would end up being the death of us, so I left them. Don't think they ever got out. Make you a bet the mobs got them. They deserved whatever they got— killin' them might be the only fair thing 'bout the night."

Vent couldn't help himself. "One more fair killin' tonight, I promise you!"

Moses turned to Vent and pointed to his spot in the elevated storage area. "Sit down. I done told you, we're gonna listen to the whole story, almost done. What happened next?"

"I got lucky and ran into Edward Heath, who is a good, smart man. He paid some folks a little money to row us across the river and we made our way to Weeksville. Been a good man ever since. Went to Liberia with Mr. Heath, kept him safe, and helped the people like we s'posed to. Remember, I only the *watch-man*—never touched her, and I never told them the boy was on the roof next door. You got to believe me!"

Moses asked, "What are the names of these men who done this to Vent's mama?"

"Never introduced themselves, and like I said, they probably died in the riots."

Ezra broke his silence. "And you think being the *watchman* makes you innocent?"

"Yes. I never touched his mama."

Vent came out of his funk. "You not *innocent*, you nothing but a raccoon, who kills your own kind." Vent slid down the center beam, pulled his knife, and started advancing toward Mackie. Moses stood in front of the tied man and told Vent to back off, and Vent peered into Moses's eyes searching for clarification and guidance—he swore to his mama he would kill the men who murdered her, yet Moses stood in his way. Ezra stepped in as well, but Moses nodded to his older brother and he backed off.

Moses turned to Mackie and said, "First of all, you not *innocent*. When you stand by and let somethin' like this happen, you as guilty as the ones who done the murder, and if you don't understand this, you lost in every way a man can be lost. The thing is—this memory haunts this boy and he thinks when he kills you, the memory goes away, or at least he keeps his promise to his mama. He don't mind you tied up, 'cause he fights dirty—dirtiest fighter I ever seen, and I'm not sure what's gonna happen to you today, but if you live through this and we don't come to some understanding tonight, you might be walkin' down the street one day and find him flying out of a tree stabbing you before his feet even touch the ground. But he's not doing any such thing right now."

Moses turned to Vent and said, "Vent put down the knife and let's you and I go to the other side of the barn for a private chat. Ezra, keep an eye on Mackie."

"Moses, he needs to pay for killin' Mama!" Vent said.

"Same thing you been sayin' since you jumped out of the crate, but you come such a long way. You learned how to move forward with your life and you need to rethink this 'I'm gonna kill everyone' stuff. You also need to rethink Miss Esther's rule. Your brother, Horace, took advantage of you, Vent—no Black man goes into Irishtown for revenge. Went to his house and told him as much, but he didn't care, so I helped you. Your brother, Horace, is a coward, like Mackie

Johnson. Horace a coward 'cause he makes you do his fighting and Mackie a coward 'cause he let something real bad happen instead of stopping it. Far as I can tell, you gettin' smarter last few years, and I think you understood Horace was taking advantage of you, so you only embarrassed the big Irish fella instead of killin' him—you made the punishment fit the crime. Real smart. Let's do the same thing right now, but you got to listen to me, 'cause I'm the one who stands up for you. Okay?"

"Moses, he killed Mama!" Vent started to cry.

"No, he didn't kill Mama directly, but he is guilty, but not the same as the men who went upstairs. Punishment got to fit the crime, Vent. Write this one in your book when you go home, 'cause I need you to remember this new rule."

Moses walked toward his brother and said, "We got some thinkin' to do, Ezra. Go fetch Edward Heath, who done spent so much time with this coward. He's a smart man and he gonna help figure this thing out for us."

-»-▶—◉ ◉—◀-«-

Ezra explained the entire mess to Edward Heath as they headed for the barn, and Edward shook his head back and forth in shock as he learned about the actions of his longtime friend. Over the years, Edward realized Mackie possessed a certain edge, but thought he understood where to draw the line. At least the Brown brothers thought to bring him into the discussion, rather than acting out of haste and revenge. Edward Heath entered the barn and walked over to Mackie.

"Moses, please untie Mackie. We can all sit around the construction table. He won't do anything rash, and I think sitting to figure this out will be the best way."

"What you mean *rash*, Mr. Heath. Nobody talking 'bout any rashes here!"

"No. I'm sorry, Moses. I meant to say, he won't do anything in a sudden way, like try to run or attack anyone."

"Okay, but next time, just say what you mean, Mr. Heath."

"Understood, Moses."

"Okay, Mackie, we gonna untie you and let you sit at the table, but I'm gonna hold this here club in my hand, and if you try to go anywhere, the end gonna come crashing down on your head for the second time tonight. You understand, Mackie? Are we clear?"

"Yeah, we clear."

Vent and Mackie sat at the ends of the long construction table, with Ezra and Edward on either side, and Moses standing guard over Mackie. Edward Heath opened. "Ezra told me the whole story, Mackie. I guess I understand for the first time why you wanted to join me in Liberia—you wanted to move as far away from this terrible act as possible. All of you should understand Mackie acted like a good and proper man during our time in Liberia by helping people, and protecting me on more than one occasion. After acting like such a coward during the riots, he started to turn his life around in Liberia, and we should keep this in mind."

Vent jumped in. "My mama never had a chance to turn *her* life around, so why should we keep this in mind?"

"You're right, Vent, but *you* did turn *your* life around. I remember how you started out in Weeksville as compared to how you are today. You got a second chance, and perhaps we can figure out some nonviolent way forward."

Moses thought this was a good opportunity for Vent to consider any suggestions with an open mind. "Vent, you got so many bad memories in your head, and you learned not to think about them so much. Now you got a pretty girlfriend, a lovin' family—mostly—and a good job, so if you do something bad, you'll be set back with new bad memories. Do you think your mama would want you to live a sad life thinking about all these bad things, or do you think she'd want you to be happy?"

"Mama would want me to be happy, but I promised to kill the men who killed her."

Edward jumped back in. "So you found the only remaining man with any involvement, but his role, the smallest. So why don't we consider some other options. Mackie, you've been saving money for years. How much have you accumulated?"

Moses complained, "Mr. Heath, you got to speak plain, what's this *'cumulated?*"

"I meant to say, how much money have you saved?"

Mackie answered, "A hundred dollars."

Edward countered, "Don't lie, Mackie. I don't think you're in any position to play games. Try again."

"Three hundred, but that's my life savings!"

Ezra reminded Mackie of his circumstances. "Already knew you were a coward and now I see you a stupid man, too. Don't you understand—right now you choosing between the two? So what you want to keep, Mr. Mackie, your savings or your life?"

Mackie grunted and looked at the ground.

Edward made the proposal. "Vent's loss of his mother is forever, so I think he should be compensated…"

Moses interrupted, "*Compensated?*"

"Sorry, I think Vent should be given two hundred and fifty of Mackie's three hundred in life savings, so he can buy some land—something which could also be forever."

Moses added, "And you must leave Brooklyn, never to come back, 'cause if you do, not gonna be Vent who does the killin'. The boy's got enough bad stuff in his brain, but I ain't got so much—gonna be me dealing with you. You gonna give Vent his two hundred and fifty, take your shit, and be gone by the morning. Vent, is this okay with you?"

Vent didn't answer and sat with his head lowered for some time. Once he raised it, Moses caught his classic look of rage and hatred, but as Vent continued to stare at Mackie's face, his eyes changed from hatred to pity and then, finally, to disgust.

Edward, disturbed by the boy's intense glare, worried this matter would end up with a violent resolution.

Mackie understood things could go either way and either his life or his savings would be taken from him.

Ezra admired his younger brother, Moses, who he'd been calling stupid for so many years, and thought, *Moses is the one with the smarts.*

Moses read Vent's facial expressions perfectly—his friend consented to the arrangement.

Vent never said a word.

CHAPTER 29

Did My Best

MACKIE ROLLED UP his pant leg, which uncovered a pouch of cash strapped to his right calf—three hundred proved to be a gross underestimation of the total. An infuriated Edward Heath grabbed the stack of bills from his disgraced friend, peeled off fifty for Mackie, and handed the rest of the stack to Vent. Moses took charge of the money, counted four hundred dollars in bills, and told Vent he would work with him to find some property in the neighborhood. In typical fashion, Vent offered no response, but the fire in his eyes dimmed. The two friends sat together and reflected on their day separately in their minds, but together in spirit. Their eyes connected and they exchanged an affirmative nod, but no words were spoken. After taking a deep breath, Vent raised his head, walked toward his friend, gave him a hug, and walked away.

Within a few minutes, Moses collected Mabel from her home, brought her over to the Johnsons', and asked her to knock on the door to bring Georgia outside for a chat. Georgia's mom, Florence, thought the hour too late for a sidewalk conversation, but she agreed to send out her daughter because she trusted Mabel.

"Miss Georgia, my name is Moses Brown."

"Vent told me about you. Is he okay?"

"Well, lots of things happened today and he ain't much of a talker, I'm surprised he even told you about me, but he wants you, Mabel, and Miss Esther to understand what happened." Moses paused and turned his attention to Mabel. "So after I tell you, Mabel, I'm askin' you to talk to Miss Esther."

Mabel responded, "Of course, tell us what happened."

Moses told the story of the full day's events and suggested Vent got away with his Irishtown adventure undetected, and might be in a better place with regard to his mother. But in his typical style, he would never speak of either thing. Moses warned both women about speaking of what happened in Irishtown to anyone, because a Black man couldn't do what Vent did and live to tell the tale.

Moses turned to Mabel and ended with a final statement. "I hate to say a bad thing to a sister about her brother, but Horace nothing but a coward. He better stay away from Vent and he better stay away from me, too. I done my part tellin' you, and Mabel needs to tell Miss Esther."

Moses turned to Georgia. "I hope you realize what a special man you got in Vent—he don't talk so much with words, but in his own way, he shows us what he made of. Today, he also showed he can control himself when he needs to. Proud to call him my friend, and I hope all this don't scare you, 'cause Vent's a good man. Yeah, he a man, ain't no boy no more—he done grow'd up."

Georgia took a moment to respond to Moses. "Not afraid, but worried. Thank you for tellin' me what happened." Moses and Mabel left in their separate directions and Florence Johnson walked out to confront her daughter. "Vent okay?"

"Yes, but tough day for him—he found one of the men who took part in his mother's death."

"Did he do something to the man? Is he in trouble?"

Georgia responded, "No, he wasn't the main one who did the killin' and they told him to leave Brooklyn and made him give up all his money, so Vent can buy some land here in Weeksville."

Florence Johnson hugged her daughter. "Thank God. I thought you wuz gonna tell me he killed the man. This the best news, Georgia, you datin' a man of with a stack of cash!"

The daughter smiled, but didn't return the snort after her mother went into her thigh-slapping routine. Florence assumed she only heard part of the story, and would get the full details one day, but not tonight. Vent, unlike anyone she'd ever met, possessed an honorable quality she liked for her daughter—but had more secrets at the age of eighteen than any one person should have in a lifetime. The thought of Georgia one day marrying Vent confused Florence as she thought, *Should I celebrate or fear this match for my baby?* She offered her daughter some advice before they went back inside. "Georgia, no need for you to tell anybody else this news 'bout Vent, not even your daddy. You leave your daddy to me, I'll talk to him now. If ever you want to tell me more, I'm here for you. Understand?"

"Of course, Mama."

⟶▬⊙ ⊙▬⟵

"Mabel, what you doing here so late? Things okay with Alex?"

"Yes, Mama. I need to tell you something."

Thomas and Horace both heard the voices and came out of their bedrooms to investigate. Mabel got right to the point as she turned to her brother and said, "Horace, I hope I'll be able to forgive you for what you done, but I can't right now. Vent is as much a brother to me as you, and he would kill to protect any of us. His friend Moses came over here yesterday to ask you to call off sendin' him to Irishtown, 'cause you the only one who could, but you refused. You think your life worth more than Vent?"

Horace refused to answer her question and responded, "Tell me what happened. Did he kill the Irish bastard?"

Esther Washington slapped her son in the face. "Your sister come here in the middle of the night and says what she just said and all you ask is, did he kill the Irish bastard? What about, what happened to Vent? What about, is Vent okay? What about, is Vent in trouble?"

Horace remained silent and accepted his slap with the hope Mabel would get to the point. Thomas Washington glared at his son in pure disgust and grabbed him by the collar. "If you think that slap hurt, you wait and see what I do to you." He released Horace and pushed him into the corner, turned to Mabel, and asked, "Where is Vent and is he okay?"

"Vent is fine. I'm guessin' he's upstairs in his room, curled up in a ball in his closet, counting in threes or fours, tryin' to make sense of the day. Some of those things might have been avoided if Horace cared at all for him."

"Some of them? Mabel, you got to start tellin' us what happened!" Esther demanded.

Mabel spent the next ten minutes describing the tarring and feathering, the escape from Irishtown, and the events with Mackie Johnson.

Horace went back to his room disappointed that Vent had only embarrassed Jimmy McGreary.

Esther returned to her bedroom concerned about Vent's state of mind and Horace's character.

Thomas walked Mabel home, thinking he gave the wrong boy his last name, and Mabel remembered the little boy who sat in the garden, playing with her and swearing to protect her at all costs. She couldn't believe her brother, Horace, took advantage of that pledge.

No one went upstairs to check on Vent, assuming he was curled up on his mat in his closet. Vent, however, was peacefully lying on the floor of his room with no need for any of his daily nocturnal rituals. On this eventful day, he learned who loved and supported him and received about as much closure as he might ever expect with his mama's death.

Vent stared out of his window at his favorite tree, and raised his head up toward the stars as he said, "Mama, I didn't kill them all, like I promised, but I think, with the help of my friend Moses, I did my best. Gonna try and move on now, Mama. Got myself a wonderful girl by the name of Georgia—real pretty, just like you, and I got me some money, so if it's okay with you, I'm gonna start looking ahead and not behind. Hope this is okay, Mama. I understand what you done for me and I think I done the best I can for you. I hope you sleep well in heaven, Mama, 'cause I think I can start sleepin' well down here. Love you. Good night."

Part III

The Bridge
1869

CHAPTER 30

The Colonel Gets the Job

THE NEWS TRAVELED fast—the esteemed chief engineer and designer of the proposed East River Bridge had died as the result of a freak accident. A few weeks earlier, a boat crushed his foot against the pier on the Brooklyn side of the river when attempting to dock. The brilliant man, John A. Roebling, who possessed strong beliefs on a multitude of subjects, refused the doctor's recommendation of amputation, and attempted to heal himself through hydrotherapy. He died a painful death from lockjaw seventeen days later. All hope for the smooth continuation of the project rested on the shoulders of his thirty-two-year-old son, Washington Roebling, who distinguished himself during the war as a bridge builder and ended his military career with the rank of colonel.

Hugh "Boss" McLaughlin rested his feet on his desk as he discussed the latest prospects for the bridge with a few of his associates. "The son should be made chief engineer, I tell ya. He built bridges on his own during the war and acted as the day-to-day manager of the large Roebling bridge in Cincinnati a few years ago. The colonel understands every detail of the plans—he's got to assume control."

The Boss didn't expect any contrary positions as his slew of *yes-men* nodded in agreement.

One remarked, "Yeah, Boss, of course, he's the only man for the job."

Another suggested, "No one better suited for the work."

The Boss continued, "No doubt, fellas, a few years from now, Brooklyn will be the largest city in the country. New York is almost filled up, so Brooklyn will be the next. Think what this building is going to mean for us!"

"Good times, Boss, nothing but good times."

The New York-Brooklyn Bridge Company confirmed the appointment of Colonel Washington Roebling as the new chief engineer and maneuvering for contracts and jobs commenced. The plans called for a bridge large enough to accommodate pedestrian, carriage, and train traffic. This massive bridge would be as wide as Broadway and make the daily commute from Brooklyn to New York, currently handled with a system of six ferries, a much simpler affair. Boss McLaughlin envisioned the day the travel would be in the other direction, once Brooklyn surpassed New York in both population and industry. The towers, which would be built close to the shore on each side, would become the tallest structures in North America and the bridge span would be over a mile long from end to end. The scope of the project was enormous.

⋅⊱⫯⊰⋅

Harold Reems called both Horace and Vent into his office, but didn't acknowledge their presence—he continued to concentrate on manipulating a glass within a large bowl of water on the table in his office. After the glass was situated, he removed it from the bowl and addressed the brothers. "Listen up, boys, I explained this to a few other people and, so far, no one understands. Hard to believe, but I think you two Colored fellas may be best able to help me bid on this bridge project, but you need to understand what they're building."

Horace asked, "What do we need to understand, Mr. Reems?"

"The engineers plan to build two massive towers to support the big cables for a suspension bridge, which, by the way, will be the biggest in the world! Those cables will support the road for the new East River Bridge. Bids need to be submitted. Horace, I need you to help me with the writing, and Vent, with the numbers. Let me explain how they plan to do this—fascinating stuff." Reems paused as he gathered his thoughts.

"The cables will be anchored on either side far inland, because the height of the bridge needs to allow the big ships to pass underneath. This means the approach to the bridge on each side needs to elevate in a gradual way, which forces the endpoints or anchors for the cables, further inland. Massive towers are going to rise out of the water on either side to create a high point, from which the cables can drop and reach their natural settling point in the middle of the river, before rising to the top of the tower on the other side, with an interior anchoring point further inland."

Horace commented, "Okay we understand this part, but how are they going to make towers rise out of the water?"

"Excellent question, Horace, and this is the part no one understands. Let me show the two of you. Look at this clear bowl of water and other materials I set up."

Vent and Horace examined the odd rectangular bowl and spotted pebbles on the bottom, followed by a kind of claylike material, followed by sand, with water up to the surface. Reems took his empty, clear glass and flipped it upside down, and put a small piece of wood, cut to the dimensions of the glass, against the open end. The glass was now fully sealed.

"Okay, boys, pay attention, this is tricky. Imagine this glass is something called a caisson—a fancy French name, but the actual one won't be made of glass. The real one will be made of wood, but by using glass in my example, you can see the inside to better understand."

Vent uttered his first words, an unusual occurrence, so Harold Reems realized he found this interesting. "Okay, so the drinking glass is the caisson, what happens next?"

"Watch this," Harold Reems directed as he inserted the upside-down glass into the bowl, flush against the first layer at the bottom, which consisted of sand. "The caisson will sink down to the rock, and form a firm foundation for a tower once filled with cement."

Vent asked, "How?"

"Another good question. They'll start by building a removable bottom on the caisson—that's what this piece of wood represents. The bottom keeps the caisson airtight and enables it to be tugged to the right location before being sunk. Next, they'll start making the caisson heavier by building tons of masonry on top. The increased weight will make the structure sink. When the caisson hits this first level of sand, they remove the temporary bottom, and start to dig so the structure can continue to sink as the weight of the tower on top gets heavier."

Reems paused for a moment and slid out the small piece of wood and started to push the glass further into the sand.

"How are they gonna do all this work under water?" Vent asked.

"This is the trick, they'll be pumping compressed air inside of the caisson. This air will keep the water out as long as they increase the air pressure the lower they go. The air pressure inside the caisson has to be equal to the pressure from the water on the outside. The air, of course, also enables the men in the caisson to breathe while they dig. At the same time, workers on top will be building the tower, which will further sink the caisson. The result of all of this work is the slow and gradual sinking of the structure through the clay, until the caisson hits bedrock and is filled with cement. The towers they plan to build will be the tallest ever!"

"Unbelievable!" Vent exclaimed. "I'm guessing we're looking to supply some of the bricks for the tower?"

"Yes, Vent, so I'll need your help estimating amounts and prices. Horace, you'll write the proposal up proper, so we can submit our quote to the Bridge Company. This might be the biggest job we ever receive. We need to do this right."

Ever since the incident in Irishtown, Vent had stopped considering Horace to be his brother. Working with him on a daily basis was uncomfortable for Vent, who thought this new bridge project might provide an opportunity for a new job, which could put more distance between him and Horace. Now that he had achieved some peace with his mother's death, Vent sought positive change in every aspect of his life. The bridge could be his chance. While he hated the nickname *Monkey Boy*, the skills that earned him this dubious distinction might also qualify him to work atop the towers. Vent smiled as he walked away from Reems's office—his plan had become clear. The life he always dreamed about seemed within his reach.

CHAPTER 31

Jimmy's New Burn

JIMMY MCGREARY'S SKIN was still raw and red from the scrubbing required to remove the tar from his body. He grabbed the armrest on his chair as another chant emanated from the street below. "Hey, Jimmy, I just finished plucking a chicken, and brought you the feathers" was a crowd favorite, but the chant "Half as Hard Jimmy" was spouted most often, and the meaning no longer related to the strength of Jimmy's punches. At first, Jimmy ran to the window with every taunt, which allowed people to gawk at his almost maroon face, but this only brought on more ridicule. After some time, he simply sat and endured the humiliation. Once able to go outside, Jimmy planned to challenge everyone to repeat the insults to his face. *Let's see what they have to say then,* he thought.

Another taunt from the street—Jimmy recognized the voice of Katie Fitzpatrick. "Hey Jimmy, always knew you were half as hard, why did everyone else take so long to figure it out? You big soft bastard!" Laughter erupted from Katie's friends, who enjoyed their daily taunts of the formerly feared neighborhood bully.

Jimmy's brother, Aengus, walked into the room, bucket and brush in hand, and closed the window. He took the seat next to Jimmy and said, "You're gonna sit here like a lumper and listen to all this bullshit."

"Can't go out yet looking like this, but I'll remember who's screaming from the streets. They'll all pay."

"Sure, Jimmy, be it what it would, but the people who got to pay are the ones who did this to you. How the fuck did this happen?"

"Me and Katie finished up in the alley, and my pants were still down. All of a sudden a rope picked me up by my feet. I remember being hit in the head from behind and then walking around with all of this shit on me and a hood on my head."

"So, you have no fucking idea who did this to you?"

"No, Aengus, I don't."

"One of my guys said a wee little boy ran away from the alley, so we chased him, but couldn't find him. Fast little fuck—he jumped over the big fence leading away from the docks and got away from us. No one else noticed him—not a good story—makes you look like an even bigger eejit. Bad enough you were made a joke in public, but if a small boy did this, your situation truly goes arseways, and I'm worried you'll never become a Cap."

"What am I gonna do, Aengus? How am I going to fix this?"

"Well, first thing, I'm going to help my little brother. I told my guy who spotted the running kid not to repeat that version of the story with the boy. A Black deliveryman we came across on the road spotted a bigger man running the other way, and this will be our story. Our new boss, Sean O'Malley, trusts me and he'll believe whatever I tell him, but we got to make someone pay for this, Jimmy. Otherwise, you're going to end up digging ditches like the rest of the Irish. So what do we do? Here's an idea, but it's going to hurt a bit and make you stay inside for at least another week."

"What's the plan?"

"Rumors are floating around about the Hook Gang—the ones who raid ships in the harbor, but we got word they might be trying to get in on our whiskey work with Devlin. O'Malley's worried about them."

"Still don't understand, Aengus, how does this help me?"

"Whenever the Hookers do a job or make a threat, they leave a symbol behind." Aengus took a piece of paper and drew a symbol formed by the combination of a colon and a question mark. "Looks like this." Aengus drew the symbol—*:?.*

"What the fuck is that?" Jimmy asked.

"I don't know, but it's these two dots and that squiggly thing, and I'm going to take some of the tar in this bucket, and put this symbol on your back. We're going to let the tar settle in and we'll scrape it off later. The outline of the symbol will still be visible for a while and we'll show O'Malley. If the Hookers came after you as a sign of war with the Caps, that's not embarrassing, but if some little boy did this to you—you're done. So, we'll blame this on the Hook Gang, and if we find the little shit of a boy, we'll take care of him too. Do you understand, Jimmy? Can I burn this symbol into your back?"

"Sure, do it," Jimmy responded as he nodded his head and peeled off his shirt. The front part of his body still showed the signs of the tar. He winced as his tender stomach pressed against the floor. Aengus picked up his brush and sketched the symbol *:?* on his back.

Captain Dill's Plan

CAPTAIN HELMUT DILL walked the streets along the harbor with his two new officers, transfers from other stations in Brooklyn. The captain pointed out where the approach to the bridge would begin and end, as well as the site of most of the initial construction activity. Dill also described what used to be in each of the parcels of land acquired from private owners to make way for both the bridge approach and the work in general. Singleton asked, "Why do we need to understand what used to be here, or what is about to be demolished?"

Dill answered, "Because your job is to keep things calm and avoid any problems. Some of the folks who gave up their land celebrated what they received, but others were angry as hell and might come back to cause some mischief."

Singleton responded, "Makes sense."

The other new transfer, Ryan MacGregor, rolled his eyes at Singleton's remark. The captain continued, "This is the area where we are most worried. They'll be hundreds of jobs at good rates. People will be fighting over these jobs—mostly Irish, German, and Italian. The Irish, in particular, MacGregor, are the ones with the greatest potential to cause trouble, so you better keep an eye on the Paddies. Understand?"

Interesting, Singleton thought. The German captain just insulted the Irish in front of an Irish officer. MacGregor smiled and responded, "Yes, sir, keep an eye out for those Paddies. Understood, sir."

At the end of the tour the three men sat in the captain's office for some final instructions. Captain Dill began, "Okay, boys—time to talk straight. Do you understand the reason for your transfers?"

Both men nodded in the affirmative.

"So you realize you built the wrong kind of reputation during your short time in the department? Both of you."

"I don't think reputation was my problem," Singleton replied.

MacGregor laughed.

The captain had picked up bad signals from MacGregor throughout their tour—time to set him straight. "The Irishman thinks his fellow officer's comment is funny? Am I right?"

"Well, sir. The Irishman, no. The Paddy, as you like to say, thinks Officer Singleton is funny. John, hasn't anyone told you about your reputation?" MacGregor paused for a moment to give John a chance to answer, but no response was offered and MacGregor began to laugh as he filled in the blanks, "You've got the reputation of a Catholic priest. Pure as the Virgin Mary!" Captain Dill motioned for Singleton not to respond and let him handle it. MacGregor added one last remark. "Singleton is the kind of cop who doesn't understand how things work in the real world."

"I imagine you understand the workings of the real world? Is that right, MacGregor?" the captain asked.

"I sure do. My father, who is your equal on the other side of the river, explained the workings to me a long time ago."

John Singleton didn't quite follow the conversation, but understood he'd been insulted. He decided the best course of action for the moment was to remain silent and let this conversation between MacGregor and the captain resolve itself without his participation.

"You little shit," the captain barked at MacGregor. "The only reason you're still on the force is your father asking for one last chance for you. You may call Singleton a priest, but do you know what they call guys like you?"

"I'm sure you're about to tell me."

"People like you are called dirty cops. You've already been caught once taking bribes and this is your last chance."

MacGregor didn't flinch at all at the unflattering characterization, sat back in his seat, and smiled. After a few moments of awkward silence, he responded, "Captain, you must have misread the official report—my small incident was deemed a misunderstanding."

"Misunderstanding, my ass. You're a crook, and so is your father."

"I beg to differ, Captain Dill."

"You can differ all you want, but this is why I'm partnering the two of you. Singleton, you keep an eye on the crook, and MacGregor, try to loosen up the priest just enough to show a little flexibility when necessary. One last thing, MacGregor, don't go running to your father. I told him if you fuck up even one time, you're out. Now shake hands, partners."

The mutual dislike between the two officers was palpable. Singleton planned to make it his business to catch his new partner doing something wrong in order to get rid of him, and MacGregor hated the idea of being monitored by a guy like Singleton. Neither officer left the room happy, but the captain was all smiles.

CHAPTER 33

A Man of Few Words

THE JOHNSONS WATCHED their one and only daughter walk hand-in-hand with Venture Simmons for another afternoon date. The couple had become inseparable and most of Georgia's conversation around the house centered on Vent—what they were going to do, where they were going to go, how strong he was, how high he jumped, and how far he threw. Florence Johnson had grown to accept the fact that Vent might be a permanent fixture in her daughter's life, but Georgia was Daddy's little girl. Florence took note of her husband's wrinkled brow and a single tear streaming down his face from his right eye.

Florence walked up to him, rubbed his back, and said, "It was bound to happen, baby, she's ready to start her own life. Vent's a good boy. Is that there a tear of joy or sadness?"

"Not sure. I know Vent a good boy, but he got some strange habits. Not sure I understand him all the time, and I thought maybe Georgia might meet a different kind of man, especially since we came back to Weeksville, where free Colored folks have lived for years."

"What you mean?"

"When we ran from the plantation in Georgia and made that long, danger-ous trip to freedom, I was hopin' our Georgia might meet someone who came from a different place—not another slave who ran like we did. I thought maybe she might find someone who grew up free in the North. Maybe someone who could give her a good start in life."

"Baby, you thinkin' 'bout this the wrong way. It don't matter what road someone took to get to the same spot. Point is, when you meet someone who makes you weak in the knees and is a good honest person, that's all you can ever ask for, 'cause everything else can be worked out."

"You sayin' Vent makes Georgia weak in the knees?"

"My God, ain't you been payin' attention at all—our girl loves that boy. Don't matter if they took the same road or if one of them took a boat—they somehow got to the same place here in Weeksville and she so weak in her knees, she can barely stand up! And she less than five feet tall, so that real important!" Florence found her last comment hilarious, as did her husband, and the Johnsons snorted and laughed until Georgia and Vent fell from their view. Florence turned to the love of her life and saw that her words had calmed his fears, and her knees buckled ever so slightly.

✦══◉ ◉══✦

"Vent, why we going to Yukaton Pond? Another base ball game? Why you being so mysterious?"

Vent didn't answer right away and waited for a couple walking in the opposite direction to pass by before responding, "Not saying."

"Venture Simmons, what do you mean, 'not saying'? I'm your girlfriend, why aren't you saying?"

"You'll see."

"If we're going to another game and come across the reporter from the *Eagle*, I don't want to sit anywhere near him. He's nothing but a bad man."

No response from Venture.

"Venture, I'm talking to you. I said if we spot the reporter from the *Eagle* at the game, I won't sit near him."

"I understand."

"Okay, so long as we're clear. I don't like what he wrote about the last game. He wrote about us like we animals."

No response from Vent.

"Listen here, Venture, I realize you don't like to talk so much, but I keep asking you these questions with lots of words and either you say nothing or you keep answering with only two words of your own. What's going on with you?"

No response from Vent.

"You better be paying attention because I'm wearing my best Sunday hat and if a ball comes and messes up this hat, I'm going to be upset. Are you ready to catch anything coming my way, Vent?"

No response from Vent.

"Venture, you answer me now, what going on with you?"

"Nothing much."

"My God, Vent. Sometimes you make me crazy. Another two-word answer! At this pace, you'll need ten hours to give me one complete thought."

Venture stopped walking, turned, gazed at Georgia's eyes, and smiled as he responded, "Could be."

Georgia found his response to be both charming and funny, and she started snorting and slapping her thigh as she said, "I can't imagine how I'm gonna ever manage carrying round all of your heavy words. Gonna break my back, I tell you. Break it clear in two!"

Vent smiled and Georgia slipped her hand into his as she scanned the area for the base ball game. The field was empty except for a few families having picnics. Georgia glanced at Vent, and he shrugged his shoulders.

"We're not here for base ball, Mr. Simmons?"

"Not today."

Georgia wondered how long he'd keep up his two-word answers and laughed to herself as she realized, *Forever.* The couple stopped at the edge of the park and Vent said, "We're here."

"I don't understand, Venture. I understand where we are, but I don't understand why or for what."

Vent wanted to speak but only managed to lower his eyes to the ground. He'd imagined this moment for a long time, but now that it arrived, he was frozen.

Georgia didn't push. "Okay, Vent, let's stand here for a while and admire the pond and think about the nice day. If you have something you want to say, maybe more than two words, you let me know."

Vent nodded, but continued to admire the grass with his head down. Another couple passed by and he waited for them to be far enough away before he whispered, "We home." Georgia peered over Vent's shoulder to the small house on the corner plot, and started to cry. She cuddled up to Vent and responded to his eloquent proposal with a kiss. The couple walked into their future home and Georgia told him where everything would go. Vent's smile grew wider with each of her decisions and reached its pinnacle when she announced the day they would be married.

Chapter 34

A Declaration of War

"Listen, Aengus, I'm in no mood for any more talk about why your brother Jimmy should be one of us," Sean O'Malley said as the two men walked up the stairs of the tenement.

"Sean, don't worry—no more talk, you need to see something I didn't spot at first with what happened to Jimmy. Just wait. He's right down this way."

The two men paused at the front door of the apartment as Aengus called out to his Ma before entering, "It's Aengus, Ma. I brought Sean O'Malley with me. We're here for Jimmy."

Bridgette McGreary rushed out to greet her important guest—the leader of the Velvet Caps. "Mr. O'Malley, thank you so much for checking on Jimmy. Terrible thing, what happened to my boy, but he's a big strong lad, and will be as good as new in a couple more days. He's right in the corner room."

The two men walked down the narrow hallway and walked in as Jimmy closed the window in anticipation of his guests.

Aengus addressed his brother. "Jimmy, seems like you're doing better. I want you to take your shirt off and show us your back." Sean O'Malley had no interest in seeing a half-naked Jimmy McGreary and started to walk toward the door.

Aengus turned to his boss and said, "Sean, I brought you here for what's on his back."

Jimmy removed this shirt and turned around. O'Malley said, "Fucking Hookers," and understood the reason for his visit. He walked closer to Jimmy to better scrutinize the symbols and took note of the prominent *:?* etched into Jimmy's back with tar. O'Malley's face turned bright red, and he directed his comments to Jimmy. "This whole thing never made any sense, but now I understand.

The Hook Gang did this and they sent us a message with this symbol on your back." O'Malley turned to Aengus for his final comment. "If they want a war, we'll give them one."

O'Malley stormed out of the room and down the hallway with a head of steam. The fucking Hookers were trying to cut into his business with Devlin and the attack on Jimmy was a public declaration of war. The new leader of the Caps learned from the mistakes of his predecessor, who became weak in his final days on the job. *The Hook Gang will dread the day they fucked with the Velvet Caps.*

⊷▭ ▭⊷

O'Malley arrived for his appointment with Devlin in the back of the bakery and walked in as Roberta McGurt left with her cake box full of cash.

"Ah, Mr. Sean O'Malley, take a seat. How about some coffee or cake on this fine day?" Devlin said.

Sean accepted the invitation by taking the seat across from Devlin. Perhaps this conversation might shed some light on why the Hook Gang targeted the Caps.

"Sure thing, Mr. Devlin. Have we another raid to plan for?"

"Yes, we sure do. Here is the location." Devlin passed the note written by Roberta McGurt to O'Malley, but pulled the paper back at the last moment and said, "You do read, don't ya?"

"Well enough to make out an address, Mr. Devlin."

"Fine. Here." Devlin slid the paper to Sean's side of the table as he said, "How are things going with the Caps?"

"Fine, Mr. Devlin, and I hope our work for you has been satisfactory."

"Satisfactory…big word, you're not as dumb as you appear," Devlin said with a smile. "But to answer your question, yes, the work of the Caps is satisfactory. Why do you ask?"

"Seems like the Hook Gang is making a move on us and I thought you might know something about that."

"Listen, you little shit, you may know a couple of big words, but when I want to replace you, you'll find out directly from me—like your last boss. Your gang bullshit is your problem, and you better take care of it quietly. I'm warning you—do not bring any more attention from the police to Irishtown. Understand?"

"Yes, sir, Mr. Devlin."

O'Malley's coffee and cake arrived but Devlin no longer desired his company and waved off the server. "Sorry for the bother, but this man has no time for cake." Devlin leaned in and grabbed O'Malley by the collar as he said, "Go take care of your gang bullshit, O'Malley, but first take care of this other problem for me, and if you can't handle my business, remember—not so hard to find someone else who can. Get the fuck out of here."

CHAPTER 35

Fick Dich

THE LINE FOR the coveted jobs on the bridge project went around the block. The attraction for most—wages of two dollars per day—much more than the typical pay for a laborer. The Bridge Company sought workers for three shifts to work inside the caisson and two shifts on top of the structure, building the tower. Members of the Velvet Caps worked the line to ensure the Irish from their neighborhood received as many spots as possible. Every Irishman who gained a spot on the line or who moved up in order understood they owed the Caps a favor, and those favors always had to be returned. Aengus McGreary paid Officer Ryan MacGregor for undisturbed access to the line, but MacGregor warned the Caps his pain-in-the-ass partner would be back within the hour.

The Caps began their work and scared off a number of Italian job seekers, but the large German contingent was difficult to intimidate and stood together as a unit. Vent tried to mix in with the Germans and kept his head down and hood on, to conceal his color.

Aengus and his cronies decided to test the Germans. "You fucking Dutchtowner's—these are Irish jobs. Get the fuck off our line."

Ten of the larger men in the German group walked toward the Caps and offered both the German version of fuck you—*fick dich*—along with the English version. Soon the entire German group was screaming "Fick dich!" Vent thought it would be too odd not to chime in as well, but his "Fick dich" sounded more like *"Fish dick,"* and caught the attention of the two Germans standing on either side of him.

One of the Germans turned to the other and asked, *"Wer ist dieser kleine schwarze Mann?* Who is this little Black man?"

Vent became the target of the *fick dichs* and the Caps, who had already backed down, enjoyed seeing the little man squirm. The entire pack of Germans surrounded Vent just as Officer John Singleton came onto the scene.

"All right, break it up. What's going on here?" Singleton asked.

Answers were offered in German. Despite the fact John had learned some basic German from his father, he insisted on getting the story in English. One of the Germans stepped forward and said, "This Black man thinks he's German and snuck in with us. We want him out."

Singleton glanced at Vent, recognized him right away, and offered a wink.

"I believe this man has been waiting as long as all of you, and you seem to be the next group they'll call into the hall to apply for your jobs. All of this fuss just moved him from eleventh in line to next. Anyone have a problem with that?"

Singleton paused as he stared directly in the eyes of the man he assumed to be the leader of the German group. He received no response and continued, "I'm walking him inside myself and all of you"—Singleton pointed to both the Germans and the Caps—"better let him be."

Vent smiled at Officer Singleton and thanked God for the good fortune of running into him during his time of need. Once inside, he walked straight over to the hiring manager.

"Quite a scene you caused outside," the manager offered.

"Not my fault—I stood in line like everyone else," Vent responded.

"We don't want this kind of trouble on the job. We think this will be more of an Irish and German job, with some Italians. We might give some jobs to Blacks, but not until things settle down."

"But I already work construction. I can walk on beams on the high floors and help with the tower."

"The tower? Seems like you understand more than most folks on the line. I'm going to take your name and address, but I can't hire you today. Down the road, however, when things quiet down, and the tower starts to soar into the skies, we could use a man like you."

Vent knew applying for the job would be tough and this was about the best outcome possible. "Thank you, my name is Venture Simmons. I can write it for you with my address."

"I'm impressed. A Colored man who can read, write, and walk on beams. You might be useful in a few months." Vent finished writing his contact information and the manager accepted the paper from him and said, "Next."

As Vent exited the office, the Germans stared him down again, and Officer Singleton was gone. Vent sensed they meant nothing but trouble, and when one of the largest men took a sudden step toward him, Vent took off in a sprint. All of the Germans laughed at the little Colored man scampering away. The Caps also found the encounter amusing and took note of Vent as he bolted past them and headed for the fence, which separated the staging area for the line and the street.

Aengus turned to one of his fellow Caps and said, "What do you think the Darkey is going to do when he realizes the gate is on the other side and he's going to need to circle back through us to actually get to it?"

"Not sure, but we'll find out soon enough."

Vent got within a step of the seven-foot fence and jumped on a tree stump, situated about two feet off the ground. He used the force of his first jump to propel his second, and he tucked his head down as he completed a perfect flip over the fence, landing on the other side.

Both the Germans and the Irish appreciated the entertainment created by their intimidation of the Colored man, as well as his dramatic escape—all the men entered the office laughing. The Caps started to head out as well and one gang member who was on the scene the night of Jimmy's attack turned and said, "Aengus, this may be the guy who got Jimmy. I remember his speed and the flip. He's also about the same size as the one I spotted running away from the alley."

"Really?" Aengus answered. "Hard to believe the Hook Gang would hire a Colored man to do their dirty work, but I guess anything is possible. Do me one favor, though—don't mention this to anyone else. This is family business. Me and Jimmy will take care of him. Are you sure about this guy?"

"Never seen anyone so small move and jump like that any other time in my life. Yes, must be him, but don't worry, I didn't say anything the last time and I won't say anything now."

Chapter 36

Thanksgiving

THE PREPARATION FOR Thanksgiving dinner took days and represented a number of firsts: the first time Georgia and Vent would host their families since their marriage in October, as well as the first time either family celebrated Thanksgiving. The Brown brothers would also be present for their very first Thanksgiving feast. Georgia reviewed the instructions with Vent for the fifth time. "Vent, I want you to greet everyone when they come in and ask them to take a seat at the table. Now this here is your house, so you gonna sit at the head, you understand?"

"No need to stand by the door and greet people. This family, let them come in and find their own seat. Why you makin' such a fuss?"

"Vent, I done told you what to do five times, why you giving me such trouble…"

Georgia stopped in midsentence because she recognized Vent's attempt at humor, which he confirmed with a smile. Georgia snorted and slapped her thigh, and said, "Good one, Vent, but time for you to take your place by the door."

The Johnsons and Washingtons arrived first, followed by Moses and Ezra Brown. Mabel and her family took their seats last. The large table, which Vent created by putting three smaller ones side by side with a tablecloth on top, appeared so perfect, none of the guests wanted to touch anything. Moses reached for a piece of bread, and everyone else followed suit. After the main meal, but before dessert, Thomas Washington clanked his fork against his glass and asked, "Why we call this dinner Thanksgiving?"

Horace seized the opportunity to demonstrate his knowledge of current events and answered, "The tradition started years ago as a harvest festival and on and off as a national holiday, but President Lincoln named it a national day of Thanksgiving and Praise during the war."

Thomas Washington didn't need so much information and responded, "Horace, why everything you say has so many words. I wanted a simple answer, like—'cause we thankful—don't need all that history. History ain't the thing for Colored folk, none of it any good. The future is what we need to think about."

Esther Washington agreed. "I think we should offer a toast to the future of these two youngen's who starting out they married life in style in this new house, which is so close to all of us. Who would have thought Colored folks could be livin' so good right after the war?"

Horace jumped in. "So good? What do you mean? We can't get the jobs we deserve and still don't vote. I'm not so thankful."

Moses gritted his teeth and put down his fork with a clang. "This the whole problem, Horace, you not thankful for nothing. Nothing but a spoiled, unthankful boy. Never did grow up and I'm tired of hearing all of your fancy history lessons. Sorry, folks, I can't listen to this boy no more." Moses got up to leave, and Ezra gawked at the hot apple pie, which was about to be served—he realized he wouldn't be having a piece. Ezra shrugged his shoulders and said his goodbyes as he followed Moses out of the front door. Esther Washington rushed out as well and called out from the doorway, "Moses, wait a minute. Please wait. I want to talk to you."

"Ms. Esther, I'm sorry if speakin' to Horace like I did bothers you, but I'm not 'pologizing. Horace no damn good."

"Moses, I understand you never forgave him and I can tell Vent hasn't forgiven him either, but this isn't why I came out to talk to you."

"What you need, Miss Esther?"

"I wanted to thank you. None of us understand about all of your businesses—you always seem to be doing something new—but I know you helped Vent buy this house. The money from Mackie wasn't enough to buy a house like this, and I wanted to thank you. After all, it is Thanksgiving!"

"No need to worry 'bout what this cost. Far as I'm concerned, Vent bought this house all on his own. He as much family to me as he is to you. I think Vent understands I added a little bit, but I'm askin' you not to say nothin' to no one else. Vent started his life in Weeksville real tough and we both realize he ain't right in the head, but he is a good man and deserves whatever help we can give him."

"You a good man yourself, Moses Brown. I better go back inside."

Florence Johnson broke the tension created by Moses and Ezra's hasty departure with a joke, which required massive snorting and thigh slapping. Esther sat back down in her assigned seat and started laughing herself, even though she missed the punch line. She glanced at Georgia, who cuddled up to Vent, and noted Vent's downward-tilting head—still a problem with eye contact—but she realized the little smile, which occasionally emanated from the side of his face, was more present than absent with the lovely Georgia by his side. The odd little boy who jumped out of a crate straight into her heart had built a good life for himself.

CHAPTER 37

Stargazing

VENT APPRECIATED THE tremendous amount of planning, labor, and luck that would be necessary to build the biggest suspension bridge in the world, and remembered every detail of the simple demonstration his boss, Harold Reems, gave him months before with the upside-down glass inside the bowl. He imagined how the weight from the tremendous tower, which would rise from the top of the glass, would sink the caisson down to bedrock. Next, a solid, cement filling would be the final touch in providing a proper foundation for the tallest tower in North America. Vent thought about how Jimmy McGreary would beat his chest in celebration after being with his Irish girl, and he wanted to do the same thing at the top of the completed tower, but first he needed to be hired.

People lined the shores on both sides of the river as if the work had become a spectator sport. The crowds were tremendous the day the caisson, towed by a steam-powered boat, traveled the short distance to its final resting place. From this point forward, the show became less spectacular, as the progress in sinking the caisson began with a rate of descent of only a few inches a week. Still, the construction of this bridge was history in the making, and Vent yearned to be part of it.

"Georgia, let me explain again. Imagine the glass upside down in the bowl, with pumped-in air, which pushes out the water, so people can be inside working. Other people will work on the top, building the tower with heavy materials in order to sink the glass."

"Oh, Vent, you and this bridge. I don't care about the *kayzon* or whatever you call this box. Explaining the base-circling thing to me in base ball would be better. By the way, when are we going to another game?"

"Not anytime soon, Georgia. Base ball is a summer game—nobody plays a summer game in the winter, but don't change the subject. One day I'm gonna work on the bridge, at least I hope to, and I want you to understand what I'll be doing, okay?"

"All right, Vent, tell me again. First, you put the glass upside down in the bowl, and second, you circle the bases and score a run, right?" Georgia's snorting and thigh slaps triggered a full Venture Simmons side-smile—he kissed her and thought of the day in the near future when people would be able to walk on the bridge, hundreds of feet in the air with boats passing underneath them as they traveled from Brooklyn to New York. Vent said to himself, *A miracle in the making, and I'm going to be part of it.*

⊷▬ ▬⊶

A few days after his visit to the construction site with Georgia, Vent returned with Moses. The two men got together at least once per week. In the beginning, no one questioned the pretense for their meetings—teaching Moses how to read. Now the two men met because they'd become family and their meetings were nothing more than a weekly check-in. Ezra always joked that Moses needed these meetings to make sure Vent hadn't killed anybody in the last seven days.

The two men stood by the shore, admiring the view of the river as well as the construction site when a large group of workers emerged from the changing area yelling and screaming.

"They can't pay me enough to go back down in the caisson. Ninety degrees inside and thirty degrees outside. Every joint in my body hurts. I'm quitting."

"Me too."

"I worked my last day as a sandhog. Never going back again."

Moses glanced at Vent and said, "Seems like some jobs opened up." Officer Singleton spotted Vent and Moses in the distance and approached from behind at the perfect moment to respond Moses's observation. "Good evening, Moses, evening, Vent. I'm sure Moses is right. About a third of the men quit every week. The conditions in the caisson are bad. Lots of people are becoming sick. The air is real thick, which is a problem. Vent, are you still interested in working on the bridge?"

"Yes, I am, but I want to work on the tower. I'm real good with heights and climbing."

Moses added, "Boy, is he ever!"

Officer Singleton didn't understand the inside joke between the two friends, but offered a smile in return.

Vent clarified, "But I don't want to be a sandhog down in the caisson. Sounds bad down below."

Moses agreed, "Yeah, better to be alive and in a good steady job even though you're not in your dream job, than dead in the *kayzon*."

"Okay, Vent, if you're still interested, I can check for you in the hiring office tomorrow. I stop by the office every day. Meet me back here around this time tomorrow night and I'll tell you what they say." Officer Singleton left the two men and continued his rounds.

Vent stared up at the moon and smiled. Moses understood, he was talking to his mama. Not an unusual thing for Vent to do—Moses had witnessed these conversations many times before—the day Vent got married, the day he moved into his house, and on many other special times of either triumph or celebration. Vent carried his mother with him wherever he went and stargazing preceded all of his maternal chats. Moses headed for the train back to Weeksville in order to give Vent some privacy.

I think I'm gonna be okay, Mama. Georgia taking good care of me, and like Moses tells me, she's real good stuff. You probably seen my house already—bought it with most of my own money. Moses helped, but he won't let me pay him back. Other good things too, Mama, like my work—I'm gonna be hired for a job working on the bridge. Once I stand on the top of the tower, I'll be so close to you in heaven you'll be able to wave hello. I'd like to see your wave, Mama. Now, I'm going home to tell Georgia. Good night.

Vent started his mad dash home, and decided to utilize his full obstacle course, which involved short sprints, fence jumping, and tree climbing. He had so much to tell Georgia and expected her to be thrilled about his improved chance to be hired. Vent neared the final stretch leading to his dream girl, who lived with him in his dream house, with a strong sense his dream job had become a reality and life was good—Vent's plan was coming together, and he again consulted the stars as he said "thank you" to his mama just as a cloud passed over the moon. Vent accepted this movement as a faint version of his mother's wave and became certain that once he stood atop the tallest tower in the world, the wave would be so much more prominent. *Good night, Mama, and thanks again.*

The Warning

"Those fucking Hookers, they're trying to squeeze us out of our deal with Devlin. The Caps outnumber them and we're going to outsmart them as well. The Hook Gang will pay for what they did to Aengus's brother. Jimmy, show the men your back." Sean O'Malley paused to give Jimmy a chance to remove his shirt. His chest had healed well from the burns, but when he turned, the outline of the symbol :? caused the men to react.

"Fucking Hookers!"

"How dare they mess with the Caps!"

The question came from Aengus, "How are we going to make this right?"

O'Malley intuitively understood this incident to be a test of his leadership. Aengus McGreary established quite a following within the Caps and if anyone would dare challenge him for leadership, he would be the one. Sean responded, "We're going to hit them where it hurts!"

O'Malley's response was nonspecific, but given that most of the men were pretty well over the bay after several shots of whiskey, the details would have been lost on them in any case. Time for another toast with some of Devlin's finest: "Hit them where it hurts!" The gang leader sensed he'd handled the issue well for the moment, but needed a plan as to what to do about the Hook Gang. His inclination: begin by talking to Suds Merrick, their leader, to determine both the motivations for the attack and any plans to encroach on Caps territory. The whole incident made no sense to O'Malley. The Hook Gang raided ships in the harbor and they always stayed within this specific line of business. The Hookers never demonstrated a leaning toward doing anything within Irishtown itself.

O'Malley's meeting with Merrick later that night might provide answers and, perhaps, a solution.

⊶⊷

Aengus sent Jimmy home, put down his glass of whiskey, left his drunken companions, and headed toward Grunding Supplies, next to the Caps headquarters by the Little Street Docks.

"Who's in charge here?" Aengus asked the small man who greeted him at the entrance of the warehouse.

"I—I'm in charge," the man stuttered. "My name is George Hinson, but we paid our monthly fee to the Caps last week—we're up to d-d-date," the manager added as his voice trembled and he continued to stutter his responses.

"Listen, Hinson. I understand you're paid up, because if not, this would be a whole different kind of a conversation. I'm here to ask a few questions."

The manager breathed a sigh of relief, and sat in a nearby chair to steady himself.

Aengus asked, "Do you know who I am?"

"Everybody knows Aengus McGreary, the number two man in the Velvet Caps."

Aengus puffed his chest out and smiled as he asked, "Do you remember hearing about a Colored man who was beaten up in the alley next door a couple of months ago?"

"Yes, I do."

"I understand he came into your warehouse before he received his beating. Who did he speak with?"

"He spoke with me. He needed to make a payment for his boss Harold Reems, down at Reems Construction."

"Do you remember his name?"

"Something like Harold, or Harry, no, no...I think Horace. Yes, Horace was his name."

"Thank you for your time, and never worry about the Caps as long as you keep making your payments and keep your mouth shut. For example, I never came in here today to ask you these questions, understand?"

"Yes, sir. I do."

Aengus got his answers and developed a lead to follow up on. George Hinson rushed back to his office, and took a long swig from his own personal bottle of Devlin's whiskey—he hoped he'd seen the last of Aengus McGreary.

⊷▬◉ ◉▬⊶

O'Malley arrived with four of his men and found Suds Merrick seated at the bar with three of his own associates. Both groups sized each other up and realized, despite the slightly uneven numbers, the outcome of a fight could go either way. Neither leader sought trouble at least at that particular moment.

Suds Merrick opened the conversation. "What the fuck does fancy Sean O'Malley, the leader of the Caps, want with me? I'm not even sure why I agreed to this."

O'Malley ignored the hostile greeting and took a seat at the bar next to Merrick. Both entourages took a few steps back and began their own little dance of posturing and intimidation. O'Malley responded after his shot of whiskey arrived. "Not here for a fight, Merrick." He paused to gulp down his shot. "Only need some answers."

"Answers about what?"

"We got your message. Do you understand what will happen if you take on the Caps in Irishtown? What the fuck are you thinking?"

"First of all, who the fuck are you to tell me what I can and can't do? If I want to take on the Caps, I will, and I'll throw all you fancy bastards into the river. What fucking message are you talking about?"

"We found your symbol"—O'Malley drew it on a napkin on the bar—"burned into the back of the brother of one of my men."

"What the hell are you talking about, O'Malley? If I planned to come after the Caps, the fucking symbol would be burned on your back, not some brother of a member."

O'Malley answered, "I'm going to let your comment pass for the moment, but you say something along those lines again, and we will have a problem. Anyone who wants a war with the Caps is a fool. I've got the men and the neighborhoods. All you have is the water, and that's not where the fighting will take place. So consider yourself warned, keep the fucking Hook Gang away from the Caps, or pay the price."

"Pay the price! Fuck you, O'Malley, you don't scare me. Nothing about a man in a velvet cap scares anyone. Right, boys?" Suds asked as he turned to his men for an obligatory laugh.

The laugh was cut short by the force of O'Malley crashing Merrick's head into the bar as he pulled a knife and put it to his throat. The rehearsed move was choreographed well, as O'Malley's men also put the three supporting Hookers in the same precarious position.

O'Malley offered one last thought before backing out of the bar. "Consider yourself warned."

Chapter 39

Awaiting the News

Vent wrapped his scarf around his neck and jogged in place to stay warm. The dramatic drop in temperature over the past few days had generated a chill deep in Vent's bones. The last bit of heat from the sun had faded thirty minutes ago, but he planned to wait as long as necessary for Officer Singleton. He trained his eyes on the pathway leading from the street, hoping to spot the officer making his way to the agreed-upon meeting place.

A row of bushes blocked Vent's full view as he detected what appeared to be the top of Officer Singleton's cap. *If only I were taller,* he thought. Vent jumped on top of the bar that framed the fence and separated the public area from the private worksite. He still needed more height for a proper view, so he jumped higher, hoping the additional elevation would let him determine the identity of the approaching figure. *Yes, it's him!* Within a few minutes, John Singleton called out to Vent, "I think I understand what Moses meant by you being good with heights—jumping up and down on a fence railing without losing your balance— quite a talent."

"Thank you, Officer Singleton, this is kind of my special thing," Vent offered with his head pointed downward. The officer thought his smile would give away the nature of his news, but Vent rarely established eye contact, so Singleton opened with, "Got some good news for you," and that did the trick—Vent's head popped up and he stood at full attention. Singleton continued, "I went to the office earlier today, as I said I would, and checked on tower jobs. They didn't seem to want to talk about tower jobs at first, but I persisted and reminded them about the fella who jumped over the fence the first day of hiring. One of the managers remembered you, and said they needed someone like you working up high. A job is waiting for you if you want it. $2.25 per day—not bad."

"You can say that again!" Vent remarked. "More than twice my pay with Mr. Reems, but I'm not doin' this for the money. Always wanted to work the tower. I like the idea of being in the clouds."

"Over the last few weeks, lots of people quit. Most of the vacant positions, however, are working down below in the caisson, but they said some tower jobs are also available. Not sure what shift, though. They need to talk to you about the choice in shifts and some other details as well. You're supposed to go to the office as soon as you can."

"I'll go in the morning, Officer Singleton."

"What about the job you have now?"

"Counted on this comin' through, so I told Mr. Reems I quit earlier today. Don't think he minded so much; we're not buildin' like we used to—mostly we just supply materials to the bridge project. I think he likes knowin' he's got one of his old men on the inside. Told me to keep an eye out for more opportunities for him. Not sure what he meant, but told him I would."

"Quitting one job before you line up another isn't generally a smart move, but I guess you realized they need men. I'm not so sure how much I helped with the job—you could have walked in the office on your own and been hired without my help."

"It didn't hurt havin' Officer John Singleton asking for me."

"After all we been through the last few months, I think you can call me John. Okay, Vent?"

Vent's head went back down, and he offered a faint nod in response. John Singleton understood he'd always be Officer Singleton to Vent. The officer offered a final thought. "Best of luck in the new job, Vent. I hope to be walking by the job site one day soon and spot you standing on top of the tower in the middle of the clouds."

Singleton walked away after his last remark, and Vent tracked him with his eyes as he disappeared into the darkness. Once alone, Vent jumped back onto the fence, inverted into a handstand on the top bar, and then flipped backward, landing squarely on his feet. He stared upward at the stars, and offered a wink because nothing needed to be said—Mama always listened. *She must be so happy. Time to tell Georgia, Moses, Miss Esther, and Mabel.* Vent skipped the obstacle course and opted for an all-out sprint back to Weeksville.

CHAPTER 40

The First Day

THE THREE HIRING managers on the bridge project met for an early cup of coffee to discuss their strategy. Many attributed the massive resignations to the mysterious caisson's disease, which brought on pains in the joints for most and severe headaches for others. The rash of recent resignations, however, related more to poor working conditions, which included the sharp rise in temperature from the frigid winter air outside to ninety degrees inside the caisson. An average of one hundred men quit per week and, unfortunately, this past week was above average. The managers needed an immediate plan to add some men to the Wednesday morning shift, scheduled to start in an hour.

The senior manager developed the basic strategy and instructed his two subordinates, "Despite all of the resignations, many people would love to be hired for one of these jobs. About one in three will quit, but right now, new candidates are still available. The ten to twenty men we hired to work on the tower starting Monday are coming in today to finalize their arrangements, let's require them to give us three days in the caisson before we move them to their permanent jobs on the tower."

The two subordinates nodded and the office doors opened. Vent arrived first, but the Germans and Irish who came after him made sure he assumed his rightful place at the back of the line. Brief conversations took place with each of the twenty potential caisson hires before the ten scheduled to work on the tower learned of their temporary caisson assignment.

The senior manager made the announcement. "We thank you for joining us in building the greatest bridge in the world. All of you will be working on the tower beginning Monday morning, but we need your help through the end of this week working down in the caisson. We are short men down below and the caisson work is as important as the work up top. Nothing wrong with a little extra pay, right fellas? Any questions?"

An Irish worker raised his hand. "Rumor is the work is terrible as a sandhog in the *kayzon*. What if I stick to my plan of starting with tower work on Monday?"

The manager hoped this question wouldn't be asked, but provided a firm answer. "You all do whatever you like, but I'm telling you, I need you down below for three days, and no matter how tough the work may be, you all can manage for this short time. Do this, and you'll be paid for three extra days. Refuse, and your name goes back to the bottom of the list. The next group who comes in here for tower jobs will likely take your place on Monday. The choice is yours."

Two Irishmen and one German left. The rest of the group received their instructions on work in the caisson as the manager continued, "Hang your clothes in one of the two large sheds set up outside the worksite. You'll likely want to go into the caisson bare-chested, wearing only your pants and the rubber boots we give you. Despite the cold outside, the temperature inside the caisson is close to ninety degrees and shirts are useless. At the end of the day, run back to the sheds, where washtubs with hot water will be waiting for you to clean up before you go home. Three days, men, only three days—you are all tower men, we're not going back on our word."

Everyone understood and walked toward the sheds. They stripped down as instructed and ran over to the entry to the caisson at the top of the structure. A few men entered at a time, and closed the top hatch. After a minute or two, the bottom hatch opened to the interior of the caisson. A number of the men squirmed when in the close quarters in the chamber, but tight spaces never bothered Vent. Once the bottom hatch opened, however, Vent started to twitch—the air coming up from the caisson seemed so heavy and dank—Vent hoped he wouldn't lose his composure and started to count in threes under his breath, "Three, six, nine, twelve, fifteen." He paused to take a deep breath, but that didn't work, so he started to take quick shallow gulps of air. A nearby supervisor, trained to detect this type of reaction, told Vent, "Slow down your breathing and try to relax. Stay up in the chamber until you are ready." Vent and two of the other new men remained in the chamber for another five minutes, and then climbed down together.

One of the Irishmen in the new group of workers turned to a German and asked, "What is this place? Are we under water?"

The German shrugged his shoulders in response.

The Irishman then turned to Vent and asked, "Hey you, do you understand this place?"

Vent kept his head down and continued walking forward, but the Irishman would not be ignored, and grabbed Vent's shoulder as he said, "Hey, Darkey, I'm talking to you."

Vent wheeled around, fists formed, ready to strike, but he controlled himself—a fight this early in his time on the job would mean certain dismissal. The fists relaxed, but the eyes burned a hole through the Irishman, who softened his approach. "I'm asking if you understand this place."

Vent explained the upside-down glass in the bowl concept, and the Irishman responded, "What the fuck are you talking about? I knew I shouldn't have asked a Darkey."

The morning supervisor called all of the new men together and they stood in the second of the chambers in the caisson. He gave the briefest of orientations. "Welcome to the Brooklyn Caisson. This underwater structure is filled with compressed air pumped in from above. This enables us to breathe and keeps the water from coming in. The folks on top of the caisson are building a heavy tower and the weight of the tower will force this caisson to go lower and lower, as long as we keep clearing out any rock or other material that might be in the way. So we keep digging out the interior while they keep building up top. All the dug-up material to be removed from the caisson should be dropped into one of two chutes on either side, where it will be taken to the top by the water pressure as well as some other equipment."

The supervisor paused for a moment as he gathered his thoughts on what else he should mention to the new workers, "Oh, one more thing. You may not realize we are standing right next to the toilet. See the man sitting over there?" The supervisor motioned to a man seated about ten feet from the group. All of the men nodded and the man waved. "He's taking a shit, probably a nasty one, but you can't smell anything in this compressed air, so we're able to stand here without being bothered." The attempt at humor brought on a little laugh, followed by a "whoosh," as the manager finished his bathroom orientation. "Ah, his contribution to the water below the toilet activated the automatic elimination feature. We've got the best engineers on this project, men; they call this the *pneumatic water closet*. The 'whoosh' sound was our friend's shit being blasted all over the East River. Time to go to work."

The third chamber became Vent's home for his first day and he took note of the odd green light that emanated from two of the corners. One of the men turned to him and said, "Those are calcium lights like the ones they use in the theaters." Vent nodded, but the theater reference didn't make any sense to him. The man spoke to him with respect, however, which Vent found unusual. Another man asked Vent to lend a hand pulling out a rock wedged under the edge of the structure. The request was polite—*quite odd*, Vent thought as he continued to be treated like an equal. After some time, he realized the green lighting, combined with his light skin color, fooled everyone as to his race. He thought how interesting this might be in a different circumstance, but all Vent wanted to do at the moment was survive the day.

The men started digging and clearing rock and walked from section to section on planks, which created pathways. A foot or more of muck greeted them when they stepped off the planks. Slime and mud covered all the walkways and beams. Vent, drenched in perspiration, felt like he had just completed a three-mile run in August.

Around noon, most of the men tried to find as dry a spot as possible to sit and eat, but the temporary caisson workers didn't have any food. Several of the other men offered some of their lunch to the newcomers, and one giant Irishman with enough food to feed a family, offered a generous portion of his meal to Vent. Another Irish worker, who entered the caisson with Vent earlier, called out, "He's a Darkey, let him starve." The large Irishman countered, "I'll do what I please with my food, thank you, and you'll shut the fuck up with this Darkey bullshit as long as you're around me. Understand?" The area cleared, and the large Irishman called over to Vent, "Come on over here, little fella. I've got some good Irish cooking for ya. My name is Connor McCloskey and I'm from County Cork." The giant extended his hand to Vent as he took a seat next to him.

Vent responded, "I'm Venture Simmons from County Brooklyn." The Irishman's laugh filled the chamber. Vent didn't realize he'd made a joke, but did appreciate, as he sat side to side with this behemoth of a man, his first Irish friend.

The day finally came to a close, and as the workers emerged in small groups from the air lock, the temperature dropped from ninety degrees to thirty degrees. Most of the men made a mad bare-chested dash toward the comfort of the employee sheds, where hot water and clothing awaited them. Several were plagued by hacking coughs, and this alarmed Vent, but his inability to run to the shed provided an even greater concern—all he could manage was a slow jog due to odd pains in his knees and ankles. After cleaning up and heading toward the train for the ride home, Vent stared up to the sky and said, "Only two more days, Mama, I'll get through it. No worries."

CHAPTER 41

The Second Day

VENT DIDN'T POP out of bed in his typical style and moved around the kitchen like an old man, not an eighteen-year-old boy. After observing for some time, Georgia commented, "This not my Vent…you not movin' how Vent moves. This how you are after only one day? Can't see how this job right for you."

"Yeah, but this not my real job. This down in the caisson. My knees and ankles hurt, but only two more days to go. A big Irishman by the name of Connor McCloskey is keepin' an eye on me, so don't worry."

"You're talkin' pure crazy. You think some Irishman gonna take care of a Colored man? Ain't never gonna happen."

"No, don't worry, he's different. He stood up for me and I can manage another two days. I'll be better later."

Vent walked out of his house and headed toward Moses's waiting wagon.

"Thought you might want a ride to work for your second day. I stopped by last night, and Georgia said you might need some help—tough day and all. You sure this job the one for you?"

"Yeah, Moses. I'm sure. Only two more days in the caisson, so I'll be okay. Thanks for the ride."

"Last time, we rode this way together, you hid down below. I think I'll let you sit up top today!"

"Real kind of you, Moses." Vent lumbered into the wagon and Moses wondered if he would make the two days. Some people tolerated the caisson well, others not at all.

⊷⊷⊷ ⊷⊷⊷

Aengus McGreary walked into Harold Reems's office like he owned the place. Reems didn't recognize him, but based on his swagger and general demeanor, the manager realized this was not a man to be trifled with. Aengus made himself comfortable—he took the seat across from Reems, plopping his feet firmly on Reems's desk. McGreary motioned for Reems to sit.

"My name is Aengus McGreary and I'm one of the heads of the Velvet Caps. You ever heard of the Caps?"

Reems stammered, "Yes, of course. I don't want any trouble. I never go to Irishtown."

"No trouble for you, as long as you prove to be helpful. Are you going to be helpful, Harold Reems?"

"Yes, of course. What do you need?"

"I need to speak with one of your employees. A Colored fella by the name of Horace."

Reems perked up in his seat, but as his posture straightened, Aengus's grimace intensified. Harold slithered back down into his chair and said, "He's the Colored man with the brown shirt sitting right outside my office."

"Good decision, Harold Reems—real helpful. So this is what we are going to do. I am going to sit behind your desk for a few minutes and you'll send Horace in here to talk with me. I don't plan to hurt him in any way as long as he is as helpful as you. Go send him in and take a walk. I need five minutes with him."

Reems did as instructed and walked out of his office. Moments later, Horace appeared before McGreary, who puffed on a cigar with his legs up on Reems's desk.

"Take a seat, Horace."

"Who are you? Why did Mr. Reems tell me to come in here? What do you want?"

"You got this all wrong. I'm the one with the questions, but I'll give some answers too. First, you sit the fuck down, and I'll tell you who I am."

Horace sat on the edge of the seat and scrutinized the outside office area through the glass window. He found no trace of his boss.

"My name is Aengus McGreary and I believe you've already met my brother, Jimmy."

Horace sank back into his chair and turned his attention to the floor. He muttered his response. "Never met you or your brother."

"Listen Horace, I'm leaning toward not hurting you because my brother almost killed you a few weeks ago. The thing is, someone tried to get even for you and caused embarrassment to my brother and my family and this must be avenged."

"I don't understand what you mean, Mr. McGreary."

"Oh, don't you Mr. McGreary me. We can do this easy and pain-free right now, or I can wait for you outside and give you another beating like the one you got a few weeks ago, and you'll tell me then. Remember, though, Jimmy is a boy and I'm a man. I won't stop with a beating, I'll kill you. Now, who the fuck went after my brother? I understand he's a small little fella."

Horace's thoughts raced. *Can't take another beating—this time he says he'll kill me. Already knows it's a small person, might as well tell him 'bout Vent. If not, he'll figure it out on his own and kill both of us. Vent is tough—he can run, but I have to give his name, and I'll warn him right away. Yeah, I'll warn him like any good brother would. Yes, as long as I warn him, I'll be doing the right thing.*

Horace responded, "My brother, Vent."

"Good boy, Horace. You made this easier than I thought it would be."

No response from Horace.

"Where can I find Vent?"

"He works the day shift in the caisson at the bridge."

McGreary laughed and took a deep drag from his cigar. "Not much of a brother, are ya, Horace? Made my morning easy. Here's the deal, you aren't going to warn your brother about how I need to *speak* with him. I'm not gonna kill the little fella, but no Darkey is going to come into Irishtown and mess with a McGreary. He'll pay a price and we'll be even as far as I'm concerned. If I find out you warned him, I'm be coming back for ya. Understand?"

Horace nodded, and returned to his thoughts. *Vent is tough. I can't warn him, but I'll be a good brother and I'll help nurse him until he's healthy. Yes, I'll even give money to Georgia to help out while he can't work. We've got to put this behind us. I don't understand why Vent took this so far. What a mess he's gotten us into, but as long as I help him mend, I'll be doing the right thing.*

⊷►●◗●◖◁

Singleton spotted Ryan MacGregor placing another envelope in his pocket but didn't recognize his latest criminal acquaintance. He walked over to his partner moments after the envelope was tucked away.

"What's in your pocket, Ryan? Seems a little heavy."

"Listen, Father Singleton, I'll make a full confession on Sunday in church, but you stay the fuck out of my business and don't concern yourself with what's in my pocket. You should be concerned about what's not in your pocket."

Singleton decided long ago he would take down MacGregor. Rampant corruption of the sort practiced by his partner was without limits or boundaries and had to be stopped.

"Enjoy your money, MacGregor. You're going to make a mistake, and I'll be there when you do."

"You're saying you would come after one of your own?"

"You and I are not on the same side. I thought at least that much was clear. You're a fucking criminal and you're on your last legs in the department."

"Be careful, Father. Don't make any threats you can't back up."

"Believe you me. That won't be a problem. Take care, partner. I'll see you real soon in the captain's office."

"Fuck you, Singleton."

⊷▬⊙ ⊙▬⊷

Connor McCloskey helped Vent walk over to the shed at the end of the shift and again out to Moses's waiting wagon on the street. Vent turned to the Irish giant and said, "This is my friend Moses. He'll make sure I'm okay. Thanks for the help." The Irishman helped Vent into the wagon and said, "You only been down under for two days and you got clear signs of caisson's disease. One more day might be okay because I'll cover for ya when you need to rest a bit, but if they tell ya to go back into the caisson on Monday, you gotta quit. You're not meant to be a sandhog."

Vent appreciated the good advice, and Moses thanked Vent's new Irish friend for his help. McCloskey threw a blanket over Vent once he'd settled into the carriage. The eighteen-year-old boy, who'd become an old man during his two-day experience in the caisson, curled up into a ball and counted by fours all the way back to Weeksville.

CHAPTER 42

The Last Day Begins

SUDS MERRICK SAT in a circle with twenty of his men—all handpicked for the burglary of a boat loaded with goods headed for Europe. Merrick understood part of the shipment included jewelry and other portable goods, which could be snatched and taken away quickly. The plan for each burglary involved two groups of men. The first created an obstruction in the street about two blocks away from their intended target. The second group gained control of the ship and committed the actual burglary. Once the second group fled, the entire gang dispersed and met later to split the proceeds.

"Okay, men, we're going after the *Hellgate*, a fully loaded ship ready to sail tomorrow morning for Europe." Suds turned his attention to his first group. "Your job will be to block all traffic headed toward the docks for about thirty to forty-five minutes. Should be plenty of time."

The most senior of the men, Tommy O'Flanahan, answered for the group, "No problem, Boss. We've done this many of times before. Do you want us to claim to be working on the roads or just flat-out refuse entry with muscle?"

"Plain old muscle this time, Tommy. You can't be out blocking the streets with shovels and picks. We're too close to Caps territory and they think we're after them, for some reason. If they recognize the Hook Gang blocking the streets, they'll likely come after us, and we need to be ready. So everyone should be armed and prepared to fight."

O'Flanahan responded, "We understand, Boss. Don't worry about those fucking Caps. They'd never mess with the Hook Gang."

"Okay. Liam, you'll lead the other group boarding the ship. O'Flanahan, you'll be in charge of the men blocking the roads. We're planning to catch them by surprise at four thirty. We understand they're letting most of the men out early to go home and pack for their trip to Europe. The evening security doesn't arrive until six."

⊷╠══◉ ◉══╣⊶

Sean O'Malley addressed his men at their Little Docks headquarters. He paced back and forth and didn't want to start with his instructions until his second in command, Aengus McGreary, had arrived, but the hour was late, so he began his remarks. "Men, another standard operation tonight—the local authorities and marines from the Navy Yard will be raiding our very own Little Docks distillery, just one block away. This is our neighborhood, so organizing the women on the roofs and the boys in the alleys shouldn't be a problem." The leader stopped, and asked for the last time, "Where the fuck is Aengus?"

One of the men offered, "I saw him heading out of Irishtown with his brother earlier today. Don't know where they went."

"What fucking good is a number two if he's not around when you need him? McGreary better have a good reason he's not with us tonight, but I think all of you can handle this without him. The authorities should be heading toward the docks, because the distillery is in the last building before the water."

The Velvet Caps hit the streets and prepared for the late-afternoon raid.

⊷╠══◉ ◉══╣⊶

Vent struggled throughout the morning and spent a lot of his day standing in the shadow of Connor McCloskey. Due to Vent's small size and the poor lighting, the supervisors and other workers assumed he was hard at work, but the pain in his joints forced him to sit for most of the morning.

Connor whispered, "Vent, a supervisor is coming."

Vent scrambled to his feet, grabbed his pick and started attacking a large rock wedged under the ridge of the caisson. The supervisor took a moment to gauge the volume of work the two men produced, and seemed pleased. Connor McCloskey could do the work of two men, which is what he'd done all day.

Vent sat down as soon as the supervisor left, and said, "Connor, you're the nicest Irishman in the world."

Connor's laugh filled the chamber. "Ah, I take it the Irish haven't been so kind to ya over the years."

Vent nodded his head in agreement.

"Not surprised. Most Irish think the Blacks are taking their jobs, but you and I know it's more than that."

"What do you mean, Connor?"

"Vent, I thought you were a smart boy. Ever heard of the word *superior*? Big word."

"Yeah, I understand what superior means."

"Well, the rest of the world thinks they're *superior* to the Irish."

"You think the same thing doesn't happen to Colored folks?"

"Ah, this is the point, my little friend, the Blacks are the only group the Irish can claim to be superior to. Human nature, Vent—people don't like to take shit, but they love to give a little bit. This is what the Blacks do for the Irish. Now let's try to lift this rock out of here—almost quitting time. You made it, my friend."

⊸►═◉ ◉═◄⊸

Aengus handed the envelope to Ryan MacGregor and asked, "You're sure you understand who I'm talking about. His name is Vent and he works down in the *kayzon* during the day shift. All I need you to do is bring him to me when he gets out of work, and find some private place for me to chat with him."

"Yes, no one else fits the description you gave me. I kept track of him the last couple of days. He stands out because of his size, his color, and the fact a large Irishman protects him."

"So, here is a little extra to make sure you bring this Vent to me without any large Irishman by his side. Understand?"

MacGregor accepted a second envelope, peeked inside, smiled, and responded, "Consider it done."

CHAPTER 43

All for Me Grog

THREE O'CLOCK—ONE HOUR before the assumed time of the raid. Often the authorities arrived later than the scheduled time, but an early surprise was always a possibility. Women with rocks sat in chairs on rooftops. Some passed the time singing songs, others knitted, and many compared notes about family and friends in the new and old country. Raid preparation brought everyone together in one unified voice for an important cause. The Irish voted together, lived together, but most importantly, drank together. The authorities often misunderstood the reasons for the organized Irishtown resistance to federal raids. John Devlin held no special place in their hearts, but his cheap, sweet poteen, did.

A tall woman stood on the ledge of her rooftop and all heads turned in her direction. O'Malley and many of his men admired her bobbing red hair and flowing arm movements as the behemoth of a woman drew in a deep breath and began singing their fight song, "All for Me Grog." Once she reached the chorus, all of the rooftop women stood up and joined her:

"And it's all for me grog, me jolly jolly grog
All for me beer and tobacco
For I spent all me tin on lassies drinkin' gin
Across the Western ocean I must wander."

After three rounds of the chorus, the women, finished with their fun, returned to their solitary pursuits and awaited the order to begin pelting the authorities. O'Malley appreciated their spirit and offered a nod from the street to the big redhead as he walked past her position.

The kids in the alley gangs needed supervision. Unlike their mothers on the rooftops, they passed time fighting and competing in any number of ways. The kids, who all aspired to become Caps, viewed these raids as their chance to show their toughness and suitability for the gang. Some of the kids created favorable impressions during these raids, but in the sixty- to ninety-minute wait in the alleys, maintaining some semblance of order presented a challenge. As a result of this, the Caps put one of their men in the mix with each alley gang so things wouldn't get out of control.

Sean O'Malley walked from alley to alley and stopped in the middle of the block as he pronounced, "Okay, folks, wait for the first street gang to attack and start the rock throwing."

The streets were quiet until three forty-five, when a group of twenty men from the Hook Gang formed a line one block from the Velvet Caps position, and started redirecting all carriage and foot traffic away from the area—no explanations offered, and no questions asked. All the Hookers flashed their guns for effect.

Sean O'Malley conferred with a few of his men. "So, the Hookers *are* trying to muscle in on our business. Someone in our gang leaked this to them. No other way they could have found out. Get all of the men out of the alleys and form them up behind me, let's take the fight to the Hook Gang. Tell the rest of the gang to circle around from behind."

The men offered no alternatives and made no verbal response at all. O'Malley would have received some input from Aengus, and the coincidence of his conspicuous absence with the appearance of the Hook Gang made O'Malley consider the strong possibility Aengus had turned on him—number two making his play to become number one.

The Caps marched like an army toward the Hook Gang, and O'Malley screamed, "You're in Caps territory. I'm going to give you two minutes to clear out."

Tommy O'Flanahan responded on behalf of the Hookers, "You don't tell us what to do. Two minutes from now we'll be standing in the same place. As a matter of fact, we'll give *you* two minutes to get the fuck out of *our* way."

O'Malley waved his hand and twenty more Caps appeared on the other side of the Hookers. The Caps surrounded the Hookers and O'Malley considered his next move. A massacre would start an all-out gang war and bring more police attention into the area. He decided to give the Hookers one last chance to comply.

"Leave, or die where you stand," O'Malley screamed.

O'Flanahan scanned the entire area and took note of the overwhelming number of Caps both in front and in back of his men. He raised his head and spotted the rooftop women tossing their rocks from hand to hand, and glanced off to the side and noted a few alley gangs ready to pounce. His only option—retreat, but as he began to instruct his men, shots rang out from behind the Caps. The police and marines had arrived to conduct their raid of the distillery and fired warning shots to disperse the crowd, which caused a chain reaction of events, and absolute chaos for the next ten minutes. Caps and Hookers discharged their guns, rocks rained down from rooftops, and two of the alley gangs swarmed into the mix.

Tommy O'Flanahan ran for the cover of the butcher shop, but many of his men lost their composure as they dodged the rocks pouring down from above. One of the Hookers dared to point his gun at a cluster of women on a nearby rooftop and he became the new primary target. The force of the rocks striking his body caused him to lower his arm and accidently discharge his weapon with a street-level trajectory. The single bullet caught Tommy O'Flanahan in the back of the head just as he reached the door of the shop and propelled him into the storefront window.

The aerial bombing stopped when an alley gang ran toward the bloodied shooter with the goal of providing him with his final punishment for daring to point his gun at the neighborhood mothers. The kids began to pummel the already incapacitated man, who was curled up on the ground in a ball. A marine attempted to fire a warning shot in the air to end the brutal assault, but the bullet ricocheted and struck one of the alley kids in the side of his neck.

The shooting of the boy seemed to take the steam out of the attack. Mothers abandoned their rooftop battle stations and took control of the street as the gangs fled. By the time order was restored, Tommy O'Flanahan's lifeless body rested against the window of the butcher shop and his messmate who had inadvertently shot him was unconscious, but still alive in the middle of the road.

The redheaded rooftop singer of a few moments earlier threw her massive frame onto the body of the dead boy and asked, "All for Me Grog?" The phrase, which had been the rousing title of the Irish's battle song, had become a somber question with no acceptable answer.

O'Malley and his men retreated to their headquarters and the leader's position on the matter went from possibility to certainty—Aengus McGreary had made a move for control of the Caps and used a rival gang as part of his plan. O'Malley gave one instruction: "I want Aengus McGreary on his knees in front of me within the hour. All of you fuckers go out and find him." Again, no response from his men, other than immediate action and strict obedience—just what O'Malley wanted.

Chapter 44

Interested Citizens

"All done, Vent. Shift is over. I hope this is your last time down below. The caisson's not for you—Venture Simmons is a tower man for sure," Connor McCloskey offered as he helped Vent make his way out of the air chamber. By the time the duo started to walk toward the employee sheds, the pain in Vent's joints had become extreme. Connor whispered, "Picking you up isn't a good idea. I don't want them to think you're not fit for work on Monday. You'll be fine once you rest up this weekend."

Officer Ryan MacGregor called out to the two men as they neared the sheds, "Connor McCloskey?"

The big man answered, "Yes."

"They told me you were a large fella, but you are a mountain of a man! Management needs to meet with you in the office. Here, throw this blanket over yourself. No time for your clothes in the shed—they need you right away."

Connor hesitated because he wanted to make sure Vent got to the shed safely and off to the train for the short ride to Weeksville. He looked at Vent and then back at the officer before he answered, "Officer, let me help him over to the shed and I'll need but a minute to put on my clothes. Okay?"

"No, they're closing the office soon and they need you. Here is a blanket. I'll help your little friend."

The officer's brow crinkled and he stared down McCloskey in such a way that both Vent and Connor understood his directions needed to be followed. Despite the building pain in his joints, Vent forced himself to straighten up, and patted the big man on his back as he said, "I'll be fine. Go take care of your business." The officer smiled as Connor departed.

Vent started to make his own way to the shed, but the officer grabbed his bare shoulder and said, "Hold still, there's something you need to answer for."

The words cut through Vent like a knife. The thing he'd feared from the start was happening—his day of reckoning. Venture remembered his conversation with Moses about needlessly worrying about dying every day, as he realized his day had arrived. Worrying wasn't going to help, however, and what to do was both the question and the issue. Options included running, but Vent could barely walk, and fighting, but the officer was not only larger but also armed. A shooting pain in his abdomen made him double over and helped with his decision. Vent fell to the floor and starting counting in threes. "Three, six, nine, twelve, fifteen…"

MacGregor didn't understand what to make of the odd reaction, but understanding the man's behavior was not his concern. The officer threw Vent over his shoulder and headed to a storehouse across the yard from the shed. He knocked three times, and the McGreary brothers opened the door. The officer dropped Vent on the floor and collected his final payment from Aengus. Jimmy didn't hold back, and welcomed Vent with a vicious kick to his stomach, which rendered him unconscious. Fifteen minutes later, a bucket of ice-cold water woke him up.

Jimmy took the lead. "How does this feel, little man? Do you remember when you strung me up? I'm sure you do, I still got burns all over my body."

The voice was nothing more than background noise. Vent realized he was strung up by his feet with a rope. But the real source of his discomfort, however, more than his upside-down orientation or the pain in his joints and abdomen, was the piercing cold, which pervaded his body.

Vent focused his eyes on the window on the far side of the storeroom. The sun retreated for the day and the stars assumed control of the sky. Time for one last chat with his mama. "Almost made it, Mama. Would have been a tower man on Monday. Almost made it…"

The mother-son conversation was interrupted by the first strike of the whip. Vent became unconscious for the second time before the last stroke of the whip hit his back ten minutes later. The McGrearys, pleased with their work, left Vent dangling upside down in the storeroom. Aengus considered this to be a life lesson for his little brother and said, "Killing someone fast is not much of a punishment. He'll die a slow and painful death before morning. Tomorrow morning, the workers will come in and find a little black ice cube hanging from the ceiling! Let's head back to Irishtown. We may be able to get back in time to help with the raid. O'Malley must be pissed at me, but no worries, he always believes my bullshit. Let's go."

Officer John Singleton noticed the two brothers coming from the direction of the storeroom, laughing and patting each other on the back. He remembered them from Irishtown and sensed they were up to no good. "What are you two doing down here?" he asked.

Aengus responded, "We're interested citizens admiring this impressive bridge—biggest bridge in the world, we understand…needed to come down to see it ourselves. Top of the evening to you, Officer."

Chapter 45

Where's Vent?

Georgia paced back and forth, peeking through the front window each time she passed by. Vent, a creature of habit and routine, should have taken the five-thirty train and arrived home well before six; now, at seven, he was nowhere to be found. Georgia had noted his deteriorating condition with each day he worked in the caisson and worried something had happened to him at the job. She refused to sit around the house any longer.

After the second knock, Ezra opened the door. Georgia asked, "Either you or Moses seen Vent? He never came home from work."

Ezra shook his head and shrugged his shoulder as he answered, "Not me, but Moses is out back. Let's check with him."

Georgia and Ezra found Moses settling his horse down for the night when they entered the barn.

"Moses, you seen Vent? I know sometimes you pick him up," Georgia asked.

"No. I couldn't pick him up today. Lots of deliveries, but the big Irishman said he'd put him on the five-thirty train. You ain't seen him yet?"

"No, Moses. I'm afraid something happened to my Vent."

"All right, you go back home and wait in case he shows up. I'm going to ride over to Miss Esther's and if she has no news, I'll go down to the construction site and check for him."

Moses harnessed his horse to his wagon and made the short trip over to the Washingtons. He found the family sitting down for dinner. "Sorry to bother you folks, but Vent missing. Any of you heard from him after work today?"

Miss Esther answered, "No. I haven't seen him for a few days."

Thomas shook his head, signaling *no*, and Horace stared at his plate. Moses turned to Horace. "What about you. What you know 'bout this?"

Horace raised his head up, but his eyes remained down. Moses jumped in. "What you done, boy? What do you know 'bout Vent?"

Horace's words poured out in rapid succession. "They were going to kill me—I had no choice. They wanted to know who attacked Jimmy McGreary—I had no choice. They said they would kill me. No choice. They told me I couldn't warn Vent either. You don't understand. I'm going to help him get better—I will…like he helped me."

Miss Esther and Thomas sat in silence as they gathered their thoughts. Moses dashed out of the house, back into his carriage, and headed for the worksite.

Thomas cleared his throat and turned to his son. "I don't even know what to say. You think like a coward and act like a scared child, not a man, and not my son. I want you to go to your room and start to pack. You're not my son anymore—you can't live in this house and turn against your own. Leave in the morning…don't care where you go."

Miss Esther's silence was a tacit endorsement of the decision. Horace walked away in disgrace.

⤜▶ ◀⤛

"Officer Singleton, you seen Vent? He never came home after work and we think the Irish came after him. Need your help," Moses pleaded.

Singleton immediately thought of the laughing McGreary brothers he'd seen earlier that night and ran toward the storeroom. Moses followed and helped the officer unbolt the door. They found Vent dangling from the ceiling, almost dead from both exposure and his terrible whipping.

Singleton took charge. "Moses, fetch the wagon."

The two men kept Vent wrapped in blankets by their side during the trip to the doctor's house. He was unconscious, but alive. The doc came out to the carriage to have a quick look and directed Moses and Officer Singleton to take Vent home, indicating he would follow on horseback. Once back in Weeksville, the doctor tended to his patient in the privacy of the bedroom.

The last to arrive was Moses's brother, Ezra, who moved a chair into the space between Moses and John Singleton. He reached for his brother's hand, who then reached for Georgia's, and by the time John Singleton held Ezra's hand, the circle was complete. Everyone lowered their head and offered a silent prayer. The doctor exited the bedroom and cleared his throat to draw the attention of the group. He offered three words, "I'm so sorry."

CHAPTER 46

John's New Friend

JOHN SINGLETON OPENED the bottle of Jameson whiskey The Professor had given him a few weeks earlier and started to drink as soon as he got home. *Maybe this will help me to understand,* he thought, as he considered the brutality he'd witnessed a few hours earlier. After all this time, John considered Vent to be a good man, even somewhat of a friend. The police hadn't protected him from the McGreary brothers. As a matter of fact, Aengus McGreary was known to have a relationship with Ryan MacGregor, who likely provided the brothers with both the access and opportunity. *What kind of job is this? We're supposed to be the good guys. At least that's what Dad always said.*

John's thoughts turned his attention to the prominent framed picture of his father in full uniform toward the end of his career, which hung on the wall across from the table, and he took a long sip from his bottle. *Yeah, I think The Professor is right. This does help at the end of a bad day.* John chuckled. His conversation with his deceased father began with the bottle about a third consumed, and entered full swing by the halfway point.

"Dad, I don't understand how you did this job for so many years. So much is wrong with the department. It's not what you said, the good guys versus the bad. You lied to me."

John drank a little more as he waited for his father's response. None came, but John's eyes began to travel again and settled on his dad's citations from the department—all framed and mounted on the wall above a small bookcase. He remembered the daily advice his father had offered during the last week of his life. "Son, when you are confused and need guidance, turn to the Bible, and when you think the department is letting you down and you need resources to push through, open the box on the bottom shelf of the bookcase, which contains the wealth of knowledge I gained from my years as an officer."

John's father repeated the same speech every morning for the last several days of his life. Given the events of the day, and the inspiration provided by the Jameson whiskey—now about two-thirds consumed—John determined the time was right for both guidance and resources. First, he reached for the Bible, and spotted an envelope addressed "John" protruding from one of the first few pages. After opening the envelope, he moved his new friend, the bottle of Jameson, next to his side so he, too, might listen to his father's words.

John,

I hope you're reading this after I'm gone. I'll do the best I can to explain some things to you, but my partner, The Professor, is the one with the gift for words, and he'll provide you with further advice.

The Professor and I formed a small group of officers who tried to make things better, but many might question the way we went about our work. It took several years for us to understand the reality of our jobs. Corrupt politicians owned the corrupt judges, who were given cases by corrupt policemen, and the system, if you want to call it that, often got things wrong. We couldn't fix things by working harder, but we found a way to make a difference by working smarter, and developing other resources to help make things right.

You're working in a job where most of the good guys are not all good, and many of the bad guys aren't all bad. We decided to find the middle ground and overlook the little things, so we might get the big things right.

Please don't be shocked or think less of me when you open the box with your resources at the bottom of the shelf. Trust my words…your dad was one of the good ones. Go to The Professor and he'll explain everything.
Dad

John consulted his friend by taking a few more sips before he reached down to pick up the box. "Sorry to see you go, my new friend," John said, as he placed the empty bottle on the far side of the table. The lid of the box, secured with string, took some time to unravel. John became impatient and pulled his small pocketknife from his pocket and cut the string. *Is this some kind of joke?* John opened the box and stared down at the very book his dad said had no answers, *The Metropolitan Police Manual.*

The temptation to throw the book out of the window and march into the station in the morning to quit his godforsaken job grew stronger by the moment. He wished his new friend were still available to offer sound advice before making such an important decision—but he was alone, and this choice would be all his to make. John sat for several moments deciding whether to toss the book or play his father's game and check what passages he circled, which represented *the wealth of knowledge he'd gained from his years as an officer.*

"Fuck it. Out the window it goes, just like this shit of a job." John picked up the manual, but sensed right away the weight of the book wasn't right. He opened the cover, and realized the center of the thick, oversized handbook had been hollowed out and held a tremendous stash of cash, upon which rested a short note, "John, don't overreact. Put this money away somewhere safe, and talk to The Professor."

John laughed as he flipped through the stack of large denomination bills. He counted fifty bills, mostly twenties and tens. *So this is what he means by his wealth of resources? All of the dirty money he stashed away over the years?* John took out his pocket watch and remembered his father's lesson about some gifts that simply had to be accepted in order to avoid being disrespectful. John always imagined this was the exception, not the rule. *Dad, I guess you never disrespected anyone.* He remained tempted to toss the book, but instead turned back to the portrait of his father and called out, "You were one of the good ones? What a joke! Look at this cash, you were no better than The Criminal Cop, Sergeant Anderson." He paused and reached for his friend, but his bottle was now empty, sitting all alone on the table, and John realized why they'd bonded so well.

CHAPTER 47

New Number Twos

SUDS MERRICK PACED back and forth at the front of the bar and denied entry to anyone outside of his gang. The proprietor fumed as he estimated his lost revenue on this, the busiest night of the week. Suds glanced at the barkeep and tossed him a wad of bills as he said, "The place is mine tonight. Take this for your troubles."

By eight, most of the Hook Gang was several drinks into the evening. Suds went to the back of the bar with two of his top lieutenants, Muddy MacAuley, or Muddy Mac for short, and Liam O'Brien. Suds opened the conversation. "Before we go out and talk to the men, I need you both to tell me what happened today. I need to find out if I missed anything. With Tommy gone, I'll be counting more on the two of you. Let's start with the operation Tommy ran. Muddy Mac, you were with him. What happened?"

Muddy Mac stood up to speak, and the stench from his filthy coat and clothes wafted in the direction of Merrick. Suds held his arm up and said, "Jesus, Muddy, take a fucking bath once in a while, you smell like shit. Now sit back down, push your chair farther away, and tell me what happened, you filthy piece of shit."

Muddy Mac never minded the comments about his hygiene and understood the constant dirt all over his personage inspired his nickname. He gave his version of events. "We didn't realize the Caps set up for a raid and went into our positions about a block away, blocking people and carriages, like you told us. All of a sudden, O'Malley shows up with one big group and tells us to fuck off, and when Tommy told him the same, another group of Caps came up from behind.

The Caps surrounded us and we needed to escape, but before we did, the shooting started."

Suds interrupted, "So who started the shooting, and who killed Tommy O'Flanahan?"

Muddy Mac was torn as to whether he should tell Merrick there was a report that O'Flanahan's death might have been the result of an accidental shot from another Hooker. He thought better of offering this uncorroborated theory and said, "We couldn't tell—too much going on."

"All right," Merrick responded. "But you can't rule out the Caps, and our men think the Caps killed Tommy, so this is the story we'll go with. O'Malley came after us a few days ago in a meeting and now they attacked us during one of our operations. The men must understand we're not standing for this bullshit— the Caps need to pay. Liam, tell me what happened on the *Hellgate*, and what you got away with."

Liam O'Brien began his explanation. "We boarded the *Hellgate* and took control with no problem, but when the police and the marines headed our way, we figured we better run."

Merrick jumped in, "You didn't answer my question, what did you manage to steal?"

"Sorry, boss, nothing much. Once the commotion started with the marines in the background, we jumped off the schooner and ran."

"Who decided to do that?" Merrick asked.

"Me. Needed to run."

"You fucking little coward, we lost one of our top men, took a load of shit from another gang, and we have nothing to show for this mess? Is this what you're telling me?"

"Well, yeah, Suds—we needed to run right after we boarded."

"All right, at least you made my decision easy. Muddy MacAuley is my new number two, and, O'Brien, if you can't handle a little pressure from the police during a robbery, you may not even be cut out to be the lead in anything anymore. Only one condition, Muddy, take a fucking bath! Can't be around me all day smelling like a dog's ass."

Suds Merrick walked out to the rest of the men and tapped one of the mugs on the bar top to call everyone to attention. "Quiet down, we've got things to discuss. Both the street and the ship operations went arseways today, and we lost a good man, my number two, Tommy O'Flanahan. So first order of business, a toast to Tommy." All of the men raised their mugs and took a hearty sip of their sweet poteen. Once the group settled down, Suds continued, "This means we need to fill Tommy's shoes and I'm making Muddy Mac the new number two." Muddy raised his arm in self-recognition, and two of the men standing on either side of him moved away. The leader concluded his thoughts. "The Caps did this to us, and if they want a war, we'll oblige. Let's take the fight right to them on Sunday night at their Little Docks headquarters. An eye for an eye, boys!"

The gang raised their mugs for one final cheer. "An eye for an eye!"

◄►═◉ ◉═◄►

The Velvet Caps held a meeting of their own a few blocks away at their Little Docks location. About ten minutes in, loud shouting emanated from the street below. O'Malley extended his neck out the window and spotted Aengus McGreary and his brother Jimmy surrounded by five of the gang members sent to find them.

"Who the fuck do you think you're talking to? I'm Aengus McGreary!"

O'Malley called out from the window facing the street on the top floor, "Send them up boys, plenty of time for a proper discussion."

Aengus expected to be able to talk his way out of his absence in today's raid, which he thought would be routine, but now he had doubts.

"Fucking Aengus McGreary and his stupid as shit little brother, Jimmy. Where the fuck did the two of you go off to today?" O'Malley asked.

Jimmy remained silent with no intention of uttering a word—he normally led one of the alley gangs, but Aengus played a much larger role.

Aengus cleared his throat, and answered, "Sean, some unexpected family business came up on the other side of town. Had I known the Hookers were in the way—"

O'Malley cut him off. "Had you known? You're the one who fucking told them. Boys, rip off Jimmy's shirt."

Three men walked toward Jimmy, who decided to utter his first words, "No need." Jimmy struggled with the first and second buttons because of his shaking hands, and O'Malley screamed, "Rip the fucking shirt off his back!"

The shirt fell in pieces on the floor.

O'Malley continued, "Turn in a circle so everyone can examine your big fat body, you lying piece of shit."

Jimmy turned full circle, but no one understood the reason for the display. O'Malley walked closer to Jimmy and asked, "Why are the burns on your front almost gone, but the Hook Gang symbol on your back is still so clear?"

Jimmy shrugged his shoulders, but Aengus suggested, "They made those burns deeper so their threat would be even more strong."

"Good try, Aengus, but I think you put the symbol on his back weeks after the attack, to start something between the Hookers and the Caps. You wanted to make me look bad either to Devlin or the men, to make a move on me."

"I'd never make a move, Sean—I never lie to you at all."

O'Malley called out to the men, "What do we think? He never lies at all or he's a lying piece of shit?"

The men chanted, "Lying piece of shit!" several times.

Aengus's right-hand man realized his mentor had lost his standing in the gang, and joined the attack as he said, "I told Aengus I saw a little man running away after Jimmy got attacked, and we got a better look at him days later at the building construction site. The man is a wee little Darkey. Aengus told me not to say anything 'cause Jimmy would seem weak, but I never understood anything about the symbol on Jimmy's back."

"Finally, the pinch of the game," O'Malley exclaimed. "You knew who attacked Jimmy, but the truth was much too embarrassing, so you tried to save your brother's reputation at the same time you made your move on me. What a plan! What do we think, boys?"

Several of the men started to call out, "Traitor! Traitor! Traitor!" O'Malley silenced the gang and added, "Okay, everything makes sense now. Our friend Aengus started this shit with the Hookers—for aught I know, they never wanted to cut in on our business; they planned to raid a ship, so they blocked the traffic like they always do."

One of the men pointed to the McGreary brothers and asked, "So what do we do with them?"

"Oh, they're dead men for sure, but I need to think over our options." O'Malley smiled and considered walking over to shake Aengus's hand. His treachery gave O'Malley the perfect opportunity to establish himself as a ferocious leader. The leader of the Caps wasn't sure who his next number two would be, but he was confident he'd be well-behaved.

CHAPTER 48

Eyes Not Okay

THOMAS WASHINGTON LEFT early to make deliveries and Esther checked on Horace's progress with his packing. She walked into her son's room and took note of his empty closet and dresser drawers. One last item needed to be packed, but Esther grabbed Horace's hand as he reached for it.

"Horace, leave the mirror. Time for you to stop looking at yourself like you some pretty little girl. You got to be a man now and learn from these terrible mistakes you done made. Even if you take another beating, you never turn on family. Don't matter if your face gets a little messed up, 'cause all we got is family, and we need to protect each other."

"Mama, they said they would beat me."

"Hush, Horace, stop talkin' like a scared boy. Time to be a man. You gonna be on your own and you need to start a new life. Your daddy might take you back one day, but only after you grow up—this mirror is holding you back. Now go and find yourself some place to stay. Send me word once you do."

Horace placed his cherished mirror back on the top of the dresser and dragged his two large satchels out of the house.

⊷◉ ◉⊶

Georgia and Mabel took turns tending to Vent. He mumbled from time to time, and often burned with fever. The doctor advised them to keep the dressings on his back clean because if the infection persisted, he would not recover. But every time they changed the dressing, however, the infection appeared worse. Venture found himself someplace in between the past and the present as he faded in and out of consciousness. He relived some difficult moments in his life through his dreams, which took him back to the early days in the boardinghouse, when he and his mom first arrived after escaping slavery in Virginia.

"Vent, Mama got to find a way to make money. Ten years may be old 'nuff to understand some important things. You think you can understand somethin' important, Vent?"

"Yes, Mama."

"Remember when the master took me up to his room most nights, and you asked me why?"

"Yes, Mama. You said—*grown-up stuff*—and not to worry myself 'bout it."

"You right, Vent. The master did the *grown-up stuff* to me real rough, but I had to let him do it 'cause he owned me. He hurt your mama, but I can't be mad at him for everything he did, 'cause he did give me one special gift."

"What's the gift, Mama? You told me he only did bad things."

"The gift he gave me is you, my baby. The *grown-up stuff* I'm talkin' 'bout is what makes babies. The master is your daddy."

"Mama, I don't understand, you said I didn't have a daddy?"

"I meant to say, you ain't got a daddy who loves you and cares for you like your mama. Remember, my little boy, nobody ever gonna love you like your mama."

Vent's eyes shot open for a moment and Georgia witnessed the rage Moses described the day he jumped out of the crate. His head thrashed back and forth, but then his lids closed, and he collapsed back on the bed. Sweat poured from his brow and Georgia did her best to cool him down with a cold rag. Soon, Vent's dreams took him back to his mama in the boardinghouse.

"Vent, I found a man who gonna help us. He a White man and he'll give us money to live in this here boardinghouse. He and I gonna do *grown-up stuff*, but he won't hurt me like the master, and I'm letting him do it with my own free will. You understand, Vent?"

"Yes, Mama, but you sure he ain't gonna hurt you like the master?"

"I'm pretty sure, but you can't be out here when he comes to visit."

"Where I going to be, Mama?"

"Only one place I can think of. Settin' you up in your own space. Yup, just the right size for my little boy. Right in here." She opened the door to the closet and Vent admired the little bed his mom had made for him. "When my gentl'man friend comes over, you go in the closet and be quiet. I'll teach you a game to make the time go by fast. Count to one hundred in twos, threes, and fours. I know how good you are with numbers. By the time you're counting by eights, I'll be opening the door to let you out."

"You want me to count and when I'm done, you'll be done?"

"Yup, and if you're worried about me, you can peek through the crack, but only at my eyes—long as my eyes tell you everything is okay, you go back to counting. If things aren't okay with my eyes, I'm gonna give you this here club, and you come out swinging. Understand, Vent."

"Yes, Mama."

Vent started to convulse as his mind went back to that fateful day during the Draft Riots. This time, however, he screamed what he remembered as he witnessed his mother's attack from the rooftop next door.

"Mama, Mama, why you didn't put me in the closet? Eyes not okay, Mama. Eyes not okay. Where's my club? Mama, eyes not okay! I let you down, Mama! I let you down!"

Vent popped up in bed and started swinging his hands as he screamed, "Eyes not okay! Eyes not okay, Mama." Moses ran in to settle him back down. A few hours later, the doctor arrived and after spending time alone with Vent assessing the advance of his infection, he emerged from the bedroom with slumped shoulders and began his report with a sigh. "Try to keep him comfortable with cool rags and keep tending to his cuts." He paused for a moment and reached for Georgia's hand. The doctor ended his remarks with the same three words he uttered after first treating Vent after the attack. "I'm so sorry."

CHAPTER 49

See You at Five

JOHN SINGLETON WOKE up Saturday morning with his face flush against the kitchen table. He strained to raise his head, but a pounding in his temples forced him to return to a resting position. John glared across the table at the empty bottle of Jameson, and recalled his classification of the bottle the previous night as one of his very few friends. *A friend with a kick*, he thought as his head began its upward journey for the second time, and the pounding became more tolerable. John relocated to his bed.

Two hours later, he woke up with clarity of both mind and purpose and headed to Irishtown.

"John, what brings you to my door on a cold Saturday morning?" The Professor asked.

"The last few days and weeks raised lots of questions, and I need answers."

The Professor glanced down at the Bible and police handbook John held by his side, and responded, "Of course, what can I answer first?"

"Was my father a dirty cop?"

"John, if this is the first question, I'm afraid the conversation won't last too long. What in your mind makes someone a dirty cop?"

"How about this?" John responded as he opened the police manual and flashed the ill-gotten cash.

"Ah, so life is black and white, no gray for John Singleton—anyone who takes money is dirty. Do you realize your father saved more good lives and put more bad guys away than anyone else I worked with during my time in the department? To most people, this makes him a good cop."

"Lining your pockets along the way with bribes takes the luster off his good deeds. My dad was a crook, pure and simple."

"John, take a breath. I hoped you'd start to understand that things aren't so straightforward. Did your father ever tell ya why they began calling me The Professor?"

"No, he didn't, but I figured you attended some college."

"No. I never attended a day of college in my life, but I did do a lot of reading, and one day after going through a bit of bad time, which seems to be your situation right now, I read a book called *The Prince* by Machiavelli, and I took away an important lesson—one I shared with your father, and a few other key officers along the way."

"What lesson?"

"The end justifies the means."

"Sounds to me like an open invitation to do whatever is necessary to get what you want," John responded.

"Perhaps, but not the way we practiced it. I led the group and your father came next in terms of rank. Your first captain in Irishtown, Arnold Johnson, and your current captain, Helmut Dill, are also founding members. A few others retired along the way, but I stayed involved even after I left the job. We needed positive change and we all decided we would cross certain lines to achieve the desired end, as long as we unanimously agreed the end was just."

"How did taking bribes help you to achieve good ends? Doesn't make any sense."

"Lots of what we did related to trust, John. The money we accepted never came from good people who we threatened in some way. Our money came from criminals, who we needed to assist us from time to time, to achieve something good. Accepting their money enabled them to trust us, and the money also provided a resource to encourage others to help in some way."

"So, none of the money went into your pockets for personal gain?"

"No, I'm not saying we were angels, and some of the money did go to us. Why do you think I drink Jameson instead of Devlin's sweet poteen, and how do you think you grew up in such a well-to-do household on a policeman's salary? Your father gave ya options to do something with your life other than become a policeman, but you wanted to follow in his footsteps, and we thought in time you'd become one of us."

"I'll never be like Sergeant Anderson—I'll never be a corrupt cop."

"Anderson's not the model, John, but your father was. Tell me what happened over the last few days, and play along with me for a bit. Let's try to find some solutions."

John walked toward The Professor's living room and tried to process everything as he settled into one of the two large easy chairs.

"Interesting, you instinctively sat in your father's seat, when he and I had these discussions."

John relaxed and realized he might be wrong about his dad; the money, however, was still a concern, and he didn't understand what other lines his father crossed. Despite all of these reservations, John had to admit he did not make a difference following procedure. He opened up and told The Professor the entire story of the McGreary brothers, the attack on Vent, and the role his partner, Ryan MacGregor, likely played in the entire affair.

"Okay, thanks for explaining the part of the story you know—I wasn't aware of what happened to your friend, the young Colored man. The things ya don't know yet came to me from Captain Johnson, your old boss in Irishtown. He's got people connected to the gangs, who we give a few dollars to now and again to tell us when something big is about to happen. Here is the additional information—Aengus McGreary planted the Hook Gang's symbol as a burn on his younger brother's back, which made the Caps think the Hookers came after them. They both had illegal operations going on last night in the same general vicinity, and because of this manufactured scratch, both gangs viewed the actions of the other as a declaration of war. The number two leader in the Hook Gang lost his life in their brief but furious exchange, and the leader of the Caps is aware of the deceit of his own number two. So, what do ya think will happen if we follow procedure and do everything as we should according to the manual?"

"Sounds like gang warfare in which several gang members will be killed on each side, and some innocent people as well."

"You're right, my boy! So is this the end we want?"

"No."

"What would a good end be?"

John Singleton started to understand how the approach his father and The Professor adopted might achieve a good end, but before he suggested his solution, he asked, "First, tell me what you meant when you said you would only move forward if the decision on the good end was unanimous? Who gets a vote?"

"At five tonight, Captain Dill and Captain Johnson will be sitting in those two chairs across from us, and if you've got a recommendation, we'll listen. We may accept it outright, or reject your idea and suggest something else. But once a plan is set, we will all vote, including you. We've been waiting for your moment—the day when your frustration would build up to the point you would be open to this approach—today is that day, John. Your father's vote is yours—we all agreed on this the moment you started on the force, but we needed you to be ready. So, tell me…are ya ready?"

John felt no hesitation. His response, "See you at five."

CHAPTER 50

Amazing Grace

MOTHER AND DAUGHTER took turns sitting with Vent, but often sat together bedside. Georgia sang all of her favorite songs while Florence sat quietly and tried to smile. When Georgia began Vent's favorite, "Amazing Grace," they sang together.

Amazing grace! How sweet the sound
That saved a wretch like me!
I once was lost, but now am found;
Was blind, but now I see.

'Twas grace that taught my heart to fear,
And grace my fears relieved;
How precious did that grace appear
The hour I first believed.

Through many dangers, toils and snares,
I have already come;
'Tis grace hath brought me safe thus far,
And grace will lead me home.

The Lord has promised good to me,
His Word my hope secures;
He will my Shield and Portion be,
As long as life endures.

Yea, when this flesh and heart shall fail,
And mortal life shall cease,
I shall possess, within the veil,
A life of joy and peace.

The earth shall soon dissolve like snow,
The sun forbear to shine;
But God, who called me here below,
Will be forever mine.

When we've been there ten thousand years,
Bright shining as the sun,
We've no less days to sing God's praise
Than when we'd first begun.

Georgia felt a sense of hope in her heart and gazed at the heavens when she sang, "A Life of Joy and Peace." Florence did much the same as she sang the first line of the previous stanza, "The Lord has promised good to me." They both hoped their prayers would be answered.

Miss Esther spent most of her time in the kitchen and the living area of Vent's home, trying to stay busy making everyone comfortable. Her visits to Vent's bedside were rare because they triggered thoughts of Horace's deceit, and a chain reaction of conclusions, which led to the sad reality—she had failed to develop her eldest son's character, and was unable to protect her youngest. *I was a bad mother, Lord,* was always her final thought and conclusion.

Horace tried to come by early Saturday morning to check on Vent, but Moses threatened to beat him to a pulp if he stepped foot in the house. Esther remembered the little boy tied in ropes, being marched into town by a man who later would turn out to love him as much as she. What an unusual beginning and what a devastating end. Vent planned to kill the world for what they did to his mama. In the end, he found some forgiveness in his heart, or at least was at peace with what happened. The world, however, ended up killing him.

Mabel stopped by throughout the day, pulled up a chair next to Moses, and cried. She too couldn't bear to spend much time bedside, perhaps for the same reasons as her mother.

Moses sat, alert and ready—he had failed to protect Vent once. It wouldn't happen again.

After some time, Esther began to worry about Moses, whose intense stare melted into resolve and determination—she worried about what he planned to do to Horace. Esther still had two sons to protect, although one had proven to be much less of a man. After a few moments, Esther broached the topic with Moses. "I know you love Vent as much as I do, but you can't be planning to do nothin' to my Horace. He already been sent away—can't be no more revenge. Both you and I understand revenge is at the heart of all of this mess."

"Miss Esther, don't want to say nothin' right now. Not in no mood to forgive and forget, and I ain't planning nothin' until things work out one way or the other. So I'm askin' you to let me sit here quiet. Leave me be."

Not the answer she hoped for.

From time to time, Ezra came by for instructions from his younger brother as to how to keep his many businesses running at least at a minimal level. Moses was the brains of all of their business pursuits—Ezra couldn't believe he'd ever called Moses stupid. He whispered to Miss Esther as he left the first morning, "Best not to talk to Moses. Never seen him like this. He's not himself."

Neighborhood folks stopped by with dishes of food for the family, but at a certain point, Miss Esther asked them to stop. All the offerings contributed to the hopelessness of the situation, and seemed premature—Vent still had a chance to survive, albeit a small one.

This Will Do

S ATURDAY, FIVE O'CLOCK. The Professor, Captain Dill, and Captain Johnson were already seated, each with a tumbler of Jameson in their hands, as John arrived and took his seat in the large chair next to The Professor, who called the meeting to order.

"All right, we first want to welcome the son of one of our founding members to our group. To John!" The Professor offered.

All four men took a healthy sip of whiskey.

Captain Dill stood and made another toast. "To peace in Irishtown in the upcoming week."

All four men said, "Here! Here!"

Johnson's toast brought the men to the matter at hand, but more whiskey needed to be poured to create the kind of deep thinking needed for issues of this magnitude. The Professor started the dialogue. "John, I briefed the two captains on the new facts you provided, and you heard their end of the story earlier today. The captains should speak first to tell us what they are worried about in their respective neighborhoods. Helmut?"

Captain Helmut Dill, who headed the station in charge of the area that included the bridge construction site, offered his assessment. "For me, the issue is a rogue cop, who facilitated a brutal beating on the grounds of the construction site. There's been no trouble of note at the site despite the fighting over jobs and typical ethnic and racial bullshit. I believe Ryan MacGregor allowed this to happen, and I warned him I would end his career once he went back to his old tricks, and now he did. Don't give a shit about his father—he's done as a policeman."

"Thank you, Captain Dill, I think your suggestion is something we can likely all get behind. What are your thoughts, Captain Johnson?"

Johnson finished his tumbler before he began his remarks—his face was absent expression as he detailed his prediction for the upcoming week. "Irishtown's gang war is based on bullshit. The Hook Gang is going to come after the Velvet Caps for the killing of their number two man. We understand the whole feud was manufactured by the Cap's number two, Aengus McGreary, but I'm looking at bloodshed—likely multiple people, including some innocent folks who'll get caught up in the violence by mistake."

The Professor thanked Johnson for his information and turned to John Singleton. "So, John, we understand you want to present an idea to achieve a good end. First, tell us what the end is and, if we can unanimously agree on that, we'll work out how to move forward."

John studied the three men, the first, his current boss, the second, his former boss, and the third, his mentor, and realized at this moment, he was their equal—they were giving him the opportunity to offer a solution. He imagined his father sitting in this chair many times over the years offering suggestions to solve problems of days gone by and realized, perhaps for the first time, he was now truly following in his father's footsteps.

John took out his pocket watch and rubbed his finger against the etching of the angel's wings and then began, "The good end will be a combination of things. Aengus McGreary pays for the beating he administered on the construction site. He also pays for his manipulation of the two gangs into war and the death of the number two on the other side. My solution to this first piece will enable the two gangs to settle their dispute without any unnecessary deaths. My second good end is for Ryan MacGregor to be out of the police department."

All four men raised their glasses in a symbol of unity—the decision, unanimous. John filled them in on his plan, which would begin to unfold in the morning. If all went well, matters would be settled by Sunday night, and while John couldn't undo the brutal beating his friend Vent received, justice would prevail.

Captain Dill offered the only note of concern. "John, your plan will require some resources because we will need to ask people to do things they will not do without encouragement."

John replied by handing the captain his father's hollowed-out police manual. "Will this give you enough in the way of resources?" Dill scooped out what he needed and handed the balance back to John as he said, "This will do."

The Professor proposed one final toast, the one that always followed a decision of this importance: "To the day we no longer need to take matters into our own hands." All the men replied, "Here, Here."

CHAPTER 52

Long Live the Priest

THE PROFESSOR'S APARTMENT was all set for the meeting between the leaders of the Velvet Caps and the Hook Gang. Captains Dill and Johnson made all of the arrangements, which included a police presence around the house and at the end of each block. The captains told each gang to approach from a particular direction and only the leaders would pass beyond a certain point with a police escort. These arrangements were their contribution to the good end, and John Singleton's resources helped to encourage the security detail to volunteer for this special Sunday assignment. Dill told his intermediaries to inform the gang leaders that The Professor, a well-known figure in Irishtown, and his new associate, The Priest, would run the meeting.

Sean O'Malley entered through the front door and Suds Merrick through the back. Officers inside the apartment checked one last time for weapons and escorted the two leaders into the living area to meet The Professor and The Priest, already in place, seated in their oversized chairs. John wore civilian clothes for the meeting and didn't realize the two gang leaders expected someone with a priestly collar.

The Professor opened the meeting. "Gentleman, please sit, and I hope you won't mind the officer who will stand between the two of you as a precaution."

O'Malley offered The Professor a nod and The Priest a smirk as he remembered the young cop from his time in Irishtown, but refused to acknowledge the presence of Suds Merrick. "Seems like you've come a long way in a short while. A pleasure to meet you, Father," O'Malley joked as he addressed John Singleton.

Suds Merrick offered no greetings of any kind—only a deadly glare directed at Sean O'Malley, the man responsible for the death of his trusted number two,

Tommy O'Flanahan. The Professor took the glare as a sign of trouble and addressed the officer situated between the two men. "Officer, we may need a little more separation between these two gentlemen. Mr. Merrick doesn't yet appear ready for a discussion." The officer motioned for Merrick to stand, but Suds waved him off as he said, "Don't worry about me right now, Sean O'Malley, but once we're through with this bullshit meeting, understand the Hook Gang is coming for ya and all of your fancy friends wearing their velvet caps."

O'Malley jumped out of his chair and needed to be restrained by the officer. John Singleton stood and addressed both men. "Sit down and shut the fuck up. We're not having a gang war in Irishtown and we're resolving this bullshit today in this room." The men sat, and The Professor took a moment to view his protégé with a new sense of admiration—he was his father's son.

Singleton continued, "First, let's clear up the thing that started all of this trouble. Suds, are you moving against the Caps and their business with Devlin?"

Merrick answered, "Not before, but now, maybe we will."

John grabbed the armrests of his chair as if he needed them to restrain him from smacking the uncooperative gang leader and said, "I'm telling you right now, stop the bullshit or pay the consequences. The police don't have the resources to shut down all the Irish gangs, but we sure can take care of one. Do you understand me, Suds?"

Suds sat back in his chair. "Yes, I do, but—"

John cut him off. "'Yes, I do' was all you needed to say. I will repeat my question. Are the Hookers trying to take over the work the Caps do with Devlin?"

"No, we're not. The Hook Gang had business on the block Friday night at the same time the Caps were out and about."

John acknowledged his clear yet vague answer, which involved the obvious difficulty of admitting criminal activity and said, "We understand." Singleton turned his attention to Sean O'Malley and asked, "Why did you go after the Hookers on Friday night?"

"We thought they were coming after our business when they burned their damn symbol on the back of the brother of one of my men as a threat."

"We never burned our symbol on anyone. Don't know anything about that," Merrick answered.

Sean O'Malley paused for a second, and realized he had no reason to admit he understood the true source of the burn. He turned to Merrick and said, "If you gave me the same answer when I asked you a few days ago, your man would still be alive."

"But he's not, and you got to pay. The Hookers demand an eye for an eye."

The Priest regained control of the conversation as The Professor remained settled in his chair, admiring John's work. "We agree, but no innocents are going to pay this price and they'll be no war. O'Flanahan was your number two and Aengus McGreary is the number two for the Caps. So this is what we are going to do—McGreary will be payment for O'Flanahan."

Merrick felt victorious when O'Malley nodded without even raising an objection. The leader of the Caps did clarify his acceptance of the deal. "I'll agree, but no Hooker is going to kill a Cap. I'll deliver Aengus McGreary dead on your doorstep by tomorrow morning."

The Priest concluded the meeting. "Gentlemen, I believe we are done." O'Malley left through the front and Merrick through the back. Both claimed victory as they explained how they dominated the meeting and put the other leader in their place. Back in the apartment, The Professor turned to John and said, "Bravo, well done, and with little assistance from me. Dill and Johnson were right—all you needed was time. Now The Professor can finally retire. Long live The Priest!"

CHAPTER 53

Sunday Collections

CAPTAIN DILL POSITIONED two of his men one block away from the entrance to the bridge construction site and kept another two by his side. No work was conducted on Sunday and the site was locked up tight. The men close to the site had instructions to take note of anyone who approached and entered the gate between the afternoon hours of one and three. Once these individuals exited the gate, they were to be detained. The captain planned to supervise this operation directly and needed to use a substantial amount of the resources given to him by John Singleton to entice these four handpicked men to join him for this unusual assignment, which was not only on a Sunday, but also an operation intended to arrest one of their own.

A storekeeper who sold a variety of illegal bottles of sweet poteen from a special shelf under his counter was the first to arrive. The men spotted him entering the construction site through a supposedly locked gate, and watched him walk to the same storehouse where Vent received his brutal beating. Ryan MacGregor opened the door in full uniform and accepted a sealed envelope from the storekeeper. He took his time and counted the bills. MacGregor smiled and tipped his hat, but called the man back after he walked away.

"Did you forget my special gift?" he asked.

The man returned, head down, and pulled a bottle of Jameson whiskey, which he provided as a final offering to the corrupt policeman. MacGregor tipped his hat again and said, "Pleasure doing business with ya."

After the man exited the construction site and MacGregor went back inside, the two officers escorted the storekeeper into an alley, where Captain Helmut Dill waited with his other men.

"What's your name?" the captain asked.

"Ian Patrick, but I'm all paid up. Can't afford any more—all paid up, I tell ya."

"Oh no, Mr. Patrick, you misunderstand. No more payments. How much did you give the officer?"

"Twenty dollars and a bottle of Jameson."

"All right, Mr. Patrick. Go back to your store and wait for one of my officers to return your money within a few hours. Now, I'm sure you are appreciative of what we are doing for you today, and I expect you will give at least a few dollars, perhaps half of what is returned, to the officer who appears at your doorstep. Are we clear, Mr. Patrick?"

"Yes, sir, and then no more payments?"

"No more payments. The reward you are offering for the return of your money is a one-time thing. A gesture for the help we gave you today. Go on, wait in your store."

By three o'clock, MacGregor had collected the last of his four payments of twenty dollars and was eighty dollars richer for his two-hour effort. He smiled as he locked the gate to the site, carrying a large burlap bag by his side, but lost his good spirits as soon as Captain Dill and his four officers approached him.

"I never realized Sunday was such a busy day," the captain said.

"What the fuck is this? I'm just checking on things on my day off—being a good cop is all."

"A good cop?" The captain laughed. "Take his bag and empty his pockets. We should find four envelopes containing twenty dollars, a bottle of whiskey, a box of cigars, a bit of opium, and, for some odd reason, a stovepipe hat."

The officers did as instructed and found what they expected plus another fifty dollars of cash in his front pocket.

"Okay, this is what is going to happen…I spoke to Boss McLaughlin, if you put up a fight, you'll be brought up on formal charges of corruption and you'll likely spend some time in jail. Remember, policemen are not so well-liked in jail. If you resign your position today, never to return to the force, we'll let you walk away, with fifty dollars in your pocket, which is much too generous on my part."

"You can't do this to me! How can you turn against one of your own? Don't you understand who my father is? He's a captain in New York. He'll never let this stand!"

"After your transfer, I warned your father this day was bound to come. He understood I wouldn't stand for this, and you'd lose your job when we caught you doing this kind of thing on a big scale. Remember, your father's influence in New York as a captain is nothing compared to Boss McLaughlin's influence in the City of Brooklyn. The Boss runs the entire city—you understand this as well as I, and he thinks making a public spectacle of prosecuting a corrupt policeman once in a while takes the pressure off the rest of us. This is the deal. Take it or you'll be arrested."

Ryan MacGregor considered his options and after a few moments responded, "You fuck, give me my fifty dollars. I am going—"

Dill punched him in the stomach before he finished his sentence and each officer kicked him while on the ground. The captain reached down and grabbed him by the collar as he ripped the badge from his uniform. "I bend rules too, but for different reasons. Come after us, and I promise you, no, we all promise you, you're a dead man. Stand up and take off the uniform. We'll let you keep your pants and your shoes, but you don't deserve to wear the uniform of the Metropolitan Police anymore."

MacGregor started to walk away in the cold December weather in his undershirt, clutching his fifty dollars in his hand. The captain called him back and reached into the satchel of gifts and tossed him the stovetop hat. "Here you go. I wouldn't want you to catch a chill." Dill paused for a moment and then offered his final thought with the best Irish brogue he could muster. "Pleasure doing business with ya." MacGregor continued his walk of shame, but stomped the hat into the street as he offered his own final thought. "Fuck you. Fuck all of you!"

The captain disposed of the opium, split the cigars among the men, and kept the whiskey for himself. Each of the four officers were provided with an address and headed their separate ways. Within a few minutes, each storekeeper offered the agreed-upon reward as well as their heartfelt thanks.

Chapter 54

A Final Prayer

Minister Sundick and his wife, Johanna, stood at the door of the temporary home of the Berean Baptist Church as they greeted the arriving worshippers. The couple tried hard to maintain some sense of normalcy during this awkward time for the congregation, and longed for the day they would once again preside over their flock at their own place of worship. Fire damage at their old location had caused the minister to find a number of temporary places for services, but regardless of their location each Sunday, he always began with the knowledge that God was with them and would see them through the rebuilding of another permanent home.

Most of the regulars were undeterred by the challenges with facilities, and attendance each Sunday remained strong. Ezra Brown addressed the minister as he entered. "Moses couldn't come today, he's stayin' with Vent. Doc says it could be any day now."

Sundick responded, "I learned of the terrible attack and we will pray for Vent today, but I'm so happy you're with us."

Miss Esther arrived soon after Ezra, and she entered with a full entourage, including her husband, Thomas, her daughter, Mabel, along with Georgia and Florence Johnson. The minister hugged them all and offered words of comfort. "We will pray for him today. Trust in the Lord. He has a plan for all of us."

The family took seats next to Ezra and they all held hands and offered a silent prayer before the service started. Horace came in a few minutes later, but sat in the back, away from the family.

The five-person choir began to sing the hymn "Amazing Grace." Florence fell to her knees and began to cry as they sang, "The Lord has promised good to me," and Georgia joined her mother when the words, "A Life of Joy and Peace," filled the room. Miss Esther cried throughout the entire hymn, the only one Vent ever loved.

After some time and a few more hymns, Reverend Sundick delivered God's message. His fiery oratory on this day spoke of God's plan and how those who are evil in this world pay the price in the end. He encouraged the congregation to find forgiveness in their hearts for those who hurt them, because God would be the final arbiter of justice.

Ezra hoped Moses would follow the minister's advice. The words resonated with Horace as well, as he realized his punishment in this life might be nothing compared to what waited for him on the other side. Horace got up after the minister's sermon and exited without making any attempt to speak with his family.

The service neared its end, and the minister skipped all of his typical housekeeping issues and announcements and asked the entire congregation to bow their heads to pray for the speedy recovery of their fallen brother, Venture Simmons. No sounds were heard for the next minute other than the sobs of Miss Esther and Georgia.

The family walked back to Vent's house after the service and wondered if today would be his last day—the doctor had advised them to prepare for the inevitable as he was unable to stop the spread of the infection. Venture's shallow breathing and fever-ravaged body neared the end of its fight. Death was imminent—time for everyone to say their goodbyes.

The family found Moses by Vent's side on his knees crying when they arrived home, and they all joined hands, forming a circle around their beloved Vent. Georgia offered her husband one last performance of "Amazing Grace" and the family joined in. After the final verse, they all fell to their knees with heads bowed. Moses looked up first, and saw Vent's eyes wide open, staring out the window to the heavens. Moses smiled, as he overheard Vent whisper, "Mama, I made it."

Part IV

Brooklyn
1876 - 1883

CHAPTER 55

The Traveler

THE *BROOKLYN EAGLE* ran the headline "Wedded" when two special ropes, connected into a loop, rose out of the water and traversed the river. This loop of rope was the starting point in laying the massive cables that would support the bridge. Engineers tested the movement of the rope, powered by a steam engine on the Brooklyn side, in a circular motion from end to end for several days. Anything attached to the moving loop would, in fact, travel across the river, hence the name assigned to the device: The Traveler.

The initial tests were successful, but The Traveler still contained some kinks and twists, which might cause something attached to it to flip over during the trek from one side to the other. Given the plan of sending a man across the river as an initial test as well as a public relations spectacle, such flipping might prove to be deadly. Once a stick attached to a section of the rope remained upright after many rotations, the engineers deemed The Traveler safe for its first human passenger.

Many men volunteered for the honor of being the first to cross the river aerially, but on August 25, 1876, sixty-year-old master mechanic E.F. Farrington made the first trip on The Traveler with tremendous fanfare and applause as he sat in a boatswain's chair, which resembled a simple swing, and made his way from shore to shore, waving his hat and blowing kisses. The public relations event, witnessed by over ten thousand people, provided tremendous publicity for the never-ending bridge project. Before the real work to be conducted by The Traveler could commence, however, a second Traveler designed to carry heavier loads, strong enough to create platforms for the men, needed to be established.

The rope used for the first Traveler went from shore to shore by boat and was later pulled up from the water and raised to the top of each tower. The second Traveler, however, could be carried over by the first, an approach that would not require cooperation from ships passing by the construction site on the East River. The weight of the second Traveler, which consisted of one light and one heavy wire rope, presented a special challenge. The two Travelers needed to be bound together as the first carried the second across the river. After every fifty feet of movement, the large steam engines stopped, affording the men the opportunity to bind the two ropes together in multiple locations in order to support the weight.

Crowds gathered for a second day after the fabulous entertainment provided by the hat-waving master mechanic on the first, and lined both sides of the river as the work on the second Traveler commenced. The binding worked well and within a short period of time, the second Traveler traversed the river. The final step was to cut the lashes, which bound the two Travelers, by hand.

Given his high-flying dexterity, the engineers had picked Vent to handle the cutting of the lashes on the New York side. His job was to cut the connection of the two Travelers between the interior anchorage of the bridge on the New York side and the top of the New York tower, a distance of about a thousand feet. Vent used a boatswain chair similar to the one E.F. Farrington used the day before, but he didn't attach any additional ropes as security—he needed to be able to maneuver as he neared each point of connection in order to cut the lashes binding the ropes.

Thousands of people in the streets on the New York side cheered as Vent launched himself off the New York tower in his boatswain chair, holding a short rope he would pull to slow his descent as he neared a lashing point. Simultaneously, another man launched himself off the Brooklyn tower on the other side of the river to perform the same job.

Vent reached the first point of connection in seconds, pulled on his rope to stop, and cut the lashing. When the heavier cable fell some distance toward the water after disconnecting from the lighter cable, Vent's chair vibrated violently, and he held on, experiencing the ride of his life. He then released his short rope again to descend further and disconnected the next section in a similar fashion.

This process was repeated until he landed on the ground by the anchorage with all lashings cut. The entire job took him less than ten minutes. The crowd roared.

Things didn't go as well on the Brooklyn side. The worker was so cautious, onlookers joked he'd be lucky if he finished within a week. Eventually, he did complete the work, but in typical New York/Brooklyn competitive fashion, Brooklyn was declared the loser of the first battle. Workers on the Brooklyn side jokingly cursed Vent, but hoped to fare better in the next round. Two other workers needed to descend from the tower on each side and cut the lashings every fifty feet until both reached middle span. Once done, the workers would use the boatswain chair for a ride back to the Brooklyn side.

A fast and efficient man descended from the Brooklyn side and made good progress from the start. The worker on the New York side, however, experienced trouble right away—a pulley jammed and he became stuck a short distance away from the tower. Vent monitored the difficulties from the top of the New York tower and figured out a plan to fix the problem. He climbed onto The Traveler, clutching the rope with his hands as well as his crossed legs, and shimmied his way past the distressed worker to the next point of connection, cut the lash, and freed up the pulley, enabling the work to continue. Vent crawled back up to the tower to another round of applause, but the man on the New York side still made slow progress. Brooklyn appeared in position to win this portion of the competition.

The fast-moving worker from the Brooklyn side passed midspan and started to make his way up toward the New York tower, cutting lashes as he went. The two men met much closer to the New York side, but The Traveler stopped moving. The engineers improvised and placed a ring with a heavy weight around The Traveler, hoping it would descend to the area where the men remained stranded about four hundred feet from the New York tower. The ring, however, stopped after moving only one-quarter of the required distance. Again, Vent came to the rescue and looped a rope around one of his legs as he scurried down toward the stranded men. Moses gazed at the scene from down below and remembered the first time he saw Vent climb like this in the wooded area just outside of Weeksville. Moses thought, *Vent was born for this job. Always knew he'd be the best tower man.*

Vent handed the stranded man from the New York side the rope wrapped around his leg and attached it to the boatswain chair. Workers on the tower pulled him back up. Vent went back up the same way he went down, with a smile on his face and nothing but pure efficiency in his movements. The Traveler started working again and transported the final stranded man back to the Brooklyn side.

The crowd cheered Vent as he returned to the New York tower and his co-workers congratulated him on his athletic feat. One of the Irishmen who worked with him in the old days started to chant "Monkey Boy, Monkey Boy," but big Connor McCloskey put an immediate stop to that with a grimace and a step in the man's direction. The giant Irishman wouldn't let anything take away from his old caisson partner's moment of triumph. "Good work, little fella," Connor called out to his friend, as he picked him up in a big bear hug. In a fleeting moment of celebration, the mostly Irish and German workers cheered Vent as one of their own and carried him off on their shoulders.

Chapter 56

A Wave from Mama

May 23, 1883—the celebration the world waited more than a decade for—would take place the next day. The president, Chester A. Arthur, headlined the dignitaries along with the governor of New York, Grover Cleveland. Hundreds of thousands of people from all over the country arrived for the ceremonies and a fireworks display that promised to be the best ever. Ships jockeyed for prime positions in the harbor and both cities became a buzz of activity as the grand moment approached—the day the Brooklyn Bridge would open to the public.

Fourteen years of construction, twenty-seven deaths, and scores of illnesses, including a number from the mysterious caisson's disease. Through it all, the work continued, and after Vent's difficult three-day stint as a sandhog in the caisson, followed by his six-month recovery from his injuries, he became the tower man he always wanted to be.

Everyone considered his heroics the day of the launch of the second Traveler to be the highlight of his work on the bridge, but Vent never appreciated fleeting moments—he valued what he could count on every day. Being up on the tallest structure in the world, out in the fresh air, warm or cold, was all he ever wanted. His job utilized all of his special skills, and he agreed with his dear friend Moses—he was born to be a tower man.

At the end of the construction, Vent made one special request of the Bridge Company and asked for a private moment on the Brooklyn tower the night before the opening. After his heroics in 1876, his request was granted without hesitation. Vent brought along his two closest friends. Moses Brown, who arguably was family, and John Singleton, who had become the captain of the Metropolitan Police station in Irishtown. Captain Singleton wielded tremendous influence in

Brooklyn and, in certain circles, continued to be referred to as The Priest. But to Vent, he was John, a friend he could count on.

The captain wanted to admire the view from the top of the world, and Moses came along because Vent never did anything of consequence without him by his side. Singleton joked as they climbed the steps leading to the top of the tower, "Moses, why does such a rich man want to exert himself with all of these steps—don't you have people to do this kind of thing for you?" Singleton laughed, and Moses offered a begrudging smile—this was a new joke for Vent, and he offered a belated chuckle once he detected the evidence of humor.

Once the three men arrived at the top and got their bearings, Singleton flashed his badge and asked the three workers who were tinkering with something by the edge of the tower to take a short break. He stayed back with Moses and admired the view. The world appeared so small from the top of the massive tower and both men found the view to be breathtaking.

John held his pocket watch in his right hand and traced the outline of the angel's wings with his thumb. He wished his father were by his side and knew he would have loved being above it all on top of the Brooklyn tower, just like he was as a policeman—the best of the best. After admiring the craftsmanship of the watch one last time, John detected a small gap between two bricks, and smiled as he slid his prized possession into the void. *A perfect fit.*

Moses achieved everything he'd ever dreamed of financially and found quiet ways to help others gain the same kind of success. His support could always be counted on for any worthy cause, but Moses felt especially blessed when someone sought him out for advice. After being called *stupid* for most of his adult life, the idea that people valued his knowledge and wisdom was one of his most important achievements. There was no one he advised more than Vent, who had become the son he never had, and Venture's success was more important to Moses than his own.

Vent walked toward the edge which faced New York and started to unbutton his shirt. After the last button was unfastened, he paused for a second, gazed out at the river, and smiled as he removed and folded his shirt neatly on the tower floor. John and Moses cringed as the scars on Vent's back from his whipping came into full view. Vent bent his knees to loosen up and John worried this trip to the top of the world might be for a different purpose, but Moses grabbed him by the arm and said, "No worries, John. Vent getting ready to do some of his crazy stuff, but he only does things he knows he can do. Told me long time ago he's not afraid of things he's sure of—only need to be afraid one day of your life—the day you gonna die. He already got by one of those days, but today is not another one, John. So don't you worry."

The wind light, and the evening sky, clear—everything was perfect, just like he imagined it would be. Vent remembered the symbol of conquest his old foe, Jimmy McGreary, displayed after each of his romantic encounters with Katie Fitzpatrick in the alley, and he pounded his bare chest with his hands. Moses and John laughed at the sight, but not loud enough to ruin the moment.

The chest pounding continued for some time as Moses and John admired Vent from the distance. They both reflected on the peculiar situations that delivered Venture Simmons into their lives. For Moses, his introduction started with Vent jumping out of a crate, and for John, his first encounter came when Vent leaped down from the side of a building in a dark alley in Irishtown. Whenever anyone thought of Vent, jumping and climbing came to mind, but a certain social awkwardness and an inability to understand basic social clues did as well. Georgia said it best—Vent was a mixed bag. Despite his social challenges, Vent had built a life for himself, and always protected those around him. He still lived by the basic codes instilled in him by Miss Esther, Moses, Principal Morel, and his mama.

Vent jumped up and down on the edge of the tower trying to get closer to the stars. John again became nervous, but Moses reassured him, "Remember, Venture only does what he knows he can do. No need to disturb him."

Vent counted his jumps and did them in sets of three. By the time he reached number twelve, a cloud passed by the moon, which rose slightly above the New York tower, and Vent celebrated what he'd long waited for...*a wave from Mama.* He screamed back, "I made it, Mama! I made it, Mama!" over and over. After some time, the waving stopped. A few moments later, the screaming subsided, and Vent sat on the edge of the tower, legs dangling, waiting for a response. Moses and John stopped talking to give Vent complete silence. A ship passed by below, which temporarily diverted Vent's attention, but he looked up just in time as another cloud passed by the moon. Venture smiled—certain Mama answered, "You sure did, baby."

Historical Notes & Liberties

Part I – Weeksville – 1863-1865

THE FIRST SECTION of the book takes place in the town of Weeksville, a section of Brooklyn dominated by free Black landowners, which was located where Crown Heights stands today. Male Blacks were able to vote in New York during the early 1860s if they owned land valued at $250 or more. Many Blacks from New York fled to Weeksville after the violent Draft Riots in 1863. These riots pitted the Irish against both the Blacks and the rich. The Blacks were targeted because the Irish were infuriated at the prospect of being drafted to fight in a war that would free the people (Blacks) who would likely steal their jobs. Blacks were beaten severely and a number were lynched by roving Irish mobs. Many homes of the rich were ransacked and some wealthy New Yorkers were physically attacked because the Irish were incensed that they were able to pay a fee to be exempted from the draft.

The initial scenes in the book take place in Fort Sumter, which was the name of the refugee camp in Weeksville. Junius Morel was actually the principal of Colored School No. 2 and Minister Sundick was the preacher at the Berean Baptist Church. The African Civilization Society, which encouraged emigration of free Blacks to Liberia, was also based in Weeksville. The newspaper mentioned throughout this section and later in the book, *The Brooklyn Eagle*, was the leading paper of the day.

Part II – Brooklyn – 1869

Another section of Brooklyn called Irishtown, also known as Vinegar Hill, is introduced in this section of the novel. This area was filled with gangs, two of which, the Velvet Caps and the Hook Gang, are featured in Part II. Suds Merrick was actually one of the leaders of the Hook Gang.

A few powerful individuals dubbed the Whiskey Kings dominated Irishtown, and they controlled the production and distribution of an illegal spirit called sweet poteen, which the Irish learned to distill in Ireland. John Devlin was one of the more prominent Whiskey Kings, and the president of the United States, Andrew Johnson, did pardon him from prison.

The federal revenue officers raided the illegal distilleries in Irishtown from time to time with the assistance of the local police and the marines from the Brooklyn Navy Yard, and the people of Irishtown impeded the raids in the hope of protecting their cheap source of spirits.

The Weeksville Unknowns (later renamed the Mutual Base Ball Club) was the local athletic team, and the name of the sport, base ball, was broken into two words during this time period.

Finally, Hugh "Boss" McLaughlin was the leader of Democratic politics in Brooklyn during this period of time.

Part III – The Bridge – 1869

The Brooklyn Bridge was built during a period in which New York and Brooklyn were two separate cities connected by a very active ferry service. New York was the largest city in the country and Brooklyn was number three. All of the information provided about the construction of the bridge is factual. John A. Roebling designed the bridge but died of lockjaw at the very beginning of the construction. His son, Colonel Washington Roebling, became chief engineer.

The towers of the bridge became the tallest structures in North America, and the caissons, which formed the base of the towers, caused a mysterious and misunderstood disease, which was fittingly called caisson's disease. This disease is now called decompression sickness. No one understood the illness well at the time, and the fear of this disease was one of the main reasons for the high level of turnover which plagued the bridge project.

Colonel Washington Roebling became afflicted with a severe case of caisson disease that plagued him for the rest of his life. He was confined to his apartment in Brooklyn Heights during most of the construction and would observe the progress of the bridge with binoculars and send his wife, Emily, to the site with specific instructions.

Part IV – Brooklyn – 1876 - 1883

The first trip on The Traveler was made by master mechanic E.F. Farrington on August 25, 1876, but the high-flying theatrics with the second Traveler the following day, which are ascribed to Venture Simmons, were actually the work of a man by the name of Harry Supple.

The celebration of the opening of the Brooklyn Bridge was one of the most festive celebrations ever in the United States and was attended by both President Chester A. Arthur and the governor of New York, Grover Cleveland, who himself would later become president.

The bridge took fourteen years to build and resulted in twenty-seven deaths, a number from caisson's disease. It is generally considered to be one of the most remarkable structures of its time.

Acknowledgements and Sources

I UTILIZED THE following sources during the research phase of writing the novel: *Brooklyn's Promised Land: The Free Black Community of Weeksville, New York* by Judith Wellman, *The Great Bridge: The Epic Story of the Building of the Brooklyn Bridge* by David McCullough, *Brooklyn and the Civil War* by E.A. Bud Livingston, *Chronicles of Historic Brooklyn* by John B. Manbeck, *Black Gotham: A Family History of African-Americans in Nineteenth Century New York City* by Carla L. Peterson, *The New York City Draft Riots* by Iver Bernstein, and *Asperger Syndrome Explained* by Sara Elliot Price. I also want to acknowledge the assistance and resources provided by the Weeksville Heritage Center.

About the Author

A. Robert Allen has published four novels and two short-story prequels in his *Slavery and Beyond* series. All are stand-alone stories connected by theme. He writes historical fiction that transports readers to times and places immediately before or soon after the end of slavery. A. Robert is a long-time higher education professional and resides in New York. The first volume in the series, *Failed Moments*, is a fictional account of Allen's ancestors in 1790 during the slave revolution in what would become Haiti and later in 1863 during New York's Draft Riots. The second volume, *A Wave From Mama*, immerses readers in racially charged post Civil War Brooklyn and gives an interesting look at the building of the Brooklyn Bridge. The third book in the series, *Minetta Lane*, takes place in 1904 in a downtown New York neighborhood that lives by an unusual race-based code. The prequel to this third volume, Minetta Mornings, takes place twenty-five years earlier. His most recent release, Living in the Middle, transports readers to perhaps the most violent and significant incident of racial violence in U.S. history, the Tulsa Race Riots of 1921. The prequel to this novel, which takes place in 1896, is entitled Ticket to Tulsa. Find out more about the author and his works at his website: http://arobertallen.com

Get Exclusive Materials

Given my trouble saying goodbye to my characters, I write prequels and sequels and provide this content exclusively for readers on my mailing list. Go to http://arobertallen.com to join and pick up this free additional content.

Also by A. Robert Allen

Failed Moments

Minetta Lane

Living in the Middle

Minetta Mornings (prequel to Minetta Lane)

Ticket to Tulsa (prequel to Living in the Middle)